Drive Me Wild

"Warren is back with another sexy, sassy romp, focusing this time on the oh-so-sensuous Rafael De Santos. As always, there is a great deal of humor, sizzling sex, and off-the-wall adventure in Warren's Others series, which makes for a truly lively, amusing read."

—*RT Book Reviews*

"Christine Warren sets the pages ablaze once again with *Drive Me Wild*!" —Joyfully Reviewed

On the Prowl

"Christine Warren brings her blend of humor, romance, and thrilling mystery to *On the Prowl*."

—*Fresh Fiction*

"Christine Warren has created an incredible, alluring world and then populated it with the most amazing heroes and heroines. Never a disappointment, Christine Warren continues to dazzle our senses with her books of the Others."

—*Single Titles*

Not Your Ordinary Faerie Tale

"Warren has made a name for herself in the world of paranormal romance. She expertly mixes werewolves, vampires, and faeries to create another winning novel in The Others series. *Not Your Ordinary Faerie Tale* showcases Warren's talents for creating consistent characters with strong voices and placing them in a fantastical world."

—*RT Book Reviews*

"Incredible."

—All About Romance

"Warren takes readers for a wild ride."

—Night Owl Romance

"Another good addition to The Others series."

—Romance Junkies

"[A] sexy, engaging world . . . will leave you begging for more!"

—New York Times bestselling
author Cheyenne McCray

Big Bad Wolf

"In this world . . . there's no shortage of sexy sizzle."

—RT Book Reviews

"Another hot and spicy novel from a master of paranormal romance."

—Night Owl Romance

"Ms. Warren gives readers action and danger around each turn, sizzling romance, and humor to lighten each scene. *Big Bad Wolf* is a must-read."

—Darque Reviews

You're So Vein

"Filled with supernatural danger, excitement, and sarcastic humor."

—Darque Reviews

"Five stars. This is an exciting, sexy book."

—Affaire de Coeur

"The sparks do fly!"

—RT Book Reviews

Also by
Christine Warren

Hungry Like a Wolf
Drive Me Wild
On the Prowl
Not Your Ordinary Faerie Tale
Black Magic Woman
Prince Charming Doesn't Live Here
Born to be Wild
Big Bad Wolf
You're So Vein
One Bite with a Stranger
Walk on the Wild Side
Howl at the Moon
The Demon You Know
She's No Faerie Princess
Wolf at the Door

Anthologies

The Huntress
No Rest for the Witches

Heart of Stone

Christine Warren

St. Martin's Paperbacks

This is a work of fiction. All of the characters, organizations, and events portrayed in this novel are either products of the author's imagination or are used fictitiously.

HEART OF STONE

Copyright © 2014 by Christine Warren.

For information address St. Martin's Press, 175 Fifth Avenue, New York, NY 10010.

ISBN: 978-1-250-01265-4

Printed in the United States of America

St. Martin's Paperbacks edition / January 2014

St. Martin's Paperbacks are published by St. Martin's Press, 175 Fifth Avenue, New York, NY 10010.

10 9 8 7 6 5 4 3 2 1

Chapter One

Ella Harrow fully supported the notion that people with
excessive amounts of money should donate large sums of
it to worthy causes, and she counted her employer—the
Vancouver Museum of Art and History—as among the
worthiest. She just wished the donors would hand over
the cash without wanting to *talk* to her first.

Five minutes after the last guest of the Friday evening
fund-raising gala had exited the front doors of Georgia
House, the historic building that housed the main museum
gallery, Ella gave in to the pressure she'd felt building all
through the evening. She rolled her eyes, blew a raspberry,
and thumbed her nose simultaneously. It was childish of
her, but satisfying.

Béatrice Boucher, the only other staff member still present, said, "Now, Ella, tell me how you really feel about
these little events."

Ella shot her boss a narrow-eyed glare. "They're my
favorites, Bea. Really."

Drinking wine and nibbling canapés might not sound
like a year in a Stalinist gulag, but having to do it in the
midst of five hundred elegantly dressed strangers while

maintaining a polite smile in the face of their inane conversations and pretending to laugh at their lame jokes ranked even worse in Ella's mind. She'd rather volunteer for the hard labor.

"I never would have guessed," Bea said, locking the heavy antique entrance doors. After rattling the knobs once to check the bolts, she turned to Ella and waved her hands in a shooing motion. "Fly. Be free. You've done your penance for this fiscal quarter. I'll hustle the caterers out through the kitchens and lock up that side. You can sneak out the garden gate the way you usually do and lock the terrace doors on your way out."

"You sure?"

"Don't look a gift horse, *mon amie*. Run while you can, before I come up with some new programs to spend all those lovely donations on and put you back to work."

"I'm already halfway home."

Ella listened to her friend and colleague's laughter follow her through the hall and into the historic mansion's stately ballroom, which now housed an impressive collection of paintings, antique furniture, and historic objets d'art. She'd worked for the assistant curator for more than two years now, and Bea knew her well enough to understand that when Ella said she hated crowds and that making small talk with strangers gave her hives, she wasn't kidding.

She scratched absently at her arms beneath her embellished cardigan—her halfhearted nod to the event's formal dress code—and stepped out into the crisp night air. Pausing on the paving stones, she took a moment to savor the silence. The solitude. For the first time in hours, her nerves began to unwind.

. For some people, Ella knew, shyness made interacting with strangers an uncomfortable and embarrassing experience, but Ella wasn't shy; she was terrified. Crowds scared her—more than spiders, more than the threat of global war, more than the boogeyman.

With people all around her, she could never predict what might happen, and the constant tension of holding on to her self-control made her head pound and her nerves fray. Being an antisocial hermit just made life easier.

Unfortunately, the hermit gig didn't pay much, and Ella was addicted to living indoors and eating regularly, so she had to work, which meant dealing with people on a daily basis. At the museum at least, most of the people she met were on their best behavior, and being surrounded by the art made the unwelcome company almost bearable. When she gave tours as a docent, she could concentrate on her speech and on the works she pointed out to visitors to the collection; when managing the gift shop, she could smile politely and use professionalism to keep people at bay.

Most days, things went perfectly smoothly. It was only at times like this, when she had to deal with a special event and potential donors, that Ella ended her day feeling as if she'd been dragged behind a car over a field of broken glass.

A few minutes of peace, she told herself. A few minutes of quiet and isolation, and she'd be fine again. The ache in her head would ease. She'd even be able to face the bus ride home; at this hour, it wouldn't be crowded, and in twenty minutes, she could lock the door of her apartment and wallow in her Fortress of Solitude.

Bliss.

Taking a deep breath, Ella drew in the autumnal scent of drying leaves and cool breezes. Her head fell back as she closed her eyes and rolled her shoulders against the tension knotted there. She'd take a minute, just a minute, to herself on the ballroom terrace, her favorite spot in the entire museum, before she locked up and headed home.

Just a minute to collect herself, to shore up her defenses for the short trip home.

The lighting out here was dim, especially with the caterer's lamps removed and the museum shut down for the night. A full moon partially obscured by drifting clouds made it possible to see, but somehow the silvery sheen it cast only made the quiet of the gardens deeper and reminded Ella of the lateness of the hour. She enjoyed these hours of the night, enjoyed the play of the moonlight on the artful plantings and graceful sculptures scattered through the museum garden.

She enjoyed that she'd survived the ordeal of the party and wouldn't have to do anything else so annoying for at least another three months. Until, as Bea had hinted, the next fiscal quarter.

"I think this is the first time I've seen you alone all evening, Ella."

Stifling a shriek, she clenched her fists and spun around.

She also jumped, the ankle straps of her black Mary Janes the only things keeping her from literally coming out of her shoes. Adrenaline rushed through her, making her heart pound in her ears and her hands come up defensively. She focused and caught sight of the person whose words had just scared her witless.

Patrick Stanley.

She should have recognized the voice. Smooth and slick, it simultaneously sent shivers racing across her skin and raised the hairs on the back of her neck. Stanley was rich, handsome, and sophisticated, one of the most sought after bachelors in British Columbia, and a third-generation patron of the museum. He had a movie star's smile and the kind of charisma that drew people to him like lemmings to a cliff face.

He also creeped Ella the hell out, especially when she caught him repeatedly staring at her the way he'd been doing all evening. She'd thought he left with the other guests. She'd thought she could relax.

"Mr. Stanley. You startled me," she managed after a minute, once her vocal cords had unclenched and restored her power of speech. "I had no idea anyone was still here. The event ended almost an hour ago."

Stanley stood less than ten feet away on the darkened terrace, which was about twenty feet too close for Ella's comfort. Normally, strangers couldn't get that near her without her sensing their presence, especially the ones who made her uncomfortable. She'd gotten very good at being difficult to surprise.

"I'm aware, but I found that there were still some things around here tonight for me to admire." He ambled toward her, his hands buried in the pockets of his tailored trousers and his attention fixed uncomfortably on her neckline.

Ella frowned. She'd worn a simple black sheath with a high neck, a modest hem, and the sparkly cardigan over the top. She'd even paired the outfit with dark hose, which she normally loathed, but she knew there wasn't an inch of exposed skin below her hyoid bone for him to look at. That made the man's fixation on her even more disturbing, somehow.

She had met Stanley for the first time almost two years ago, shortly after she started working at the museum. He'd come out of a meeting with Bea and the director, Bea's boss, just as Ella was ending a tour in the mansion's front hall.

When Ella's guests had scattered, Bea waved her over and introduced her to both Dr. Maurice Lefavreau and one of the museum's greatest benefactors. Even with her mental shields still up from interacting with the tour group, something about Stanley had slipped through Ella's defenses and convinced her that this was a man she'd much prefer to keep at the greatest possible distance in the future.

Until tonight, she thought she'd been doing a pretty good job of it.

Suppressing the slight, irrational discomfort the man's presence always inspired, she lifted her chin and pasted on her best professional smile—the one with no actual warmth anywhere near it.

"We do have a collection to be proud of," she remarked distantly, "and the new exhibit of Légaré landscapes is particularly worth an extended study. You should make it a point to come back on another day. The natural light does make quite a difference to the viewing."

Turning, Ella moved toward the French doors, gesturing for him to join her. "Allow me to walk you to the front, Mr. Stanley. I believe Dr. Boucher has already locked the doors, but I'd be happy to let you out."

She made a concerted effort to keep Stanley in her vision, but the man seemed more amused by her tactics than inclined to play along with her. He stood where he was until she drew even with him; then with a speed she hadn't anticipated, his hand darted out and grabbed her arm. He jerked her to a stop, nearly upsetting her balance.

"Don't be in such a hurry, Ella," he purred, holding her closely enough that she could feel the clammy heat of his breath against her cheek. "It's a beautiful night. Surely you can spare a few minutes to enjoy it. With me."

Her stomach heaved.

At the best of times, Ella avoided touching strangers. Even when she kept her guard up, sometimes she could sense things about them. Right now, she sensed a sickly sort of malevolence that made her want a swift escape and a long, hot shower.

Frozen like a field mouse facing down a hungry fox,

she stared into Stanley's handsome features and fought not to let the panic overwhelm her. This was another of the reasons why she worked so hard to keep people at a distance, because she could never tell when the slightest touch would rip open her senses and let the buffeting whirlwinds of the unnatural energy that surrounded her threaten to send her spinning into the eye of the storm.

And when Ella got swept into the eye, very scary things happened.

Dizziness threatened, but Ella ruthlessly pushed it back. She blinked to clear her vision and concentrated hard on seeing only the stark reality of the objects around her— Stanley's intense, predatory stare; the majestic old elm tree that overhung the space between the garden stairs; the protective, crouching presence of the medieval gargoyle statue looming in the background.

A hysterical laugh bubbled up in her throat when Ella realized that if that ancient French sculptor had really wanted to scare people, he would have carved a statue that looked less like a demonic guardian and more like a feckless, morally bankrupt billionaire. No monster had ever scared her the way this human man was doing.

Swallowing hard, Ella forced back the nausea and fought for control. Her head spun and her ears buzzed with the low drone of a thousand bees, signs that she'd let her guard down.

She could tell herself that she couldn't have known she wasn't alone out here, that the museum was closed, and that Patrick Stanley had no business lurking in the shadows when his invitation to Georgia House had expired the minute the fund-raising event ended. None of that, however, did her any good.

Pulses of restless energy battered at her weakened barriers, but she refused to let them overwhelm her. If they did, not only would she be unable to fend off Stanley's advances, but she'd also find herself barely able to function for days, if not weeks, to come.

And that wasn't even considering what other things might happen here in this place full of history and artifacts. Old things, especially old things full of talent and beauty, held power of their own, and they could be destroyed if she was so weak as to lose control. If she couldn't hang on, those same things could feed the madness.

Ella couldn't let that happen.

Frantically, she reinforced her defenses, plugging hole after hole that the black, poisonous energy rolling off Stanley tried to slip through. She could only be grateful that the cardigan she wore had kept his skin from touching hers. If it hadn't, she'd be halfway to comatose by now.

"Mr. Stanley, I'm not sure what you're suggesting, but it's very late, and the museum is closed." Her voice sounded more like a tortured croak than a confident dismissal, but she plunged ahead regardless. "Dr. Boucher and I have each worked a very long day, and I, for one, would like to return home now. Please let me go."

Stanley's eyes, pale blue and cold, hardened along with his grip. His fingers dug into the flesh of her upper arm with enough force to leave bruises. "I'm sure Dr. Boucher would be the first to tell you that alienating one of this museum's largest benefactors is a poor way to do your job, Ella, my sweet. But even if she were shortsighted enough not to, I'm more than happy to correct her oversight."

His other hand shot up and curled around her throat, nearly cutting off her air supply. What his fingers couldn't quite accomplish, his mouth did. It attacked hers with brutal force, crushing her lips back against her teeth until she tasted blood.

Then she tasted fury.

For an instant, her control wavered. The unmuffled

touch of this man's tainted skin on hers opened her up to the most intense surge of murky energy, and she could feel the dark, vicious nature of him trying to infiltrate her defenses.

Part of her—that dark, secret part she kept imprisoned behind thick stone walls and heavy steel doors—wanted her to just let go, to stop fighting so hard to control the strange ability she'd always both feared and hated, to just let whatever wanted to happen, happen. No one would blame her. She was only defending herself.

As she felt the familiar, stomach-churning sensation of the energy welling up under her skin, she toyed with letting go, letting it not just bubble to the surface, but explode. The power inside her would stop Stanley in his tracks.

It might also stop *him*. Permanently.

The temptation of it shook her. Memories of what happened the last time she'd given in to the temptation flooded her. She recalled what it meant to stop fighting, when she'd been just a child and the energy battering at her had left her feeling overwhelmed, alone and hopeless, a freak of nature with a decidedly unnatural talent.

The power crawled over her skin, and she fought to pull it back. She couldn't let that happen again.

Without warning, Stanley jerked away, releasing her mouth and leaving her with the taste of her own blood in her mouth.

His hand shifted on her throat, forcing her head up, angling it to the side until the moonlight caught and illuminated her features. His eyes glittered with lust and fury.

And something else, something that frightened Ella more than even the assault. It twisted his lips and carved lines into the surface handsomeness of his features, transforming them into a macabre mask of evil.

He stared at her for a disconcerting moment, tracing

each line and expression on her face. Speculation lit his eyes, along with a dark, flickering flame Ella's instincts immediately identified as madness.

"Well, well, aren't you a surprise, little Ella." His voice hissed in the darkness, soft and sharp and unctuous. "I never would have guessed you might have such . . . hidden depths, my dear. I see now that I'm going to have to get to know you a great deal better."

Her stomach churned, and her senses rioted in protest.

The sharp bite of bile rising into her throat brought Ella back to reality. The bitter taste reminded her that she had made herself strong enough to fight back the electric energy crawling along her skin. And if she could withstand that siege on her control, she could certainly break free from one lecherous man's clumsy attack.

Without resorting to anything scarier than a little judicious violence.

Stanley gripped her around her left upper arm and her throat, leaving her right hand conveniently free. She knew attempting to break his grip would be impossible; he was a good seven inches taller and fifty pounds heavier than she was, but her maneuver of choice wouldn't require strength, just accuracy and the element of surprise.

She wiggled for effect and tried to scream out a protest from behind her clenched teeth, but that was just a distraction. Her blow, when it came, seemingly out of nowhere, involved the flat of her hand connecting hard with the side of her attacker's head.

She boxed his ear. Viciously.

The shock and pain made him jerk back and curse, and the hand around her throat moved abruptly to cup his ringing, throbbing head. "You bitch!"

"And you're a disgusting creep," she countered, trying to wrench her arm completely out of his grip. "Now, get your hands off me!"

If anything, his fingers tightened, making Ella whimper involuntarily. "Oh, I don't think so, whore. I've got plans for you now. You're going to make a tasty little treat for—"

"Is everything all right out here? I thought I heard someone shout." Bea's voice was like a chorus from the heavens in Ella's ears.

Quickly, she shifted from behind Stanley's taller frame until she could see her boss standing in the doors that led from the back hall onto the terrace. She flashed a smile she knew lacked a certain sincerity and used her free hand to gesture to the man still holding her in place.

"I admit I got a little bit of a scare from Mr. Stanley here," Ella said, her voice tight but determinedly cheerful. The last thing she wanted was some kind of nightmarish scene involving lodging a complaint about the lecher's behavior, or even worse, filing some sort of assault charge with the city police. "I didn't think there was anyone still here but you and me. He startled me."

Bea's dark gaze moved from Ella to Stanley, making note of the tiny details her keen eyes would never miss, like the way the man gripped Ella's arm, the disheveled wrinkles in her cardigan, and the bright red hue of Stanley's left ear.

The assistant museum director raised her eyebrows and pursed her lips. "The two of you certainly startled me," she said. "I knew you were out here, of course, Ella, but I was afraid you might have hurt yourself."

"No, no. I haven't been hurt, just shaken up. Actually, I was just offering to show Mr. Stanley to the front doors. I know you locked up when the last of the guests left, and I didn't want him to think he was trapped."

Stanley frowned and released Ella's arm to straighten the lapels of his evening jacket. "Béatrice, I think you should know what really happened here. I—"

Bea lifted a hand and firmed her lips. "And I think you should know that we've been acquainted for more than five years now, Patrick. I understand very well what happened here, and I honestly don't think it would do anyone any good if we discussed it further."

Stepping aside, she gestured toward the ballroom doors. "Now, seeing how late it is, please allow me to walk you out. Tonight was a wonderful success for the museum, and I'm certain Dr. Lefavreau will express his gratitude to you the very next time he sees you. Shall we?"

Ella watched as Patrick Stanley weighed his options. She knew his pride was wounded, not to mention his eardrum—for the sake of her lifelong desire not to be sued, she just hoped she hadn't ruptured it—and any man as arrogant as he was couldn't possibly be happy about having his plans thwarted.

She also didn't doubt he was surprised to have his incipient lie about being the injured party in any circumstances involving her burst like an overinflated party balloon. She could practically see his desire to scratch the itch caused by her refusal to cooperate with him, and Bea's untimely interruption.

If the man hadn't just attacked her, she might even have been moved to sympathy.

Or at least morbid humor.

At the moment, though, she just wanted him gone and a little time alone to get a hold of herself. The aftermath of the adrenaline flood in her system had started her hands shaking, and her mental shields needed a serious tune-up, but there was no way she was taking her eyes off Stanley until she knew the man was locked firmly on the other side of the museum's heavily carved wooden doors.

After a long moment of crackling tension, Stanley admitted defeat. Sort of.

He gave Bea a curt nod and stalked across the terrace, pulling out his cell phone on the way. "I'm suddenly more than ready for this evening to be over. My driver will pick me up out front. Let Lefavreau know I'll be calling him in the morning."

Stanley focused on his phone as he composed some sort of text message, so he missed seeing Bea's eyes narrow at the threat.

By the time he glanced up, the woman had mustered a sharp smile and waved him forward. "I'm sure he'll be more than happy to listen to whatever suggestions you have for the museum's future. Ella, I'll lock this door as well." She glanced back at Ella. "You head on home now. Mr. Stanley and I will leave by the front door."

Ella caught the final hate-filled glare the man shot her way and could just imagine what kind of suggestions Stanley would make tomorrow; first would be firing the museum's gift shop manager, but she'd have plenty of time to worry about that later. After she got a hold of herself.

Left alone, she felt the tension drain from her in an abrupt rush, leaving her dizzy and weak-kneed. She needed to sit for a minute and remind herself how to breathe.

Carefully, she crossed to the far side of the terrace to perch at the feet of her favorite work of art in the museum's entire collection. Its familiarity and looming presence comforted her, made it possible for her to think and be and regain her balance.

Affectionately known by the staff as Sir Arthur Conan Gargoyle, the enormous sculpture crouched atop a pedestal of polished black slate, its furious gaze trained over the rear of the building as if daring any evil spirits to attempt a breach of its domain.

Too bad it hadn't noticed Patrick Stanley.

Technically, the statue was a grotesque, not a true

gargoyle. Sir Arthur had been carved from a single block
of dark French limestone sometime around the beginning
of the eleventh century. Because he was solid through and
had never been intended to channel rain water away from
the sides of a structure, he couldn't be correctly called a
gargoyle, even though his appearance brought the term to
mind as soon as anyone laid eyes on him.

Standing erect, he would have easily reached seven feet
tall, and the spread of his huge, batlike wings would likely
have tripled that. He had horns like a ram curling backwards from his broad forehead, and thick, lethally sharp
claws tipped each of his fingers, as well as the eerily pre-
hensile toes on his raptorlike feet. He wore a frozen snarl
on his chiseled features, exposing long fangs beneath curled
lips.

What had always fascinated Ella about the statue,
though, were the contradictions the artist had carved into
the fierce predatory beast he had sculpted. His face didn't
look like the face of an animal. In spite of the faintly flattened nose and the threatening fangs, Sir Arthur appeared
remarkably human, more like a fallen angel than like a
devil. That impression drew support from the exquisite
detail of the cherubic curls adorning his head, clustered
around the base of his horns and even dipping over his
forehead. His cheekbones gave him the look of a warrior
king, and despite his thickly muscled tail, the bulk of his
physical attributes painted him as more man than animal.

Ella liked to think the artist had seen him as she did—a
fierce guardian, willing to battle evil on its own terms, determined to protect his charges against any harm.

From what Bea had told her, Ella knew that the sculpture had a long and slightly murky history. Obviously
French in origin, it had likely adorned the battlements of
some abbey or castle for centuries before making its way
to England during the Enlightenment, and subsequently

along a convoluted trail that had finally delivered it into Western Canada.

Everyone who caught a glimpse of it marveled at its condition, for nearly a millennium of exposure to the elements had smoothed away remarkably few of the details that made it such an impressive work of art. The museum's director had supposedly gloated for weeks after acquiring it a couple of years ago, and frankly, Ella couldn't blame him.

It was not only her favorite piece in the collection, but also her favorite sculpture in the world. And if there was something almost alive about it, something that made her sixth sense prickle and tested her resolve to remain always in control, she was happy to ignore it for the chance to simply stare at its angles and curves. She never tired of looking at it.

Hence, all the ribbing she took about being in love with Sir Arthur. The comments might have bothered her, if she hadn't dated infinitely worse male specimens.

If Bea hadn't interrupted a few minutes ago, she'd have become way too closely acquainted with another one. Suppressing a shudder, Ella closed her eyes, blocked out the memory, and focused on regaining her composure.

It took a few seconds for the quiet sigh of inhale and exhale to deepen and relax, and another minute before her hands could fully register the cool, smooth texture of the slate at her sides. When she felt normal again, she tilted her head back to gaze up at the underside of the statue's sharply angled jaw.

"You know, that pleasant little scene never would have happened if you'd been doing your duty," she griped half-humorously to the silent guardian. "You're supposed to repel evil. Talk about lying down on the job."

With her chin up and her eyes on Sir Arthur's corded throat, Ella never saw the shadow moving toward her, never heard the footsteps approaching. But she did hear the loud crack of reality fracturing all around her.

Along with the stone shell of a suddenly very animated inanimate gargoyle.

Chapter Two

He had slept for so long that he nearly forgot what the world sounded like. A human scream, however, jarred him back to consciousness.

One moment he crouched poised on his pedestal, frozen in the same position he had occupied for more than a thousand years, and the next, he heard the crack of stone as he lifted himself to his feet.

Kees—that was his name, he remembered—shifted and flexed muscles too long unused. With a half beat of his unfurled wings, he launched himself into the air above the human, landing easily a few feet in front of her. Between her and the evil now attacking her.

For some reason, the woman only screamed louder.

Kees ignored her. All his attention focused on the man moving toward them. The darkness of the terrace didn't bother him; he'd been designed to see in the night as clearly as a human saw in the day. More clearly. He had no trouble making out the rage-twisted face of the attacker, or the dark, pitted blade of the dagger the figure clutched in one fist.

Damn cultists never cared properly for their weapons.

The man darted to the right, trying to skirt around Kees to reach his target, but gargoyles had a lot more "around" to them than most creatures. With a shift of his shoulders, Kees spread his wings and used one sweeping motion to send the attacker through the air. Also unlike gargoyles, humans tended to land with a splat.

This one added a thud, then lay still. In the battle between the stones of the terrace and his skull, the stones had predictably won.

Turning to the woman whose screams had woken him, Kees examined her curiously. Her distress should not have been enough to penetrate his magical slumber and draw him back to consciousness. Only the threat of great, demonic evil unleashed on the mortal world should have done that.

So what was he to make of this ordinary human?

She was smallish, the way humans always looked to him, though he judged her even smaller than most, barely a couple of inches over five feet. Her features were soft and even, her lips bow-shaped, her hair light brown and fine. Skin fair enough to glow in the moonlight framed eyes wide and gray with no hint of blue or green to muddle their purity. And in that moment, they stared at him in pure, frozen terror.

Lifting a hand, he stepped forward. "I won't hurt you."

Even to his own ears, his voice sounded harsh and coarse from centuries of disuse. It rumbled out of him like the growl of a primitive beast, and he cursed himself when her expression filled with panic.

"You are safe with me." He took another step, wincing when his thick skin scraped across the terrace like stone on stone. He had regained movement, but he still retained his hard armored shell. It would take a while longer for his skin to soften to something more natural. "I mean you no harm."

Briefly, he let himself hope that her silence and stillness meant she intended to listen to him. He had sensed the magic in her; he knew she couldn't be ignorant of it in the rest of the world. If he could ask her a few questions, she might be able to tell him how she had woken him, what battle he needed to fight.

Then she spoke, and his hopes plummeted.

"I have to wake up," she muttered to herself. "Why can't I wake up? This is a nightmare. It can't possibly be real. None of this can be happening. Maybe if I pinch myself."

Kees watched, half-impatient and half-confused, as the woman lifted a hand to her opposite arm and twisted a fingerful of flesh.

She yelped and stared up at him. "Holy shit. I'm not dreaming, am I?"

In spite of her words, her eyes did have a glazed appearance. Perhaps the man who had attacked her frightened her more than Kees had thought?

He glanced over his shoulder to see the still-unconscious human slumped where he had landed. He really hadn't been much of a threat. Then Kees recalled what he remembered of humans from his last awakening and bit back a sigh. Some of them did seem to be as cowardly as field mice.

"No, this is no dream," he growled, scowling down at her. He needed to know why he had woken and would prefer to waste no time in finding out. For that, he needed the human awake and aware. "This is, however, a serious matter, and I require answers from you, human. How did you awaken me? Where is the creature I must slay?"

"*Slay?*"

Her squeak even sounded like the noise a mouse might make. Kees sighed. Aloud, this time.

"Where is the threat, human?" he demanded. When she only continued to stare, he stepped forward once more only to see her expression blank and her jaw drop open. Like the animal he'd compared her to, she scurried backwards and watched him as if he'd grown cat's whiskers and a hungry expression.

He made a concerted effort not to swish his tail.

"As I have said, I am no threat to you," he sighed, reading her disbelief in her wary and still dazed appearance. "Come, I will prove it. Take my hand."

He reached out to her, not even noticing the way his thick, razor-sharp talons caught the moonlight and glinted, looking almost liquid in the silvery light. Almost like they'd been coated in blood.

But the woman apparently did notice, because her next squeak turned quickly into a full-fledged scream, and she nearly fell over her own feet as she scrambled away from him.

Damn it, he didn't have time for this.

Muttering a curse, he closed the distance between them in one long stride and seized the woman's arms in a careful grip. He intended nothing more than to stop her from fleeing, but perhaps she misunderstood, because the moment that his rough skin touched her, she raised her hands and blasted him with raw magic.

I have. Lost. My. Mind.

Ella's first thought upon realizing she was about to be attacked for the second time in one night seemed perfectly reasonable to her. What other explanation could there be?

She should have been safe inside the secured confines of the museum property—at least once Patrick Stanley had been escorted from the premises—because she should have been alone. A man with a knife certainly shouldn't have emerged from the shadows and come gliding toward her like a slice of walking evil.

Most of all, though, she should not have just witnessed

a thousand-year-old statue springing to life in her defense, because things like that simply didn't happen. Not in the sane world. Statues didn't move, they didn't fly, they didn't knock would-be muggers unconscious, and they certainly didn't speak to people who had not just slipped over the edge into the land of certifiable lunatics.

Therefore, Ella had lost her mind.

Simple, really.

She was almost ready to close her eyes, click her heels together three times, and head back to Kansas when the statue turned away from her unconscious attacker and held out a hand.

"I won't hurt you," it rumbled.

As if it wasn't a freakin' *gargoyle*!

Him, her impertinent mind quickly corrected. Even with the scrap of fabric masquerading as a loincloth covering up the evidentiary bits, the statue was unquestionably a him. Male. From the top of his horns to the tip of his tail.

Horns!

Tail!

Panic robbed Ella of her voice, so that all that emerged of her intended scream was a strangled, high-pitched chirp. Her heart formed a knot in her throat, and her eyes goggled, staring helplessly as the monster in front of her leaned forward, cutting off the light, the sky, the world, until all she could see was him. Chiseled features, sharp fangs, and eyes like pools of starless night sky.

She nearly passed out.

Fortunately, she caught herself before the edges of her vision could go more than a bit hazy.

Ella had no intention of being the dumb blond girl who got eviscerated before the end of the first act. Not only wasn't she blond, but she was also not dumb, and she was not helpless; and if she found herself almost as scary as she found her present situation, at least she knew that this time, she wouldn't be hurting any innocent bystanders.

Fifteen years ago, Ella had sworn to herself never to open this door again. She had slammed it shut and mentally nailed it over with stout boards. What was inside it, what was inside *her,* had never brought her anything more than fear and pain, but tonight, it might just bring her freedom.

Turning her head away from the sight of the monster who threatened her, she clenched her teeth, braced herself, and reached for the door handle.

It slammed open with the force of a Category 5 hurricane.

Ella tried to steel herself against the screaming. Now she could close her eyes. Now she *had* to close her eyes. She couldn't watch what would follow.

It didn't matter how many times she told herself that she had no choice, that it was her life at stake, that it wasn't like the last time. Last time had been an accident. She hadn't known what would happen, hadn't even recognized it when her control snapped and her world ended. Then, her loss of control cost her everything. This time, she had nothing left to lose.

If she could have stepped out of the stream of energy and run screaming, she would have, but since the badness flowed straight through her, all she could do was to wait for the monster to let her go, and pray that it happened fast. Then she could start forgetting. Again.

She knew her mind replayed the echoes of old screams, and she concentrated on blocking those out. She frowned when she realized that without the memory-screams, the room sounded oddly quiet. The waves of energy created a rushing sound in her ears, like a constantly incoming tide, but nothing sharp or shrill rose above the steady whoosh. No one was screaming.

Cautiously, she opened her eyes and peered through the fringe of her lashes. The creature who held her hadn't moved, hadn't run away, hadn't disappeared into an explosion of light and smoke. He also hadn't been killed, wounded, dismembered, beheaded, or otherwise driven insane. Instead, he just looked annoyed.

Well, annoyed and curious.

"Are you planning to stop anytime soon, or do you plan to exhaust yourself into unconsciousness, human?"

The question startled Ella so much, the energy cut off as if a switch had been thrown. The gargoyle simply continued to loom over her, looking not a bit worse for the wear. Come to think of it, if anything, he looked mildly irritated.

He underlined the impression by glaring down at her and snapping, "Are you finished?"

Ella wondered. Her head was spinning—a side effect she knew came from letting down her barriers and unleashing the darkness inside her—but she couldn't use that to explain why a gargoyle was currently speaking to her. He'd started before she attacked him.

And she *had* attacked him, so why was he still standing?

As if triggered by the thought, Ella's knees gave out, and suddenly *she* was no longer standing. She would have ended up tailbone first on the hard stone terrace if the monster in front of her hadn't moved faster than she could blink and gripped her elbows, catching her weight and easing her down to a sitting position on the pavers.

"Thanks," she mumbled reflexively.

He waved away her gratitude. "I told you that I mean you no harm, but I have questions that I must ask you. Are you well enough to answer?"

The gargoyle had crouched down beside her, but Ella still had to look up to see his face. Maybe that explained the touch of hysteria in her small laugh.

"Me? I'm just fine. I'm hallucinating, because it's either that, or I'm talking to a real live monster at the moment, but other than that, I'm perfect. Ask away."

His mouth firmed, lips pressing together in what Ella guessed was probably not his amused face; then he blew out a breath that sounded like exasperation.

"It disturbs you to look at me? I appear as a monster to you? Fine. Is this better?"

It took Ella a good thirty seconds to remember her name.

Somehow, watching while the monstrous, terrifying creature in front of you aimed a put-upon expression in your direction and then proceeded to transform himself into a vision right out of the pages of *Studs Monthly* could really knock the wind out of a girl.

The thing from a French artist's long-ago vision of might and menace had just become the most blatantly attractive man Ella ever laid eyes on.

Standing at a huge but realistic human height of six feet and three or four inches, the man now crouched in the spot the monster had just been had the heavy, chiseled musculature of a bodybuilder. Not the thick-necked Arnold Schwarzenegger type, though. Even as powerful as he looked, he still managed to appear lean and graceful, as if every muscle in his body hadn't been artificially enlarged, but worked and honed to peak efficiency.

Underneath the jeans and long-sleeved T-shirt that had appeared during his transformation, Ella could see the ripple of contained force and found herself wishing for a better look at all that masculine perfection.

What was she thinking? Ella mentally slapped herself. This was a monster, not a man. Ogling males of other species was a creepy habit she had no intention of developing.

But without the distraction of fangs and horns and, you

know, *wings,* Ella found herself admiring the nearly an-
gelic clarity of his features. His face had actually changed
very little from how it had appeared in his stony form. A
little softer, perhaps, the angles a little less steep, but over-
all he looked nearly the same. She couldn't call him beautiful exactly—his face was too forcefully male for that—but
even so, the combination of the sharp, high cheekbones;
the long, narrow nose; and the hard, tapered jaw shadowed
with the hint of evening scruff threatened the natural balance of her hormones.

And that was before she took into account his eyes.

Monster, El. Not hunk—monster.

Deep and intense, his eyes shone with an inner fire that
burned so clearly, Ella was tempted to reach for a skewer
and a marshmallow. It flickered and flared in pools so
dark, they appeared nearly black, just the barest hint of
gold ringing the centers to distinguish iris from pupil. His
eyes held secrets and power and magic unlike anything
she had ever seen before, anything she had ever imagined.
They caught and held her like a rabbit in a snare, leaving
her feeling just that vulnerable.

Just that tasty.

She shivered, tore her gaze away.

His voice rumbled between them. "Is this form better
for our conversation?" he asked again.

Ella nearly choked on her own tongue. "Ah, yeah. Sure.
You look great. I mean—er, I mean, it's great. The body.
I—that is . . . I mean—" Her cheeks reached approximately
five million degrees. "Uh, it's fine. Thanks," she finished
lamely.

Mr. Studmuffin didn't appear to notice her bout of oral
diarrhea. He nodded once and leaned his forearm on his
knee. "Good. I am called Kees."

Ella dragged her attention away from his body and back
to his words. He had told her his name, because he had a

name, which she supposed shouldn't surprise her now that he was moving and breathing and talking and turning himself into a human. She had to stop thinking of him as a statue.

"Kees," she repeated cautiously. "Rhymes with 'peace.' Ironically enough."

He nodded.

They stared at each other through a stretch of silence, one long enough for the last of Ella's immediate fear to melt away. Logic dictated that if the monster—Kees, she reminded herself; he probably wouldn't like being called "the monster"—had wanted her dead, she'd be halfway through his digestive tract by now.

He had scared the hell out of her and totally altered her understanding of reality, but he hadn't hurt her. That meant the possibility existed that he had no intention of doing so.

Maybe it was time to relax. A little.

Realizing that she sat on her butt with her knees pulled up and the night breeze blowing directly up her skirt, Ella scrambled into a more dignified position. Tucking her legs to one side, she cleared her throat.

"So, uh, Kees . . . Now that we've been introduced, I should thank you, I guess. For, um, leaping to my rescue."

He eyed her. "Only one of us has been introduced."

She flashed him a smile so fake, a bouncer would have tossed it right out the club door. "Oh, right. In all the confusion of losing my mind, I forgot to mention my name, didn't I? It's Ella. Harrow."

"I have many questions that need answers, Ella Harrow, not the least of which is how my slumber has ended with no scent of demon in the air."

His voice in this form sounded only slightly less bass and rumbling than in the other. It tickled her senses like sandpaper, or the rough, warm tongue of a cat. She had to force herself to focus on his words.

"Such questions appear only to confuse you, however," he continued, "so perhaps we might start with something simpler. What is the name of your mentor?"

Ella frowned into his patient expression. He looked like he was making an effort not to intimidate her too badly. She could tell by the way he constantly smoothed out the glare that threatened to pull his dark brows down and together. That, however, didn't make his words any clearer to her.

"I have no clue what you're talking about," she answered, "which is one of the few things reassuring me that you're not a figment of my imagination at this point."

"Your mentor. The one who has been doing such a poor job teaching you to use your powers. What is his name? If he is a member of the Guild of Wardens, he might be able to explain what has awoken me."

"You're still not making any sense to me." She frowned, reaching up to rub her temple, which only served to emphasize the pounding that had begun behind it. "I haven't had a mentor since I left the foster system; the only quote-unquote power I have is the kind I pay BC Hydro for every month; and everything I know about guild systems, I learned in my medieval art classes. Maybe this really is a hallucination. Or one of those really bizarre dreams people have when they eat spicy food before bed."

This time, Kees was unable to smooth away his scowl. "If you give me the name of your mentor, perhaps I can ask my questions of him. He might also be able to explain why you required assistance in dealing with one poorly armed *nocturnis* when even a novice should have been able to dispatch him easily."

Ella tried with all her might to make sense of the words coming out of his mouth. She felt as she had the first time she heard a native Parisian speak to her in French; it was close enough to the Quebecois she was used to for her to make it out eventually, but she had to concentrate. Hard.

"I can't give you the name of someone who doesn't exist," she said. "I told you, I don't have a mentor, and if *nocturnis* is some new term for mugger that I haven't heard of yet, I'd like to know just how I was supposed to deal with a guy coming at me with a knife. Do I look like G.I. Jane with the kung fu grip to you?"

She figured he might have begun to understand, because his expression went from scowl all the way to glower.

"You truly do not understand at all, do you? You honestly mean that you have had no training whatsoever. Not even the most basic shielding and grounding work." He shook his head as if he couldn't believe her ignorance. "No wonder the *nocturnis* thought to seize you with a single kidnapper. It would be no harder than seizing a sleeping kitten."

"Whoa, there. *Kidnapper?*"

Ella felt as if she'd just taken a punch to the solar plexus. The unconscious guy on the terrace hadn't just been a garden-variety mugger? He'd wanted to kidnap her?

"You can't possibly know that's what the guy wanted. He probably just wanted my wallet, not that it would have made him very happy once he'd opened it. But why would anyone want to kidnap me?"

"How is it that a human with so much potential has been allowed to go unnoticed by the Guild?" He muttered to himself and pushed to his feet. "Something must be very wrong for such an oversight to have occurred."

Turning to face her, he placed his hands on his hips and fixed her with a level stare. "I can think of two very important reasons why this scum would want to kidnap you, human. One, he is of the *nocturnis,* and they live to do evil for the sake of evil. And two, you are an untrained Warden. To one like him, and to his masters, you are like a fresh battery, an untapped well of magical energy they could feed off for days, perhaps even weeks. That he has failed to seize you will make this fellow's masters very unhappy indeed."

Ella still didn't fully comprehend what the gargoyle man in front of her was talking about, but she understood enough to make her very uneasy. She didn't see how what he described was possible, but it certainly sounded unpleasant. And there was that word he'd used. That word made her particularly nervous.

"Masters?" She squeaked, "What do you mean, 'masters'? The guy is some kind of slave?"

"He is *nocturnis,* enslaved to the will of one of the Seven, the vilest powers ever known to visit this earth. A demon of the Darkness." His dark eyes seemed to drill into her. "If the *nocturnis* came to kidnap you, it was because his master commanded it, and without training, you have no hope of evading capture. For that, you need me."

Chapter Three

If she lived to be a hundred—something she hadn't really doubted was possible before a gargoyle informed her she was being hunted down by demonic minions—Ella would never forget the trip from the museum garden back to her apartment.

And not for lack of trying.

When a muffled moan had come from the mugger-cum-kidnapper on the terrace, Kees had pointed out that they might not want to still be around when he woke up. Ella had suggested that she would be more than happy to head home and wished the gargoyle a good night.

Like that had worked.

"You think this attack was some sort of aberration? That the demon who sent the *nocturnis* after you will now give up on the idea of finding you and draining you of power until your heart lacks the energy to continue beating?" He had glared down at her like a guardian angel on a bad day, obviously disgusted with her. "You cannot be so naïve. You are in danger, more danger than you know. I will not leave you unguarded until we can be certain you are safe."

No argument she put forward had swayed him. Heck, none of them even looked like they so much as ruffled his hair. Kees remained determined, and eventually Ella had surrendered to the inevitable. She'd invited him home with her.

To be fair, when he asked for her address, she'd thought maybe he would get them a cab, or maybe he had a statue of a car tucked away somewhere that he could bring to life to drive them home. She certainly hadn't expected to see him transform back into his gargoyle form, sweep her up into his arms, and launch them both into the sky.

She'd been forced to muffle her screams against his chest. With her eyes closed and her fingers clenched in a death grip behind his neck, she didn't even have the presence of mind to appreciate the feel of his chiseled muscles wrapped around her, or the way his strength made her feel small and feminine and delicate in his arms.

She was too busy praying she didn't die.

So busy, in fact, that she didn't even notice they had landed until Kees bent down and set her feet on the familiar metal surface of her apartment fire escape. He had to reach up and pry her fingers loose from around his neck, and Ella wasn't ashamed to admit she whimpered once before she let go.

She managed to force her eyelids open with an extraordinary force of will, only to narrow them furiously on her unwelcome mode of transportation.

"Unless I am trapped in a burning building and all the doors and windows have been nailed shut by a homicidal arsonist," she hissed through clenched teeth, "don't you *ever* do that again, do you hear me? I will kill you before you clear floor."

Kees shrank down before her eyes, assuming his human form and a puzzled expression. "I do not understand. How did you propose that we return here from the other location without being seen by any accomplices the *nocturnis* might have had waiting? To fly was the only logical choice."

She could see for herself he believed that. Maybe even when he looked like a human man, his head was still made of stone.

Muttering to herself, Ella spun around and headed for the stairs down to the alley beside her building.

A hand closed over her elbow. "Where are you going? I have said you are not to be alone."

"I'm going downstairs so I can let us into the apartment through the front door. I have no intention of smashing my bedroom window and crawling inside over broken glass."

"Of course not. That would be needlessly destructive."

Reaching out with his free hand, Kees pushed casually against the window sash. The new—and formerly sturdy—lock snapped like a dry twig and the window slid up as if it had been recently oiled.

He waved at the wide opening. "No glass. And this way, no one is likely to see where we have gone."

Ella didn't waste time glaring at him again. She just scrambled inside and got out of the way while he followed close behind her. When he closed the window, she reached for the dowel she had used until the new lock was installed and wedged it between the top frame and the bottom sash in a low-tech but mostly effective security device.

"Is there anything else you'd like to break at the moment? Or can we call it a night? I'm a little bit exhausted." She couldn't quite manage to keep the snark out of her voice, but she was trying very hard not to think about the fact that the most attractive man she'd ever seen now stood right beside her in her darkened bedroom.

If only he'd been human.

Kees shook his head. "We still have many things to

discuss. I have questions that must be answered, and I have been considering the best way to keep you safe. I can guard you for the moment, but while you remain untrained, you will always be in danger. You should be under the care of the Guild. Once we discover what threat I have been awakened to destroy, my duty as a Guardian will take priority over watching you."

And there he went, back to speaking his Parisian French. Ella sighed. "If you're not going to let me sleep, I need to get out of sight of my bed. I can hear it calling to me."

She would not mention that not all the suggestions she heard it make had to do with slumber.

After leading the way into the living room of her small apartment, Ella curled up on one corner of the sofa and waved Kees to a seat. "As long as we're up, maybe you can start making some sense for me. For instance, what is this Guild you keep talking about, and what do you mean when you call yourself a Guardian?"

"I find it difficult to believe that someone as talented as you has had no training and seems so ignorant of matters such as the Guild and the Guardians."

His voice rumbled as he sat not in the chair she had pointed out, but on the other end of the sofa. Too close for comfort.

"It makes no sense for it to be so."

Leaning back, Ella grabbed a throw pillow and clutched it to her chest like armor, eyeing Kees warily—and wearily—over the top.

"Yes, well, in my world, it makes no sense for me to be sitting here talking to someone who used to be a museum display, so I guess shit just happens, huh?" His words registered a second late, and she frowned. "And there you go again. What kind of talent and training are you talking about?"

He turned so that he mostly faced her across the sofa

cushions. "The magic you possess. The power that drew the *nocturnis* and his masters. The talent for it is obvious, and I cannot possibly be the only one ever to have witnessed it."

Ella felt her stomach clench. There were no witnesses to what could happen when she opened that door inside her. None living, anyway. But did that mean what poured out of her when she let down her guard was magic? Real, honest-to-God, change-a-pumpkin-into-a-fancy-carriage magic? Could she Petrificus Totalus people now?

"That's magic?" She croaked, "What comes out when I—? That's magic?"

"Of course, and at your age, it seems inconceivable that the Guild has not approached you and completed your training."

Ella sighed. Did he actually think the words coming out of his mouth amounted to a clarification of anything? "Um, not to be rude here, but you're going to have to break this down even further. People get training for this? Do they go to Hogwarts or something? Or do they go to this Guild you keep mentioning? You're going to have to explain that, because as far as I know, the guild system of work and apprenticeship went out with the Middle Ages."

"I am aware that the world operates differently in these times. I have seen the changes even while I slept. But the Guild of Wardens does not change. It cannot, not while the Guardians remain sleeping under their watch."

He must have caught her glare, because he kept going.

"I am a Guardian. I was created centuries ago to protect humanity from the threat of the Darkness."

"Wait. Created? Like, out of thin air? Or did someone actually carve you out of stone with a chisel and everything?"

"No, I am no carving imbued with life, like some mythical golem. I am a Guardian. A mage summoned me to fight the demon, and I answered."

"Summoned you from where?"

He frowned. "From where I existed."

"And where was that?"

"Somewhere else."

" 'Somewhere else.' Which is where, exactly? Outside Tampa?" The look on his face told Ella he didn't really understand what she was asking, or that she was joking. Or what a joke was. "Never mind. Just go on."

It took a second for him to start again, as if he had to search his memory for the place where he'd left off. It wasn't the first time she'd had that effect on someone. "Mages summoned us in the beginning to battle the demons—"

"Us? You mean there are other statues out there coming to life and scaring the crap out of innocent bystanders?"

The look he gave her summed up his feelings on her latest interruption. "I am one of seven, and we are not statues. We are Guardians."

"But you look like statues. Or are the other six of you somehow more outlandish than living gargoyles?"

" 'Gargoyles' is not our favorite term." His expression darkened like a thundercloud, and Ella clutched her pillow tighter.

"It's better than 'grotesques,' right? 'Cause, technically, that's what I should be calling you."

"You should be calling us Guardians."

His voice held enough growling irritation to have her nodding her agreement, whether she'd intended to or not.

"The Guardians were summoned by the first mages of the Guild. Those mages banded together to share knowledge and gather information on the demons we battled, and thus formed the Guild. They share that information with us, tell us what the evil forces plan, assist in battling against them, warding us against their evil. They monitor the activities of humans who are enslaved or seduced by the dark powers, and fight against their expanding influence. They bid us to slumber when the threat of the Darkness is defeated, and they recognize when the danger returns, waking us in time to foil its plans. They are the Guild of Wardens, and even when we slumber, they have always stood vigilant."

Ella tried to process all that, sifting through the story's details for its bones, and then gnawing on them for a minute. "So, you and your six buddies are some kind of demon hunters? And this Guild you keep talking about is like . . . the Alfreds to your Batmen?"

He just stared at her.

Apparently, he hadn't been waking up periodically to catch up with the DC Universe since—

Sheesh, when had he been crea—er, first summoned? And did she really want to know?

"They're your assistants," she clarified, watching his expression carefully. "They handle the research and pesky material details while you do the hunting and killing thing."

"Demons cannot be killed. They are immortal. All we can do is force them to use up their power until they weaken and then banish them from this plane."

"Ah, so that's why you were just sleeping through the centuries and not back wherever it was you came from." Was she finally beginning to understand him? And what did that say about her sanity?

"They also recruit and train the next generation of Wardens. Unlike the demons and the Guardians, the Wardens are humans with the ability to harness magic. They do not live forever, so they must pass their duties on to a younger mage when they near the end of their lives. Some pass the duties down through the family lines, to their sons and occasionally their daughters, but when a mage has no offspring, he will recruit an unrelated human with proven magical talents. One like you."

Ella could think of several reasons why a bunch of mages charged with helping avert the end of the world wouldn't want to trust someone like her with the job. The biggest one still echoed in her head whenever her "magic" spilled out of her control.

She forced out a casual shrug. "Huh. Guess there weren't any job openings around here. Wait. Are the other, um, Guardians here in Vancouver? Is this where the Guild is based?"

"No. I couldn't say where each of us is stationed today. Clearly, while we sleep, we can find ourselves moved to new locations. My brethren could be almost anywhere. But the Guild always remains in one place. Our individual Wardens will travel along with us, but the base of the Guild has for centuries been in Paris."

"France?"

"Of course."

Ella blinked. If she thought about it, she supposed it made sense. If these Guardians had been around for centuries, Europe was the logical place for them to have begun. Well, Europe or the Orient or Africa, but Kees's appearance, in either form, was distinctly Western. And Paris's collection of gargoyles and grotesques had made the city famous for hundreds of years. Still, it was weird to think of this man being French. He spoke English, after all, with no trace of an accent. She supposed a thousand years or so of practice could take care of that kind of thing.

"Right." She drew a breath and forced herself to focus back on the here and now. "Well, I've never been there. Heck, I've only barely been to the U.S., so it's not a big surprise that a group of guys from Europe didn't scoop me up for their secret club. I probably just never ran into one."

"You have enough magic that they should have noticed you long ago. They monitor for such things, and even with no Wardens ready to retire, you would have been sought out for training at the very least, and possibly a support role within the Guild. Standing against the Darkness requires constant vigilance and many keen eyes. No, something clearly is not right with the Guild. I need to discover what it is."

"So how come you're sitting here talking to me and not spreading your wings toward Paris?"

While he'd been easing her into this crazy new world of his, his expression had remained aloof and cool, like a professor instructing a class full of not-so-bright students, but when she asked that question, he turned his gaze on her. Suddenly those black eyes glinted sharper than an obsidian blade.

"Because none of that explains what woke me from my slumber, little human. For that, I suspect I must look to you."

Ella felt her chest seize and reminded herself to remain calm. Having all that inhuman intensity focused on her was not a comfortable experience. She wanted to deflect it somewhere else. Anywhere else.

"I don't know what you think I have to do with anything. I mean, clearly if I didn't know you existed until after you, er, woke up, then I'm not the one who woke you up. If you Guardians are big defenders of evil, then maybe you woke up just to defend me from that nocturnal guy. I did scream pretty loud when I saw him."

"No, it is impossible. The Guardians slumber until one of the demons of the Darkness stirs. If I am awake, there must be something very grave afoot. I cannot sense a demon directly, but perhaps my earlier theory is partially correct." He eyed her with speculation. "Perhaps the *nocturnis* are working toward summoning one of them, and they think to use you and others like you to feed the creature and restore its strength once it has reappeared."

Oh, this just kept getting better and better.

"Maybe you should just go ask this Warden of yours. I'm sure he'll be more helpful than I am, and you don't need me for that."

Kees made no move to leave, not by the door and not by the window to the fire escape where he'd come in. In fact, he didn't stir from the sofa. The only movement he made was a slow shake of his head.

"No. Of course, I will find Gregory and ask him many questions, but I have no intention of letting you out of my sight. You clearly had something to do with my awakening, and the Guild will want to know what that was. They will want to meet you."

"Um, no offense or anything, but I don't particularly want to meet them."

He watched her so intently that she squirmed— literally—under his gaze.

"Look, I had nothing to do with you waking up. Just because I was there, doesn't mean I had any effect on you whatsoever. And frankly, this is all a little much for me to deal with. I'd be a lot happier if you just went off to find your buddies and save the world, or whatever, and forgot all about me. That's what I'm going to try to do."

Kees frowned, and she tried to ignore the way that made her want to squirm some more.

"I do not believe you have that option, little human," he said. "What you have learned cannot be unlearned, and having met you, I must inform the Guild of your existence. I've never met a human who needed training more than you."

She glared at him. "I'm not a dog. 'Training' can go screw itself."

"You lack any sort of control over your magic. Such recklessness could lead to dire consequences. Your inability to control your power could harm another human. And if you do not learn how to use the energy, you will always be vulnerable to those like the *nocturnis* and their masters, who would seek to feed off your power. Is that what you want?"

Ella's stomach knotted up like an old-fashioned telephone cord. She didn't want that. She'd never wanted that. Not now, and not when it had happened the last time. She just wanted to be normal: safe, sane, and harmless. Was that so much to ask?

"I'm not going to hurt anyone," she protested, her voice as tight as her jaw. "The magic doesn't have to come out. I can keep it locked up. If I never use it, it can never hurt anyone." Again.

"It can hurt you." His eyes narrowed as he watched her intently. "I think it already has hurt you, and you cannot keep it locked up forever. If you try, one of two things will happen: either the magic will build up to the point where it will explode through any barriers you attempt to use to contain it—and in that case, people will undoubtedly be hurt—or it will stop attempting to move through you and will begin consuming you instead. Magic is like a river coursing through stone; eventually it will eat away at the rock until a canyon is all that is left.

"Is either of those what you want?"

She squeezed the pillow so tightly, some poor goose probably felt it up in heaven. "I don't want any of it. I don't want the magic at all."

"The magic is part of you. You don't have that choice. Unless you would prefer to have it drained from you by the *nocturnis* and their masters. Of course, I'm afraid that is one experience you would not survive. Is that your choice?"

At the moment, Ella didn't feel like she had any choices worthy of the name.

"The only way forward is for you to enter the Guild, little human," he continued, rolling right over her objections in a manner that was starting to feel a bit too familiar. "They can teach you how to use your power, and how to contain it when you are not using it. A little knowledge will go a long way toward ensuring both your safety and the safety of those around you."

It was the one thing he could have said to keep Ella from digging in her heels and sprinting for the nearest exit. As much as she wanted to ignore his words, as much as she wanted to close her eyes and pretend that the events of this night had never happened, she'd wanted that for only a couple of hours. She'd wanted to keep from harming people for most of her life.

For the last twelve years, she'd wanted it more than life itself. Could Kees and his Guild really give that to her?

She forced herself to keep her tone level and reasonable. "So how would that work? You make a phone call to Paris and give them my e-mail address, or something?"

"No, little human. I take you to my Warden, and then we find out not only how well you can control your magic, but why after a thousand years, you were the one to draw me from my slumber."

"And keep me from being kidnapped and sucked dry by the bad guys, right?"

"We can but try."

"Try really hard."

Chapter Four

When she spotted the crowd gathered in front of the museum an hour before opening on an ordinary Sunday morning, Ella realized she'd forgotten one very significant detail about the events of the past several hours. Namely, that another museum employee with a keen eye and sharp intellect might perhaps notice the unexplained disappearance of a half-ton limestone statue from the terrace. And such a disappearance had the potential to make people wonder where said statue might have disappeared to.

She kind of doubted anyone would guess he was standing right next to Ella as she drew to a stop a few feet short of a police cruiser complete with flashing lights parked at the curb. Crap. What was she supposed to do now?

"Ella!"

Before she could make a decision, she saw the crowd on the sidewalk part and Bea come rushing through to her side.

"I've been watching for you," the assistant curator said, sounding agitated and more than a little worried. "I tried calling your apartment this morning, but you must have already left for work. I was so worried! I thought something might have happened to you last night after we parted. I was ready to kick myself for agreeing to let you take yourself home."

Ella returned the woman's spontaneous hug and realized she should have taken a drama minor in college. She was going to have to act as if she had no idea what was going on despite the sinking feeling in her stomach and the knowledge that she had, in a way, just committed a major art heist.

"No, no, I'm fine," she assured Bea, mustering up an expression of puzzlement. "What's going on? Why are the police here?"

"We've had a robbery." Bea pulled back, her expression a mix of grief and anger. The woman treated the pieces in her collections like her own children, with a combination of pride, love, and possessiveness. "Someone stole Sir Arthur."

"Sir Arthur? How is that even possible? He must weigh at least eight or nine hundred pounds. Somebody would need a forklift just to get him off the pedestal."

"The police are already back there looking for tire tracks, footprints, anything they can think of, but heaven knows what they'll find. I certainly can't explain how it happened. All I know is that when I came in this morning, I let the gardener out the terrace doors and he turned right around and shouted that our gargoyle had flown the coop."

It took a supreme act of willpower for Ella not to cast a sideways glance at Kees, who remained still and quiet beside her. Luckily, he still looked like a human and not the very statue that Bea had told the police was stolen.

"Wow, I can't even believe that," she murmured, shaking her head for effect.

"You're not the only one. If not for the big space and empty pedestal where he used to be, I don't think the police would believe it either." Bea stepped back and her glance drifted over to Kees. Her brows shot up and she looked from the gorgeous, towering male to Ella's petite form. "I'm sorry, I'm being rude. Ella, is this a friend of yours?"

Oh no, he's just my mythological kidnapper slash cross to bear.

Ella opened her mouth to offer some sort of explanation— heaven only knew what it was going to be—but Kees beat her to it. He smiled easily at the other woman and held out a hand.

"I'm Kees, Ella's . . . companion," he said, the pause implying a whole bunch of levels to the relationship that Ella would truly have preferred not to visit. "It is a pleasure to meet you."

"The pleasure is all mine. As is the surprise," Bea said, slanting Ella a sly, sideways glance. "I don't recall Ella mentioning you. She must have wanted to keep you all to herself for a while."

Kees grinned and slung his arm across Ella's shoulders, drawing her close against him. "The feeling is entirely mutual."

Ella wondered if the pain would be mutual when she elbowed him in the stomach. "We haven't actually known each other that long, so there really hasn't been a lot to tell."

"Hm, looks like there's enough for the man to be walking you to work in the morning. I think that's pretty telling."

Bea's teasing tone set Ella's nerves on edge. She knew her boss didn't mean anything but friendly humor, but being pressed up against Kees's side like a cold compress didn't strike Ella as funny. It struck her as . . . deeply disturbing.

Her eyes told her that the gargoyle's human disguise

remained flawless. No one looking at him would guess him to be anything other than a drool-inducing hunk of a man, the same as any other movie-star handsome guy walking down the streets of Vancouver. But Ella knew that under that tan skin and rippling muscle was a creature with horns and wings and fangs, the kind that stepped straight out of a nightmare.

So why did her skin tingle when he touched her? And why did her heartbeat speed up as if her teenaged crush had just passed her a note in study hall?

Ella attempted to pull herself together and offered Bea a rueful smile. "It should tell you that he's a guy and that he had to come to the area this morning on business anyway. Right, Kees?"

His hand tightened on her shoulder when she tried to slip away, and under the friendly upturn of his lips, she read both his warning not to move and his humor at her desire to do so. "You know I can never argue with you, little one."

Her surprised choke of laughter probably struck Bea as part of a silly exchange between lovers. Ella meant it as punctuation for the seven thousand things they'd fought over in the last eight hours, from whether or not he intended to kill her, to the fact that she had no intention of letting him sleep in her apartment last night, to the fact that he should stay out of sight while she was at work and wait for her to bring the information regarding the address he'd come from to him at the end of the day.

So far, the only argument she'd won had been the one about her not dying, and really that was only because he'd never wanted to kill her in the first place. Technically, he'd let her win that one.

Bea looked from one to the other, smiling in obvious pleasure. She'd been nagging Ella for months about dating more and meeting a nice man, and she was obviously inclined to like Kees just for existing. At least, while he stayed in this form, she was. Of course, even an inclination couldn't suppress Béatrice's instinct to mother.

"Business," Bea repeated, fixing her gaze back on the gargoyle in human's clothing. "What kind of business are you in, Kees? If you don't mind my asking."

The steel underlying her tone implied that she didn't really care if he did.

Ella stiffened, but Kees seemed to take the question in stride. His expression remained friendly and relaxed as he replied, "Not at all. I work in private security."

Bea's brows rose. "So you're a bodyguard, then? That sounds exciting. You protect famous people from crazy fans?"

"Something like that, at least part of the time. Not that I work with celebrities, or anything exciting. There's actually more standing around and waiting for things to happen in my line of work than most people think."

The urge to haul back and kick the huge monster's shin nearly overwhelmed Ella. He sounded so casual and easy answering Bea's questions, as if he'd done the same thing a thousand times before. No hesitation, no searching for a plausible cover story, and not even any whopping lies. He *was* in private security, if you counted keeping the world safe from demons—and even Ella had to admit that probably did count—and protecting people from the ultimate evil. Even his comment on there being a lot of waiting around in his job rang with truth. He was being completely honest.

And it drove Ella out of her mind bonkers.

But maybe she was just feeling a little tense.

Bea nodded and glanced back over her shoulder at the people milling in front of the museum. The crowd didn't appear to be thinning, but now there were some uniforms mixed in with the spectators, and Ella could see

Dr. Lefavreau standing at the top of the steps near the door, speaking with a tall man in a sports jacket.

"Well, I shouldn't keep you from your business, Kees," the assistant curator said, turning back to face them with another smile. Ella thought this one looked forced. "And Ella and I will need to speak with the police and our director. Everyone who works for the museum will need to be interviewed, and it will likely take some time. In fact, I would not be surprised if the decision was made to close the museum for the day, so I can't even offer a tour of the exhibits to distract you until Ella can be swept off for a romantic lunch."

Kees nodded politely to indicate he heard Bea's words, but Ella could see he had his gaze fixed on the figures on the steps. When his eyes narrowed, she noticed a flicker of movement inside the open doorway and saw Patrick Stanley lurking in the shadows like a rat. Or a vulture. Something stinking and carrion-feeding and potentially rabid.

She cursed under her breath.

"What is it?" Bea asked.

Ella pointed.

This time, Bea cursed. In French. "Just what we need to make an unpleasant situation unbearable."

Ella watched as the other woman stalked off, and stepped out from under Kees's arm. "You should go. The police are going to want to talk to me, and there's no way to tell how long this will all take."

She dug into her purse, pulled out her cell phone, and handed it to him. "Here. Take this. I'll try to find a way to get into the files as soon as I can, and I'll call you, either when I know something or when they kick me out. Or haul me off to jail."

Turning, she moved to follow Béatrice toward the museum. It took about two steps before she acquired a large male shadow. The glare she sent his way had no impact on him whatsoever, and they reached the group gathered near the door before she had time to tell him to bugger off.

"Ella." Dr. Lefavreau greeted her in his usual serious tone, but she could detect no hint of extra disapproval in his voice. Maybe Stanley hadn't had time to sufficiently embellish his story about last night. "How are you this morning?"

"I'm well, sir, thank you. And you?"

He certainly didn't look like a very happy man. Maurice Lefavreau was a white man in his sixties with a thick head of white hair, even thicker black-framed glasses, and the barrel-shaped torso of a man used to fine food and French wines. He looked as much like a banker as a museum director, but his knowledge of and appreciation for art made his dark eyes dance with excitement whenever the museum acquired a special new piece. Ella had always liked him, and he tended to treat all the members of the museum staff as if he were a benevolent uncle to each of them.

"I'm distressed, Ella, very distressed." He frowned and clasped his hands behind his back. "I take it that Béatrice has filled you in on our terrible misfortune?"

Ella schooled her face into a mask of dismay. It wasn't difficult, considering it was a feeling she'd spent a lot of time with since last night. "She said that one of our statues was missing, sir. The terrace gargoyle? But I can't imagine how someone could have simply made off with a piece quite so large and heavy."

"Neither can I, my dear. Neither can I. That's why I'm hoping the police can shed some light on the matter. This is Detective McQuaid. He will be heading the investigation for us. Detective, Ms. Harrow is the manager of our gift shop and one of our most popular docents. She was working last night at our fund-raising event, along with Béatrice."

If Ella had tried to conjure up an image of a police investigator, Detective McQuaid would not have been it. She'd likely have gone with someone older, a world-weary man in his fifties, graying hair, soft around the middle. In contrast, McQuaid appeared to be in his thirties, Caucasian, with sandy-colored hair, the build of an athlete, and the rugged features of a high school football star all grown up. Instead of ingrained cynicism, his expression appeared open, and his blue eyes glinted with humor.

And when he looked at Ella, there was a definite spark of masculine interest.

Then he held out his hand, and his gaze flicked to Kees. Understandable, considering that the minute the detective had shifted closer, the gargoyle once again placed a possessive hand on Ella's shoulder.

She ignored it and shook the detective's hand. "Detective McQuaid."

"Ms. Harrow. It's a pleasure to meet you." He shifted his gaze back to her face and flashed her a smile that could only be called charming. Maybe boyish. "I understand you were here late last night. After the event officially ended?"

"That's right. Bea and I were the last ones here."

"And did you notice anything unusual?"

Kees felt Ella stiffen under his hand. He'd learned enough about the little human in the last few hours to know she must be biting her tongue to keep from responding to that question the way she wanted to. In her eyes, she'd seen nothing but the unusual.

Instead of giving in to the snort he half expected, she replied with calm sincerity. "No, nothing at all. Once the guests left, everything was quiet. Perfectly normal."

"You didn't see anyone who didn't belong at the museum?"

"No."

"And you left the museum with Dr. Boucher?"

She nodded.

The door to the museum opened further and a man shifted forward. "I'm not certain that's quite the truth, Detective," he sneered. "But maybe Ms. Harrow has trouble telling the truth about many things. I saw Dr. Boucher leave the museum a little before one A.M., and Ms. Harrow definitely did not accompany her."

Béatrice, the woman who had first greeted Kees and Ella upon their arrival shot the man a pointed look. "Do you really want to get into what happened here last night, Mr. Stanley? Right here on the museum's front steps? Should we do that now?"

Kees heard the hostility and the challenge behind the woman's frosty civility and took a second look at the man in the doorway. He appeared smooth and sharp and oozing with arrogance, and his eyes glinted with hunger and violence whenever he looked at Ella. He was the man on the terrace last night, the one who had attacked the little human.

Kees felt his lip curve in a snarl. He couldn't help the low sound that rumbled in his chest.

"Perhaps Béatrice is right," the museum director said, stepping forward to cut through the rising tension. "I'm certain we can do this more comfortably in my office. Or perhaps, since there are so many of us, in the ballroom."

The detective agreed genially, and the group moved forward, Kees sticking to his human like pine sap and ignoring her surreptitious pokes to his rib cage. He had no plans to leave her alone, not with the mortal authorities and the human male from last night each posing a threat to her safety. Not only did he need Ella to help him locate Gregory Lascaux, his missing Warden, but something about her brought out all his protective instincts.

The group moved into the ballroom, or what had once been a ballroom and now served as the museum's large West Gallery. Kees felt the museum director's gaze on him and offered him a questioning look.

"Forgive me, but I don't believe we've met." Lefavreau frowned and glanced from him to Ella. "Ella, will you introduce me to your companion?"

The little human stifled a groan, but Kees's sharp hearing detected the quiet rumble.

"Dr. Lefavreau, I'm so sorry. Kees, this is Dr. Maurice Lefavreau, the director of the museum. Doctor, this is Kees. He's, um . . ."

"I am a close friend of Ella's. I was walking with her to work this morning when we saw the commotion outside."

The older man nodded shortly. "I'm certain you'll understand if I insist that only the museum staff be involved in this morning's business. With the nature of the matter at hand, strangers just . . ."

He trailed off when he saw Kees's expression go stony.

"I will stay with Ella." Kees purposely kept his tone low and allowed a hint of menace to creep into his tone. He had no intention of allowing his little human out of his sight in company like this.

The group stopped and congregated around the two wooden benches positioned in the center of the open space. As soon as they halted, Stanley turned to face Bea, going immediately on the offensive.

"Yes, I do want to talk about what happened last night, Béatrice. I warned you I would be bringing the incident up to your employer," he snapped before he addressed the museum director. "Maurice, I'm uncertain what either of these . . . women may have told you about our interactions last night, but I—"

The detective interrupted. "Before anyone starts going into details about last night, I'm going to stop you. I'd

prefer to hear from each of you individually. Dr. Lefavreau, if I could accept the offer of your office to do that?"

"Of course, of course." The doctor waved a hand to indicate McQuaid should follow him. "Allow me to escort
you there."

"Appreciate it." McQuaid turned and smiled at Ella.
"You mind coming first, Ms. Harrow?"

Kees definitely didn't like the hint of suggestion lacing
the detective's smile, and when Ella nodded and moved to
follow the two human men, Kees kept right on her heels.
McQuaid caught the movement and his smile faded.

"I'm afraid I need to speak with Ms. Harrow alone," the
man said, straightening his shoulders and still falling at
least three inches short of Kees's imposing height. "You can
wait out here."

Baring his teeth in something close enough to a smile to
lie about it, Kees dug in his heels. "I go where she goes."

"Look—"

Ella put her hand on Kees's arm. "It's fine, Kees. Really. I'm sure this won't take long. Just *wait for me here.*"

Not what Kees wanted to hear, but the intensity behind
her words was hard to miss. He knew she was determined
to keep him at arm's length—she'd been attempting to do
so since the moment he first moved from his pedestal
(though at that point, he doubted her arms had been long
enough to suit her)—but he disliked that idea. He couldn't
protect his human if she wouldn't let him stay with her, and
somehow the compulsion to protect her was strong. Stronger than he'd ever experienced before.

Normally, humans as individuals meant little to him.
He had been summoned to protect the species as a
whole, but it wasn't his job to go around rescuing them
one by one. He kept the demons at bay so that they could
live their lives, however long or short those might be. He
barely noticed that they differed from one another, let

alone cared what happened to any one of them. How could he, when Guardians didn't fall prey to the burden of human emotions?

Oh, Guardians experienced anger—rage against the demons gave them strength to their purpose—and certainly, he had experienced frustration at times during his long slumber or when a demon didn't go into exile so quickly as he might like, but he'd never felt any of the more human emotions. He felt a brotherly bond with his fellow Guardians, but he didn't suffer from fear or jealousy or possessiveness.

And he certainly didn't consider himself capable of caring for a human. So what was it about Ella Harrow that made him react so differently than he had in the past? It was something he might have to ask Gregory.

As soon as they found him.

Ella squeezed his arm tightly, and he scowled down at her.

"Fine." The word sounded less than sincere, but he had led the other humans to believe he was Ella's lover, so if they believed him to be irrationally jealous or possessive as well, so be it. It didn't make it true. "I will wait for you. But if you have need of me, call out, and I will be by your side in an instant. Do you understand?"

She looked up at him with a combination of surprise and wariness in her gaze. It made the gray depths of her eyes darken like storm clouds.

She nodded. "I understand."

A strange impulse grabbed Kees, and he found himself grasping her around the waist and tugging her against him. She had to crane her head to keep her eyes on his face, and he took advantage by swooping down and sealing his lips against hers.

She stiffened in his arms. Her hands went up to press against his chest, and he tightened his grip in warning.

Let her think he feared the detective and the others seeing through their act. In reality, he simply wanted to savor the moment.

She felt soft and sweet against him, a sweetness that was mirrored in her taste, all warm sugar with a hint of spring violets. Her lips even felt like the petals of a delicate flower, and they bloomed open when he traced his tongue along the plump surface of the lower one. Diving in, Kees forgot all about their audience and continued kissing her for the simple pleasure of it.

He experienced a surge of desire that took him by surprise.

Desire? For a human? When he pulled back, she looked up at him through hazy eyes, her brows drawing together in confusion. He understood the feeling.

"Go answer your questions," he murmured. "I'll wait right here until you return."

And maybe while she was gone, he'd be able to figure out just what the hell was going on, why she made him feel more like a man than like a monster.

She offered an uncertain smile and turned to follow the museum director and the detective down a hall toward the rear of the house. Kees watched her go, ignoring the curious looks of the other humans. None of them could possibly be more puzzled by his behavior than he was.

What had the little human done to him?

What in heaven's name had the gargoyle done to her?

Ella sat in Lefavreau's office facing his desk and the classically handsome police detective perched on the corner. The director had told them to make themselves comfortable, handed McQuaid a file containing all the museum's paperwork on the provenance of the missing statue, then returned to join the others.

Ella knew she should be focusing on ways to get a

good look at the information in that folder, but her attention lingered back in the ballroom. More specifically, on the lips of a certain male monster who seemed determined to throw her off balance at every turn, first by not killing her, and now by pressing on her the most intensely sweet kiss of her life. What in God's name was going on?

"Guess your boyfriend's the possessive type, huh?"

McQuaid's voice broke into her thoughts and dragged her attention back to the present. She felt her cheeks flush.

"I don't—I guess. I mean, we haven't been seeing each other very long," she stuttered, her gaze sliding away from his. How was she supposed to explain something she didn't understand herself? "I'm not even certain how serious it is."

"Well, looked serious for him, at least. Not that I can blame him for feeling possessive over such a lovely woman."

Before Ella could decide if that comment was flattering or uncomfortable, McQuaid looked down at the folder in his hands and flipped through the pages. Then he set it aside and drew a small notebook from his jacket pocket. Finally, something she expected a detective to do.

"Dr. Lefavreau said you and Ms. Boucher were the last two people in the museum last night. Is that correct?"

Ella met his gaze and nodded. "That's right. We shut things down behind the guests, made sure the caterers got everything cleared away and cleaned up, then locked up once everyone was out. I think it was around one o'clock."

"But Mr. Stanley said you didn't leave together."

Her mouth tightened. "No. Béatrice left by the front doors, locking the house and setting the alarms behind her. She encouraged me to go out by the back gate in the garden. I'm fond of the gardens, so she knows I leave that way a lot. She wouldn't need to check that gate, because it locks automatically behind whoever goes out that way."

The detective studied her, his expression still open, but his blue eyes sharp. His mouth curved in a small smile. "You and Ms. Boucher aren't big fans of Patrick Stanley, are you?"

"To be fair, he's not wild about us, either."

"There some sort of history to that?"

The question sounded casual, but Ella debated with herself before she answered. "I'm assuming you were paying attention when he and Bea had words outside?"

McQuaid's mouth quirked. "Kind of my job."

"Right. Well, I don't know Mr. Stanley well. I've only met him a couple of times, and always at museum events or when he stopped by to talk to Dr. Lefavreau, but he . . . makes me uncomfortable."

The detective said nothing, and Ella paused. Patrick Stanley was a wealthy and powerful man. She would have to choose her words carefully and not make any direct accusations. She didn't have the money to defend against a defamation suit.

"After the event, when Bea and I thought we were the last ones here, I was on my way across the terrace toward the back gates, like I said, and Mr. Stanley just popped up out of nowhere. He startled me. I thought the gardens were empty. He attempted to start a conversation, but I just wanted to go home. It was late, and I was exhausted."

"Understandable."

"I tried to move him along. I offered to escort him out front to unlock the door for him, but he . . ."

How could she say this delicately?

"He hit on you."

Ella started to nod, then caught herself. That way there be dragons. "Excuse me?"

McQuaid laughed. "It's not hard to figure out. Attractive young woman. Dark garden. No witnesses. And Mr. Stanley is known to appreciate attractive women."

That was one way of putting it.

Ella just shrugged. She had no intention of confirming that for the record. Did they still have debtor's prisons?

"Mr. Stanley made a few comments that I found inappropriate, but Bea came out of the house and interrupted. She showed him out the front, and I stayed back on the terrace to regain my composure."

"This is the terrace where the statue was located?"

"Yes."

"And it was there during this whole time?"

She nodded. "I actually sat down on the edge of the pedestal while I pulled myself together. I remember tilting my head back and looking up at it. It's always been one of my favorite pieces."

"You said this was a little before one?"

"Between twelve thirty and one. I wasn't checking my watch, but the party ended at midnight, and the caterers were super-efficient. I do remember it was about twenty after twelve when they climbed into their truck."

"Okay, go on. You were alone on the terrace for how long?"

Until the missing statue came to life and left the museum of its own accord?

"Not very, I don't think. It was late, and you might say I had a stressful night. Once I got a hold of myself, I didn't hang around."

McQuaid watched her steadily. "Why didn't you go with Ms. Boucher and leave where she could keep an eye on you? Wouldn't that have made you feel safer?"

Ella grimaced. "To be honest, I needed a minute to myself, and I didn't want to spend another second in Mr. Stanley's company, even with a chaperone. The altercation had shaken me up, and I've always found the gardens peaceful, especially the terrace. Like I said, the gargoyle statue was my favorite, so I used to hang out there occasionally."

"Okay."

"I spent about five, maybe ten more minutes just taking deep breaths and pulling myself together. Then—" She caught herself as she recalled what had happened then. How reality had tilted on its axis and Sir Arthur magically sprang to life. But that was exactly what she couldn't tell the police.

She finished with a shrug to cover her hesitation. "Then I made my way through the garden and out the back gate."

McQuaid jotted down additions to a couple of his notes, then glanced up at her. "After leaving the garden, did you go straight home?"

"Yes." Hell yes. At top speed. A couple of hundred feet above the skyline.

"How far away do you live? You take the bus?"

Ella hesitated, then carefully edited events. No reason to make him talk to bus drivers in vain. Obviously, none of them had seen her. "Usually I take the bus. My apartment's about twenty blocks from here, but last night I went on foot."

The detective looked up, his brows lifting. "What made you decide to do that?"

Um, the monster who scooped me up didn't give me much choice.

"I guess I needed more time to clear my head." Which was true, even if the rest of her statement wasn't. Precisely "When I hit the bus stop, there wasn't one in sight, and at that hour, I didn't feel like waiting around. I just wanted to get home."

"Well, at least you made it safely. What did you do with the rest of your night?"

"I stayed in. Got cleaned up, went to bed."

"And was anyone with you at your apartment?"

"Um." She hesitated, then nodded. "Yes. Kees stayed the night."

McQuaid just hummed and acknowledgment and made another note. "Anything else you can remember? Did you see anyone suspicious on the street when you left the museum grounds by the back gate?"

Ella had been too far above the streets to notice much of anything. Even if she'd had her eyes open. And hadn't been praying for her life. "Not that I can recall. It was late, though, and I was kind of in my own little world. I just wanted to get home and get to bed."

Where she could hide under the covers. Too bad that strategy hadn't worked.

"Okay. Well, if you thin—" A shrill chime sounded from the detective's pocket, and he reached in for his cell phone. "Excuse me." He poked at the screen. "McQuaid."

Ella watched while he listened to someone on the other end of the connection. Then he held up a finger, muttered something into the phone, and stood.

"Gotta take this. Just give me a second." He stepped out of the office and clicked the door shut behind him.

She wasted half a second wondering at the stroke of luck before good sense kicked in and she grabbed the file folder off the desk. Rifling through the papers inside, she skimmed quickly through the information before she found what she was looking for. Committing a name and partial address to memory, she placed the folder back where she had found it and resumed her seat a second before the door opened and McQuaid stepped back inside.

"Sorry about that." His boyish grin flashed again.

"No problem." Ella smiled. "You had more questions for me?"

"No, we're finished, but I wanted to give you this." He pulled a business card out of his shirt pocket and handed it to her. "This is where I officially tell you that if you think of anything else, you should call me at the station."

Ella stood and took the card between her fingers, but

the detective didn't let go. Surprised, she glanced up at him.

His smile widened, and his eyes warmed. "Unofficially, I'm also going to tell you that if you ever find yourself without that possessive boyfriend, you should also call. I'd love the chance to take you to dinner sometime."

Shock made her do a double take. The police officer was flirting with her? That meant he'd believed her story and she wasn't a suspect, right?

"I—um—I mean, thank you."

McQuaid released the card and reached around her to open the door to the small office. "Thank you, Ella. If you wouldn't mind, ask Dr. Lefavreau to come up next. I want to clarify a few things about the statue with him."

She agreed and stepped outside, trying not to appear to hurry. On a normal day, she would have wanted to dash to Bea's side for a little girl talk about the attractive cop who'd asked her to call him. Personally. But today, the only thing on her mind was getting back to Kees to share the information she'd found in the file.

What in heaven had the gargoyle done to her?

Chapter Five

Ella hated to drive. She actually hated even riding in cars, which was one of the reasons she chose to live in the city, where walking and buses and trains could get her wherever she needed to go. Unfortunately, the address in Kees's file couldn't be reached by bus, and walking there would take approximately a day and a half, along with superior wilderness survival skills. A car was the only option, and Ella didn't own a car.

The rental made her grit her teeth and wince. Not only was she not comfortable driving anything bigger than the compact little Ford she'd used to test for her license years ago, but the idea of all the paperwork and insurance claim forms she would have to fill out if she damaged the hulking SUV during their trip did little to improve her mood either.

Nor did the way her mind kept straying back to *The Kiss*.

She italicized it in her head, as if it were the painting by Klimt. How something as simple as a kiss could have rocked her world on its axis astounded her. And unnerved her. Especially since the man who laid it on her hadn't so much as mentioned it since she rejoined him in the museum ballroom post-interview. No, he'd been too focused on the information she had to give him. She might as well have become a computerized information kiosk, for all the attention he paid her. It was like he had no emotions at all.

Maybe she should remind herself that he was made out of stone, after all.

Too bad his lips hadn't felt like rock. They had felt like sex, all smooth and hot and hard as they moved over hers, urging them apart, urging her to feel things she'd never felt before with a man, let alone a monster.

Yeah, she'd used the *M*-word again. She had to; it was becoming her only self-defense mechanism. The things she felt when Kees kissed her, or touched her, or, you know, so much as looked at her had her hormones and her brain chemicals spinning little stories about lust and passion and all sorts of other things it was completely inappropriate to associate with a member of another species. She needed to remember that.

And she needed to keep her legs crossed, which wasn't really possible while she was driving north out of Vancouver toward the small village of Lions Bay.

Kees sat beside her in the passenger seat, his huge form taking up every inch of space even inside the behemoth SUV that had been the only available rental on short notice. He had his arms crossed over his chest, and his gaze slid constantly back and forth between Ella and the road ahead of them. She didn't mistake his intense scrutiny for personal interest, though. She knew very well what he was up to—studying her every move so that when it was time to head back to the city, he could make a case for getting behind the wheel.

The gargoyle wanted to drive.

"Forget it," she said, keeping her eyes on the road. "I already told you, you have to have a special license in order to drive a car."

She'd also had to repeat it—loudly—several times before they had left the rental lot. She understood how a man as take charge and dominant as Kees would prefer to be in control of a vehicle, but there was no way she was going to let him operate one. Especially not when he admitted this was as close as he'd ever been to one. Her nightmares traumatized her enough already.

"It does not appear complicated." Kees tilted his head to the side and gestured toward her feet. "Already I have deduced that the objects beneath your feet control this vehicle's momentum. Your right foot moves to the right when you wish to move faster, and to the left when you wish to slow down. Simple enough for a child to master."

"Yeah, well, we don't let children drive, either. You need a license."

"No one has asked to see this license of yours since we took the machine away from the people at the desk. I don't see how anyone would know whether or not I possess one of those plastic cards."

If they hadn't been moving, Ella would have banged her head against the steering wheel. Damn, he was persistent.

"They'll know if we get pulled over." She glanced at him and sighed before explaining. "The authorities have the right to make us stop if we disobey any traffic laws, of which there are thousands that you aren't familiar with, or if we appear suspicious. When they do that, the first thing they will ask is to see the license of the driver. If you were driving, the fact that you don't have one could get both of us in serious trouble."

Kees frowned. "I would not wish to cause trouble for you with your human authorities, but perhaps later we could see about obtaining one of these licenses for me. I would like to operate this machine for myself. It appears . . . very interesting."

"It's not that simple. There are tests you have to take about the laws I mentioned, so you'd have to study. It's not a simple process. Trust me. Now, can we change the subject? I'm kind of over this one."

As soon as the words were out of her mouth, Ella felt the temperature in the interior of the SUV go up about ten degrees. She could sense Kees's gaze on her. Hell, she could almost feel it, like hands against her skin.

"And what should we talk about, little human?" His low, rumbling question sounded disturbingly close to a feline purr, full of arrogance and satisfaction. "Perhaps we could discuss the moment we shared inside the museum earlier, hm?"

Ella gritted her teeth and tried to pretend that her cheeks weren't glowing hot enough to cook an egg.

"Or we could not." She shot him a glare. "Unless you want to talk about what the hell you were thinking back there. What was that lover boy act all about? Do you just get your jollies from embarrassing me?"

Kees's expression went from teasing back to stony. He shrugged. "It seemed a logical way to explain why I had accompanied you to your work this morning. It also explained why I would not leave when requested. A male does not leave his mate in a situation in which she could be vulnerable or in which she feels unsettled."

"Yeah, well, the only thing unsettling about this morning was you, and you put me in an awkward situation. Now Bea is going to keep asking me about you like we're in some kind of relationship. And I had to tell the police you were at my apartment all night."

"We are in a relationship of sorts, at least until I locate my Warden and you are placed with an appropriate Guild mentor." He shifted to look toward the road. "And from what I understand of this age, a young woman spending the night alone with a man she is attached to will make no one think twice, not even the police."

He was right, but Ella was still unsettled. "What do you know of this age? You've been asleep for, like, a few hundred years, right? You think you understand modern relationship paradigms?"

"I slumbered," he agreed, but Ella could hear the caveat in his tone. "However, we Guardians require little enough sleep when we are awake and active. After the first few years of dormancy, we actually spend very little time in sleep. We might refer to it that way, but it's more a sort of meditative state. A trance, you might say. We are still aware of the world around us. We can still hear what is going on, and sometimes we can catch glimpses of it as well. Not only does it ensure we will wake if a threat reemerges to menace the world, but it allows us to keep track of changes in humanity so that we understand our surroundings when we do wake. When faced with a threat from the Darkness, we cannot waste time in finding ways to communicate with our Wardens or the rest of the world."

"Right. So you always wake up savvy and horny. Got it."

Silence filled the car for a long minute.

"That is not entirely accurate," he rumbled, the gravel of his voice abrading against the tension between them. "We wake with much knowledge, but it does take time to associate what we know in our minds with the reality of the physical world. Like this vehicle, for instance. I knew of them, even caught glimpses of them, but this is the first time I have experienced one in this manner. It makes my knowledge much more complete."

He didn't mention anything about being horny. Ella couldn't decide if that was good or bad. On the one hand, she should be grateful not to ease on down that particular road, since all it was likely to accomplish was acute embarrassment and almost certain regret. On the other, it would have been nice to hear that he had a reaction to her even a tenth as strong as her inexplicable reaction to him. At least then, her misery would have some company to love.

Opting for the better part of valor, she cleared her throat and watched the road. "So, um, when was the last time you . . . woke up? You made it sound like you were, er, summoned for a particular battle. Have you been asleep since you won that one?"

"No, I have woken a few times since. We were summoned to battle at first when the Seven last attempted to join together, and to prevent that is our ultimate calling, but whenever any force of the Darkness gains sufficient power to threaten mankind, one or more of us will wake to fight it. The last time I fought was in your year 1703."

Ella paused. It took a second for that to sink in. "Really? Um, my knowledge of history is limited to knowing that was the transitional period between Baroque and Rococo, but I don't remember learning anything special about that year in school. What happened?"

"One of the Seven escaped its prison. It emerged in the south of England and attempted to bring the sea in to devour the land. My brother and I stopped it, but the battle lasted for days near the close of the year. Many human lives were lost to the sea before we prevailed, but we vanquished the demon and banished him again from this plane."

He spoke clinically, no emotion wrapped through the words, as if he recited some sort of multiplication table. Ella found herself wanting more. She wanted to know how the experience had felt to him. Had he been frightened? Exhilarated? Did the accomplishment leave him feeling proud and satisfied? Or angry and exhausted?

He so rarely showed anything resembling emotion. Those rare glimpses of humor when he teased her, or the glint of possessiveness and hunger when they had kissed. Those were the only times she felt she understood this man-creature. The rest of the time, he might as well have been truly carved from stone.

She just wished her hormones would remember that. It was becoming harder for her to remind them that in spite of the suit of gorgeous Kees wore in order to fit into a vehicle designed for human physical dimensions, he wasn't really an ordinary man.

He wasn't really ordinary at all.

Her brows drew closer together, and she bit back another question. She didn't need to know what made Kees the gargoyle tick. Better to focus on the task at hand. Find out where his Warden was hiding, put the two of them back together, then go back to living her sane, boring life. With hopefully a new trick or two up her sleeve to keep the magic inside her from harming anyone else ever again.

With her hands on the steering wheel, she jerked her chin toward the road in front of them. "That's Lions Bay up ahead. Once we're through, we continue a little bit north and a fair bit east and we should run into the address from the file. We'll be there soon."

And be that much closer to the end of this crazy internal turmoil.

Or so she could only hope.

Kees felt the confines of the automobile pressing in on him. Despite all the windows letting in light and the view of the forest and land around them, he felt trapped. It was not a feeling he was accustomed to, nor one for which he felt any fondness. He did not believe he would ever be a fan of this human mode of transportation. He would much rather have flown.

That desire could also account for a bit of his claustro-
phobia. He'd remained in his human form since changing
last night to reassure Ella, and his skin felt too tight,
stretched and itchy and confining. He needed to switch
back to his natural shape, stand at his full height, and
stretch his wings. With Fortune's blessing, they would find
Gregory in this remote location, and Kees would get the
chance to do so soon.

Of course, the small car and the small shape could not
entirely explain away the tension eating at Kees. No, a
portion of the blame for that lay just a foot away to his
left. Ella Harrow had him tied into knots he simply didn't
understand.

Kees could never claim to be an expert on human beings. Despite his many centuries of life in their world, he
had spent most of it separate and apart from the race he
protected. Most of the humans he had had contact with over
the years had been Wardens, and they, too, lived somewhat
separated from their non-magical counterparts. The talent
to feel, harness, and shape magical power set the Wardens
apart. Most of them were born to magical families and
lived their entire lives knowing that there was more to the
universe than met the human eye.

Ella, though, wasn't like that. She had magic inside
her—huge, glowing, reservoirs of it—but she had shown
herself ignorant of not only how to mold it, but even where
it came from or what purpose it served. It made Kees want
to protect her and educate her, to show her how special she
could be compared to those surrounding her.

And therein lay the root of his problem.

Kees reacted to the little human in ways he had never
before imagined, let alone experienced. Just being in her
presence made him feel protective and possessive and alive
with an intensity he had never previously felt. His mind

told him she was simply one of many of her race, perhaps distinguished somewhat by her magical talents, but in the end, human through and through. The instinct to protect her race was logical, natural; but to want to protect her, specifically—Ella of the ordinary brown hair and extraordinary gray eyes—made no sense whatsoever.

Neither did the surge of electricity that pulsed through him when their bodies touched.

Guardians were summoned, not made or born. They numbered only in the dozens, as far as he knew. He and his six brothers, the largest and strongest of their kind, existed to protect against the Seven, but there were others—smaller, less powerful—who battled the minor demons and fiends that occasionally escaped into the human realm.

The lesser guards spent more time among humans, never confined in the sort of slumber Kees had known, sleeping only during daylight hours and patrolling each night against the smaller threats of evil. Their kind came in both male and female forms and reproduced with each other, but as far as Kees knew, his kind could come into existence only when summoned by a full circle of Wardens. They did not mate, since no females of their kind existed. They had no need to mate, and should feel no desire for it.

So why did desire for the little human Ella threaten to set his stone on fire?

The question both intrigued and terrified him. Desire was an emotion, something Kees had always assumed belonged to the weak and fallible human race. Guardians needed no emotion. They served one purpose in this plane, and that was to battle against the forces of the Darkness. To do that required no emotion, only power and brute strength. Emotion, in fact, could be a weakness. Fear might lead to mistakes, pride in victory to arrogance and conceit, also a certain path to defeat.

Guardians could not afford to feel, and before he had laid eyes on Ella, Kees never had.

He tried to recall the other awakenings of his long existence, and he realized with a jolt that not one of them had felt anything like this. During none of them had he ever really experienced emotion. Again and again, he was discovering that something about this time differed from all the others. He only hoped Gregory could help him understand.

Kees had little opportunity to brood on the situation. Only fifteen or twenty minutes outside the small town of Lions Bay, Ella steered the car between two tall gate posts. Lamps of glass and wrought iron arched from the top of each over the gravel drive, and against the worn brick of one, weathered brass numbers indicated an address.

"This is it," Ella murmured. "Good thing the gates are open."

At this point, Kees wouldn't have allowed the tall bars of iron to stop him, but he admitted it was easier not to have to rip them off their hinges. They stood wide, pushed back on either side of the lane against the thick trees that blocked any view beyond the bend ahead of them. Kees glanced at the gate on his side of the car and felt a jolt of satisfaction.

"That's a Guild symbol."

Ella shot him a sideways glance. "What's a what?"

Kees nodded toward the right-hand gate. "The medallion in the center of the gate, with the sun rising over the mountain peak. That's a symbol used by the Guild. We're in the right place."

Ella blew out a breath and steered the vehicle slowly down the narrow drive. "Well, that's something, I guess."

Her words were noncommittal, but Kees felt the surge

of energy from her hidden excitement. He just wished he could tell if she felt excitement over successfully moving forward toward their goal of locating Gregory, or if it was excitement over the prospect of washing her hands of his company.

Damn it. His existence had been much easier before he'd begun to care about the answers to such questions.

It took several minutes to leave the thick woods of the gate area behind and to pull forward into a lush green expanse of lawn and garden. Surrounded by more forest and capped by breathtaking views of the mountains beyond, the cleared pocket of open space encompassed an enormous, intriguing house of wood and stone.

Kees heard Ella murmur in appreciation when she caught sight of the building. He didn't recall this place, felt a twinge of worry that perhaps he'd never been here before, but then he pushed it aside and surveyed the scene with fresh eyes.

The house somehow managed to appear both rustic and elegant. Huge wooden beams ran in heavy lines along the eaves and through the walls, and rough slabs of stone called to mind both the fortresses of Kees's first home and the untouched mountains in the background. Not quite a chalet, and a long way from a manor house, the impressive dwelling seemed to create an architectural style all its own, one that could very well have grown from the earth exactly where it stood.

"It's gorgeous," Ella murmured, opening her door and sliding from the vehicle. "I was expecting a big house, if the person who lives here used to own you, but this is . . . this is amazing."

Kees climbed from the car, his own pleasure at seeing the structure somewhat soured by the woman's choice of words. "No one has ever owned me, human. I was Warded, not owned."

"Right. Sorry."

She didn't even bother to tear her gaze away from the house to deliver the apology, which made Kees doubt its sincerity. He resisted the urge to sniff and folded his arms across his chest.

Finally, she turned to him and gestured toward the front porch. "Come on. Let's go see what we can find out."

Still stinging, Kees followed her up the wide steps to a front porch large enough to host a cotillion. Hell, you could practically quarter an army on the huge expanse of weathered cedar. Ella glanced around her, soaking in every last detail on their way to the ornately carved oak doors. Again, Kees noticed the sun and mountain symbol, along with several other subtle references to the Guild cunningly worked into the details of the carving. His sense of anticipation slowly built.

Ella pressed a small button next to the doorframe and stepped back. Kees heard the faint sound of chimes from inside. A bell. She had rung the doorbell.

They waited in silence for several minutes. As the time slipped past, he noticed signs of Ella's growing impatience. She first shifted her weight from one foot to the other, then back. Then she tapped her fingertips against her legs and began to look around for a window to peer through into the front hall.

When she raised her hand to press the button a second time, Kees reached out to stop her. He could hear quiet footsteps growing louder.

"Don't. Someone is coming."

Ella frowned at him but dropped her hand. A few seconds later, the left-hand door opened, and a woman of middle height and middle years frowned out at them.

"Yes? Can I help you?"

Kees eyed the woman from head to toe and scowled.

He could detect not the faintest trace of magic on her person. She clearly was not connected to the Guild. Had the journey here been just a waste of time?

Ella smiled at the woman and held out her hand. "I hope so," she said, her tone friendly and confident. "My name is Ella. Ella Harrow. I'm with the Vancouver Museum of Art and History."

The woman's frown cleared, though she continued to appear slightly confused. "Oh. Oh, I'm sorry. I'm Greta Mikaelsen, the housekeeper. Did you come about the paperwork?"

The two women shook hands.

"The paperwork?" Ella asked, confusion clear in her words. "Actually, I was hoping I could speak with, ah, Gregory."

Greta looked startled and shook her head. "Now I don't know who's more confused, you or me. Come on inside."

She ushered them into a large wood-paneled hallway and picked up a rag from a round table, clutching it familiarly. She didn't fit the stereotypical notion of a Scandinavian housekeeper of the kind Kees remembered from his past. Her hair was short and curled, not pulled back into a tight bun, and she wore no apron or large ring of keys dangling from her belt. Instead, she was dressed in a simple cotton T-shirt and a pair of faded denim jeans. Only the dust rag in her hand indicated she might engage in domestic work.

Ella appeared nervous as she looked around at the richly detailed architecture and gleaming expanses of walnut. A wide, heavy staircase hugged the left-hand wall, then turned to climb the rear before opening into a balustraded hallway along the second floor. In the corner of the stair, a pedestal held an exquisite marble nude draped in diaphanous fabric. On the high wall below the hallway railings, three small but masterful landscapes showcased the mountains and countryside of Europe in summer, autumn, and the depths of night.

For someone who worked in an art museum, Ella appeared nearly awestruck before she mustered another smile and turned back to the housekeeper. "This is such a beautiful house. Who lives here now?"

"No one. Not since Mr. Gregory died. It's been almost three years now, and the lawyers still can't decide if the estate can be sold, whether it can go in pieces or has to stay all together. Who knows when they'll finally make a decision. But until they do, at least I have a job."

Kees stiffened when he heard Gregory's name. Dead? Was the woman referring to the same Gregory they had been searching for? Was Kees's Warden really dead?

Ella tilted her head to the side, her smile turning quizzical. "Mr. Gregory? Sorry, when I said I was from the museum, I should have mentioned I was just a minion."

"Mr. Gregory Lascaux. This was his house."

Damn. The same Gregory, then. Kees wondered how he could not have known of his old friend's death, not have been introduced to the other man's replacement, as was customary.

"He owned that sculpture the museum purchased a couple of years ago," Greta continued. "He was quite an art collector. I thought that's why you came. I left a message for the director of the museum a few days ago that I had located some additional paperwork related to the statue and offered to mail it to him. I never expected someone to show up to collect it in person."

"Oh, right." Ella nodded as if all her questions had just been answered, and Kees found himself admiring his little human's dramatic talents. "Honestly, it was kind of my idea to come out here. The statue is one of my favorites, and I always wanted to see where it came from. I guess

I was expecting a house more like some medieval castle or something, with more just like it lurking in the battlements."

Her laugh invited the housekeeper to join in. "No battlements, I'm afraid, but Mr. Gregory did have quite a collection. That was the only gargoyle that I know of, but there are plenty of other sculptures and paintings that haven't been sold off yet."

"Sold off?"

"Mr. Gregory never had children. I know he was married at one time, but from what I know, she died years and years ago. I never met her. When he died, there was quite a bit of confusion because no one could locate a will, so no one knew what to do with the house or the art or anything. It finally turned out that everything had been left to Mr. Gregory's nephew. Well, great-nephew, I think. His sister's son's boy, or something like that. I've never met the man, personally."

"What is his name?"

Both women looked at Kees, startled, as if they had forgotten he was there. Ella recovered first and gestured from him to the housekeeper.

"I'm so sorry, Greta. This is my friend who agreed to keep me company on the drive today. Kees, uh—"

"Kees Livingston." He cut in smoothly, extending his hand for a shake. "It's a pleasure to meet you."

"And you," Greta murmured, her gaze skimming appreciatively over his tall human form. "I'm sorry, but what was your question?"

"The name of Mr. Lascaux's heir. Do you know it?"

"Actually, I can never remember it," the housekeeper admitted, covering her obvious embarrassment with a half laugh. "Like I said, I've never met him, and I'm not that good with names. I have it written down somewhere, but he's never visited, and we don't speak. My paychecks come from Mr. Gregory's lawyers, which I guess the nephew must be using now, too, so there's really no need for us to talk. Frankly, I'm good with that. If he did want to speak with me, I'd assume it was to let me go. If he winds up selling the house, there won't be any reason to keep me around."

Ella nodded, her expression sympathetic. "Hopefully, he's forgotten all about you. Although—" She paused and looked around her. "—I don't see how anyone could forget about a place like this. Especially with this amazing artwork. It's like another kind of museum. How much of the original collection is still here?"

"Oh, almost all of it."

Kees could almost feel the way Ella's ears pricked up at that answer.

"Really?"

Greta nodded. "Like I said, the lawyers are still trying to sort out what pieces of the estate go together and that sort of thing. I imagine it has to do with the misunderstanding of not locating the will right away. But in any case, the only pieces the nephew was able to sell were the gargoyle statue and a few bits of antique jewelry. Those were the only things the will mentioned outright."

A few pieces of jewelry and a statue of a gargoyle. Those sounded to Kees very much like himself and the ritual accoutrements of a Guild Warden. Something about this situation didn't sit well with him.

"Well, the museum was very lucky to acquire the statue," Ella said. "I hope those papers you found don't call the purchase of it into question, or anything. I think that would give our director a heart attack."

"Oh, no—not at all. It's just some bits and pieces Mr. Gregory had jumbled up with the other paperwork on that junk pile he called his desk. Some journal pages he wrote about it, a few photos, and some bits about where it came from and who had it before him. I just thought the museum might like to have it. I know sometimes they tell stories about the history of paintings and things like that."

"We do. I'm sure whatever you've found will be a real thrill to go through. Dr. Lefavreau will be very excited when I bring it back for him."

"I have it all back in my office. It will just take me a minute to fetch it." Greta started to turn, then hesitated and glanced back at them. "The pride of Mr. Gregory's collection is still on display in the downstairs gallery here. Maybe you'd like to look around while you wait?"

"Put a bow on that, and I'll call it Christmas." Ella nodded, her eyes gleaming with anticipation.

The housekeeper laughed. "Right this way, then."

She led them out of the foyer and down a short hall at the front of the house to a long, open room with a second-level balcony and gleaming expanses of dark, polished floors. Art hung from every wall and decorated the tops of podiums and pedestals scattered about the room. Even the pieces of furniture positioned here and there qualified as historically significant works of art. It certainly was as much of a museum as the one where Ella worked.

"Oh, wow. This is amazing," Ella breathed, looking around her with wide eyes and an open mouth. She twirled on her heel just like a little girl on Christmas morning. "Take your time finding those papers. I could spend months looking at all this."

Greta laughed. "It won't take me that long, but enjoy yourselves."

Kees watched the woman leave with a frown. "She's very trusting to leave two strangers alone with such valuable treasures."

Ella rolled her eyes. "We might be strangers, but we told her our names, and she knows I work at the museum. If something went missing, it's not like I'd be hard to track down. Plus, your Warden friend wasn't stupid. If you look closely, you can see the security cameras pointing in strategic directions, and some of the wires for a pretty hefty alarm system. Museum standard."

"You are right. Gregory would have left wards. Spells, too. Three years is not so long without maintenance that they should not still be active."

"You mean there's magic in here?"

Kees lifted a brow at her surprised tone. "Of course there is. Can't you feel it?"

"I don't know. I'm used to blocking that stuff out, not trying to pick up on it."

"Try now."

He watched as uncertainty flickered over her features, chased away by budding curiosity. After taking a second to focus, she closed her eyes and her brow furrowed in concentration. An instant later her eyes popped open and her gaze flew to him.

"There's not just magic in here," she said quietly, as if she didn't want to be overheard. Which was silly. They were the only two beings in the room. "There's something else."

Alarmed, Kees stiffened and opened his senses. It took only seconds to understand what she was talking about. He cursed his own lack of attention. He should have noticed before she did, and she was the only thing he could blame. The human distracted him, and that was not something he could allow to happen.

In addition to the solid silvery blue glow of Gregory's remaining protection spells and wards guarding the artwork, Kees now saw the splinters of broken wards surrounding the windows at the front of the house. Mixed in with the scattered pieces of Warden magic, something thick and black and pulsing tainted the air around it.

Kees recognized that vile residue. It trailed behind

wherever the agents of the Darkness had passed. He cursed quietly, but long and with great originality.

Ella eyes him warily. "You felt it, too, didn't you?"

"I saw it. It is not good."

"Yeah, that much I figured out for myself."

The sound of footsteps on wooden floorboards warned them of Greta's approach. Kees and Ella had been sensitized to any person drawing near. Any *thing* drawing near.

"Found it," the housekeeper said with a smile. She carried a large manila envelope in her hands. When she looked up as she drew near, her expression turned quizzical. "Is everything okay? You look . . . unsettled."

Ella's laugh sounded forced to Kees's ear, but he wasn't certain the other human would pick up on it. "No, no. I'm fine. I was just imagining how much time and devotion went into assembling a collection like this. It's so sad to think that the man who went to so much effort over such a long time is no longer here to enjoy it."

Greta's face softened. "It is sad. I was very fond of Mr. Gregory. I worked for him for more than fifteen years, and I don't think I ever met a kinder, more generous man. A little eccentric, certainly, but so sweet. Everyone who knew him mourned his passing."

Kees took advantage of the opening. "How did your employer die, Ms. Mikaelsen? I don't think you mentioned."

"The coroner said it was his heart, but none of us had any idea he might have problems with it. He was an older man, but he seemed quite vigorous, right up until the end. I came in one morning and found him. Here in the gallery, actually. He must have had a heart attack sometime during the night. So tragic. And so sudden, really. None of us saw it coming."

Kees felt a rush of ice that solidified inside him at her words. He might not have spoken to Gregory in many,

many years—not since the human had assumed the mantle of Warden in the middle of the last century, but an unexpected death combined with the broken wards and the traces of Dark magic in the room led to only one conclusion—it was a good thing Kees had awakened.

"That's a shame," Ella repeated, and beneath the sympathetic tone, Kees could hear the rising note of concern. "I'm sure everyone who knew him misses him."

"We do."

Ella accepted the envelope from the other woman with a smile. "Well, we'll get out of your hair now. Thanks so much for handing this over to the museum. I'm sure Dr. Lefavreau can't wait to go through it."

"You're very welcome. The gargoyle was one of Mr. Gregory's favorite pieces, so I'm sure he'd want everyone to know as much of the story surrounding it as they can."

Kees and Ella trailed after the housekeeper back to the front door of the sprawling old house. This time, Kees kept his senses open, searching for more traces of Dark magic. He found nothing. The wards here were intact, covering the bottom of the stairway, as well as each door leading off the front hall. Curiously, nothing warded the main entrance. Had that ward been entirely uncast, or had Gregory for some reason not laid one on the door to his mountain home?

Had he felt that secure here? Or had he been attempting to lay some sort of trap? Maybe his death hadn't surprised him as much as it had his friends and employees.

They shook hands with Greta on the front porch and crossed the short distance to their vehicle.

Ella slid behind the steering wheel and pulled her door shut with a solid thunk. "So."

The word encompassed an encyclopedia of meaning—puzzlement, uncertainty, questioning, exhaustion, wonder, frustration. Kees let it hang between them as he reviewed everything they had just learned. Gregory was dead, and Dark magic had likely killed him. He had all but invited it into his home, yet once inside, he had probably thought he would be safe. Not one of the Seven, then. Even an experienced Warden would not think to face a demon that powerful without a Guardian or two at his back. What, then?

A thought occurred, and Kees felt a creeping sensation of unease move across his skin. Could the Order be stirring to life once again?

Impatiently, Ella humphed and glared from the seat beside him. "Well? What's going on in that head of yours, O ancient and mysterious Guardian man? Your friend is dead, so there goes having your Warden explain what's going on. So what do we do now?"

"You drive." Kees pulled the safety strap she had called a seat belt away from the car door and fastened it across his chest. "I need to think."

Ella stared at him for a moment, her eyes narrowed and her mouth open in an expression of disbelief. Then her jaw snapped shut and she was turning the key in the ignition, bringing the engine of the huge SUV to life.

"I could tell you what you need," she muttered under her breath as she turned the vehicle back up the drive toward the iron gates and the road beyond, "but I don't think they stock rubber hoses and vise clamps in the backs of rentals these days."

At another time, in another place, Kees would have laughed at the little human's bloodthirsty imagination, but right now he didn't feel like laughing. He still did not know what had awakened him, but he was beginning to fear that whatever the cause, the purpose was about to come clear.

A battle approached. Now the question became, did Kees have the tools he needed to fight it and win?

He'd never faced the enemy without a Warden by his side and his brothers at his back. If he had to do it now, would he survive the challenge?

Would the world?

Chapter Six

The hour-and-some minutes' drive back to Vancouver convinced Ella of two things: one, in spite of his human size and shape, Kees could still do a pretty damned fine impression of a mute, motionless statue; and two, curiosity probably hadn't actually killed the cat, just driven it to suicide. Ella certainly intended to kill something if she didn't get answers to at least a few of her questions pretty damned quick.

She unlocked the door to her apartment and led the way inside, tossing her keys onto a side table. Flipping the locks behind her, she turned to find the Guardian standing in the middle of the living room floor, stretching his long arms to the ceiling like a puppy that had just woken from a satisfying snooze.

She contemplated punching him right in the taut, washboard stomach.

Knowing her luck, she'd probably break her hand.

"Okay, you've had more than two hours to think or plan or process or whatever the hell you've been doing while you haven't been talking to me," she bit out, planting her feet wide apart and glaring at him. "I have been more than patient. So, spill. What the hell did we accomplish with that little trip, and where the hell are we supposed to go next?"

Kees looked at her and dropped his arms to his sides. "I have grown increasingly uncomfortable with this confining shape I wear. Will it disturb you if I shift into my natural form?"

"I don't care if you shift into fifth gear and become a half-dead wallaby, I want answers."

Ignoring the growl in her voice, the Guardian stretched again and blurred, and in an instant, the space before her overflowed with fanged, winged, horned, gray-skinned gargoyle.

Ella stumbled an instinctive step back.

Kees frowned. "Surely you realize that if I intended to cause you harm, I would have done so by now."

Pressing a hand to her stomach, Ella marshaled her courage and tried to quiet her animal instinct to run. Run and hide. And scream. This was Kees, she reminded herself. The same man she'd driven to Lions Bay with. The same man who had slept in her apartment the night before. The same man she'd kissed in the ballroom of the museum. He wasn't a monster.

No matter how much he looked like one.

"No, I know. It's fine," she said, proud when her voice didn't quiver the way her stomach was doing. "I just forgot, that's all. I forgot how . . . big you are."

And she had. She felt tiny next to his human shape. In this form, she wanted to break into a rousing rendition of "The Lollipop Guild." Kees was lucky that her apartment was in a historic building with twelve-foot ceilings. As it was, if he stretched again, he'd easily touch them.

Kees rumbled something noncommittal and took a seat on the sofa. He made it look like dollhouse furniture. Ella watched in fascination as he settled his wings around him before turning his attention back to her.

"You should sit," he instructed. "There are things I must explain to you."

"It's about time."

He waited until she sat. With him taking up so much of her sofa, Ella dropped into the only other available seat, the battered armchair to his left, and tucked her legs up underneath her.

"I told you before about the Guild of Wardens and the other Guardians like myself. I explained that we were summoned to battle the Darkness, that the Guild of Wardens assists us and watches over our slumber, waking us when there is a threat to this world. I also told you that the Guardians defend against the Seven demons, while lesser threats are dealt with by other guards who do not sleep as we do."

He waited until she nodded. Yeah, she remembered all that. It made her head spin, but she remembered it.

"What I did not tell you was the story of the Darkness, and why the Guardians stand ever vigilant against its servants."

"Well, I kinda figured that 'the Darkness' was your way of talking about evil, and I figured that staying vigilant against evil was pretty much a given."

"Matters are not quite so simple."

"Why do I feel like that's my new life story?"

He ignored her grumbled question.

"The Darkness is not just evil, it is *the evil,* the sum of all that is evil and all that evil is. It has existed since the dawn of time, and in all those ages, it has sought to devour all life that stands against it. It is eternal and relentless and indestructible."

"Indestructible?" Ella swallowed hard. "If it's the all-powerful embodiment of evil, how come the world isn't dead and gone already?"

"Because the Universe abhors the Darkness."

His clawed fingers tapped on his thigh as he spoke, reminding Ella that when resuming his natural shape, he'd also assumed his "natural" clothing, which basically amounted to a cross between a loincloth and an abbreviated kilt. And she really shouldn't be staring at the thigh muscles of a guy from another species. No matter how much she wanted to lick them.

Down, girl!

What the hell was wrong with her?

"Now even the powers of the Universe cannot destroy the Darkness, but they could weaken it, and so they did, by dividing it into Seven pieces. Seven slices of pure and utter evil whose only desire is to reunite and destroy all life and light in existence."

Ella forced herself to focus and remember what he had already told her. "Seven pieces, huh? That number seems like a pretty big coincidence."

"It is no coincidence. The Seven demons my brothers and I guard against are those same Seven pieces of Darkness. We fight to keep them apart and to keep them off the mortal plane, because when they are here, they can feed off the chaos and destruction they cause and become stronger. Banishing them not only keeps humanity safe from their evil, but it also weakens them—however, they never stop looking for ways back into this realm."

"So you fight the demons and banish them. The Wardens keep watch and call you when they slip away from wherever they go in the meantime. You wake up and banish them again, and it's some kind of never-ending cycle?"

"Put simply, yes."

"So how do they keep finding their way back here? Can't you banish them permanently?"

"They are powerful. And cunning. And there are those who would seek to aid in their return."

Ella felt her eyes widen. "Humans?"

Kees nodded.

She shook her head and tried to wrap her mind around that concept. Were there really human beings out there who would want the ultimate evil to be unleashed into the world? *Okay,* she told herself, *dumb question.* Of course there were. But why on earth would anyone want to do that? *Who* would want to do that?

"Just like the Guardians are served by the Guild of Wardens, the Darkness draws to it servants of its own. They are known as the Order of Eternal Darkness. We call them the *nocturnis.*"

"And these are humans who . . . what? Aid and abet the Seven demons?"

"They serve the Darkness in any way they can. They attempt to summon the Seven forth from their prisons, and if they succeed, they work to feed the demons and make them stronger. Ultimately, they hope to free all Seven at once and see them unite once more into the Darkness."

"I don't understand. Why try to help something that has no purpose other than to wipe out life as we know it? I mean, eventually it's going to run out of innocent people to kill and turn on its own allies, right? Isn't that the definition of pure evil?"

Kees shrugged, his expression stony. In more ways than one. "They seek power, and they naïvely believe that the Darkness will give it to them. For a time, they may be correct, but ultimately, even they will be consumed."

"Well, duh."

The gargoyle's mouth quirked.

Ella took a moment to think. When they first took their seats, she had expected Kees to explain what the energy they both sensed in the gallery of his Warden's house had meant. She hadn't been expecting a more in-depth lecture on what he and his Warden had been created to protect against.

But she was coming to understand that the gargoyle was a supremely logical creature. If he believed this was what she needed to know first, he had a very good reason for drawing that conclusion.

"Are you trying to tell me that that stuff, the icky stuff I sensed in the gallery earlier . . . Did that stuff mean this Order of Eternal Darkness had been inside Gregory's house?"

Kees fixed his black gaze on her, his expression grave. "That 'stuff' was magic, but Dark magic, the kind used by the *nocturnis* and their masters."

Ella shuddered. And here she'd been afraid of her own magic all these years. Compared to that nasty, black ooze, her own uncontrolled surges of blue-white energy seemed like fresh water in contrast to sewer sludge.

"Do you think the Order—the *nocturnis*." She corrected herself. "Do you think they killed your Warden?"

"I am certain of it."

She wrapped her arms around herself and bit her lip. The expression on the gargoyle's face had barely shifted since he resumed this form, but Ella could see tension and anger in the banked flames in his eyes.

"I'm sorry," she said quietly. "I'm sorry he's dead, and not just because he can't help answer all those questions you wanted to ask him. Were you . . . close?"

His huge head shook side to side. "We met and spoke only once, at the ritual where he took up the mantle of his father's position as Warden. Since then, there has been no grave threat. I slept uninterrupted until now. But that I knew him only slightly is of no consequence. He was mine."

Ella heard steel behind the words, or maybe it was stone. Either way, she knew Kees would find justice for his fallen comrade. She found herself wanting that for Kees. Maybe if she concentrated on what she wanted for him, she could stop thinking about what she wanted from him.

She had breathed a sigh of relief when he shifted back to his monstrous form once they returned to her apartment. Surely, she had told herself, seeing the true shape of the distractingly gorgeous man she'd spent the last night and day lusting over would cure her of that little obsession.

No such luck.

In reality, Ella couldn't make herself think of Kees as a monster. Somehow, her eyes just wanted to skim over the small ram's horns that curled back above his temples and the fangs that flashed whenever he spoke. His long claws made for a bit of an extreme manicure, but she'd dated men who wore nail polish, so who was to say what was normal?

Okay, so his feet made her a little uncomfortable, looking like a cross between the feet of a man and a giant raptor, but she wasn't into feet anyway. She figured her own stubby toes and pale skin and bony ankles couldn't exactly be called alluring, so she shouldn't judge.

The tail was easy enough to ignore, and honestly, the wings . . . well, those she found oddly comforting.

Maybe she was losing her mind, but the wings soothed her. They made her want to climb into his lap and curl up against his chest. She could almost feel the warm embrace of them fold around her, shielding her from the outside world, creating a perfect cocoon of peace and tranquility. It would be like a giant hug surrounding them both, sealing them off in their own private nest.

She shivered and hugged herself tighter.

God, she had to drag her mind off his body and force it back to the matter at hand. Especially since he hadn't so much as indicated he remembered her gender since they got out of the car at Gregory's house.

Ella cleared her throat. "So, um, since Gregory's gone and he can't answer any of your questions, what are you going to do now?"

What she wanted to ask was what were *they* going to do, but she tamped down the impulse. She could fight that battle later if he actually tried to exclude her from their next move. She could always remind him of the magical training he had told her she needed. After hearing of the Warden's death and sensing the nasty stuff left behind by whoever had killed him, she was inclined to agree that the idea of learning enough magic to protect herself had merit.

"I am starting to believe that the questions I had intended to ask have ceased to be important," he told her. "I think I know why I have woken, even if the way in which it happened remains unclear. I think it is more important now to contact the Guild directly. If Gregory has been dead for three years as Greta indicated, a replacement should have been named long ago. I need to find out why this was not done, and see how much they know about the threat that killed him. If the *nocturnis* are active again, the Guild must know about it. They will be able to tell us if matters have become serious enough to warrant waking another of my brothers to defend against it."

Able to tell "us," he had said. Ella tried to ignore the warm glow his words caused. Seriously, she was becoming a sap.

"That makes sense," she said, careful to conceal her satisfaction. "How do we do that?"

"I told you, the Guild always remains in one place. It allows for continuity in spite of the long stretches of time during which the individual Guardians might sleep. Their base in Paris has been there for hundreds of years. They designed and built the structure specifically to be an eternal stronghold from which to fight the long war. We will go to them there."

"Um, seriously? Don't get me wrong, I think contacting the Guild is probably the right move, but Paris is a long way away, and plane tickets are expensive. You know, since I don't have wings of my own."

Kees shook his head. "Traveling to Paris would take too long. We will have to contact them. We can use a telephone, yes?"

"Sure, if you remember the number." She paused. "Although, I don't know if phone numbers work the same way now that they did the last time you woke up. Wait, if you last woke in 1703, they didn't even have telephones."

"The last time I battled one of the Seven was in 1703, not the last time I woke. I had to interrupt my slumber briefly each time a new Warden succeeded into my service. So the last time was approximately sixty-five years ago."

Ella thought for a minute, and then shook her head. She just kept remembering old movies from the '40s and '50s when people would pick up the phone and ask the operator to connect them to Bumbleford 8173, or something.

"Still not sure anything you remember will work. I don't suppose their number is in the book, is it?"

"What book?"

"You know, listed in a public directory. Like, can I call the phone company in Paris and ask for a number to connect me to the Guild of Wardens?"

"Ah." Kees indicated his understanding with a small gesture. "I do not think so. The Guild has become much more private over the centuries since it was founded. Only those whom they wish to hear from know how to contact them."

"Hm."

Ella pursed her lips. An unlisted phone number did present an obstacle in the path, but not an insurmountable one. There was more than one way to skin a cat. Or a gargoyle. She thought about asking Kees if he knew the physical address of the Guild's building, but even that wasn't likely to prove helpful. Cities, especially major ones, had changed dramatically over the centuries, and streets got renamed all the time. An old address, whether it was three hundred years old or sixty-five years old could very well lead them down another dead end.

An idea occurred to Ella, and she began to smile. It was true that cities changed, but if the Guild had its base in a truly historical building, chances were, it had been the subject of architectural curiosity and historic preservation movements through the years. And that meant that it would be well known, probably featured in guide books and photographic studies of a city as famous and often visited as Paris.

Yes, Ella decided, pushing up from her chair and heading toward her desk in the corner of her unused dining room. It was definitely time to introduce a medieval gargoyle to the wonders of the modern world.

Look out, Google. Here we come.

Kees's jaw had dropped when Ella first opened the wonders of the Internet. He had heard of such things during his slumber, of course, but to witness the enormous wealth of information so easily accessed so quickly and efficiently . . .

His mind, as Ella would put it later, was blown.

Not that finding a single ancient building in a city as old and crowded as Paris was easy, of course, but Ella had determination on her side. With the help of several maps, both modern and historical, she first had Kees point out which section of Paris the Guild has settled in. Then, armed with the number of the corresponding arrondissements, Ella began the laborious task of drawing up a list of historic buildings so she could find photos for Kees to look at. Once he identified the correct building, a little Internet sleuthing should tell her the current street address. With that, finding the owner and some contact information would be only a matter of time.

It took four hours to find the building. When she showed Kees the digital photograph of the classical stone façade with Gothic detailing and decorative sculpture recessed in niches along the walls, his eyes narrowed and he grunted in satisfaction.

"That is it. That is the headquarters of the Guild of Wardens."

"Good," Ella grunted in return. "Now, let me get back to work."

She did, while Kees got back to the refrigerator.

They had eaten lunch together about two hours ago, Ella munching her sandwich while still hunched over her keyboard; Kees plowing through four times the food on the other side of the desk. The gargoyle, though, said he was hungry again. Apparently, it took a lot of fuel to keep those enormous muscles performing. Ella tried not to think about them. At least, not while she was working.

Another two hours passed and Ella squealed with triumph. "I got it!"

She leapt out of her chair, ignoring the protests of her stiff muscles, and did a little victory dance in the fading light from the dining room window. She loved solving puzzles, and this one had been a doozy.

Kees looked up from where he had been sitting on the sofa, studiously examining her remote control. "You have a number to call? What is it? Where is your telephone?"

"Whoa, hold on, big guy."

Ella held up a hand, which Kees walked right into as he stalked around the sofa to the computer.

"What is the number? We must call immediately."

"I said, hold your horses."

He growled. Ella felt the sound rumbling under her

palm, but instead of frightening her, the sensation fascinated her, as did the warm, rough-smooth feel of his skin beneath her hand. She had to force herself to pay attention.

"I found the listed owners of the building, not the phone number," she explained, reluctantly dropping her hand and raising her gaze to his face. "It's a trust, which I suppose makes sense if the Guild has been operating for centuries and intends to continue doing so. But more importantly, I found the names of the trust's managers, a law firm in Paris."

"Then why are we wasting time? We must call."

"We'll call once I dig up the number. It should only take a few minutes, but you do realize that's it currently about two o'clock in the morning, Paris time, right?"

"The hour does not matter. Find the number. We will call the Guild immediately once you do. Trust me, someone will answer."

"All right. Give me five minutes. Ten, tops."

Ella settled back into her desk chair and tried to ignore the feel of Kees's dark gaze boring into her while she typed and scrolled and clicked. The man proved a potent distraction just being in the same room. Having him actively watching while she worked wreaked havoc on her concentration.

She returned her focus to her Web search and reread the text of a news link. Her heart took a nosedive into her stomach, and she read the words a third time. She bit her lip as she clicked on the link.

"What is it? What is wrong?"

That was the other problem with Kees staring at her while she worked. He knew immediately when she found something and he always demanded she share that very instant.

Her expression tightened as she waved him forward.

"This is a news article from an English-language news site in Paris. I didn't find it right away, because it was published more than a year ago, so it got buried under more recent results."

She shifted aside so he could see the screen more clearly. Kees leaned over her shoulder and focused on the headline that filled the computer monitor:

23 DEAD, NO SURVIVORS AS CATASTROPHIC FIRE CONSUMES HISTORIC BUILDING

The Guild of Wardens no longer inhabited the shell of the old structure in the ancient quarter of Paris. No one did, according to the article.

The Guild had been destroyed.

Ella felt the silence take over the room. It covered everything like a blanket, making the atmosphere heavy and claustrophobic.. She even found herself turning her head to look at Kees, just to make certain he hadn't turned back to stone. He held himself too stiff and still she worried for a minute until she saw his chest expand when he drew in a breath.

"Read the article to me." His voice sounded tight and fierce as he barked the command. He pushed himself away from Ella's desk and began to pace, his tail swishing behind him like an angry cat's. "Tell me everything it says. Tell me exactly what happened."

Ella's heart ached as she turned back to the screen and read about the destruction of Kees's strongest link to the human world. She knew the loss of those twenty-three lives must represent the loss of centuries and centuries of friendships and families and a community that was all he had, a rock the stone-skinned sentinel could lean on during his long ages of sleep. And now it had been ripped away from him.

Ripped away more than a year ago, and he hadn't even known.

The story couldn't possibly make him feel any better, but Ella read it anyway. He deserved to know. According to the news article, the fire had started in a "file room" in the old building, feeding quickly on dry paper and books. The Guild headquarters was described as the home and offices of a "private research society" concerned with "historical and political philosophy," a description Ella thought dry enough to burn all on its own.

The blaze broke out at night, the first bad sign, when society members and employees were sleeping. Outdated wiring took the blame for fire alarms failing to sound, and the age of the building was cited when the report mentioned exits had been blocked by fallen debris, trapping victims in the flames. By the time other residents of the street noticed the flames and called the fire department, the inferno already raged out of control. Officials made the decision to concentrate their efforts on saving neighboring buildings, and the Guild headquarters burned until nearly noon the next day before the blaze was brought under control and finally extinguished.

As of the time the article was written, the cause of the fire had not been determined, but authorities were "investigating."

Kees listened to every word in silence. Ella felt a flash of surprise when she realized that even in his enormous natural form, he made hardly a sound as he paced across her wooden floor. Of course, considering how gracefully he moved at any size, she shouldn't wonder at the quiet.

She did wonder about what he was thinking, though. His expression had turned back to stone, even if the rest of him remained awake and alive, and she couldn't detect so much as a hint of emotion behind the carved mask of inscrutability.

When she finished reading, Ella swiveled her chair to face her companion and twisted her hands in her lap. She wanted to reach out and touch him, wanted to comfort him, but she didn't know how. Didn't know if he would let her. Right now, he looked as forbidding as he had the first time she saw him move in the museum gardens. This time, he didn't frighten her, but that didn't mean she felt confident in offering him her sympathy.

She couldn't keep silent, though.

She stayed in her chair, but her eyes followed him across the room.

"I'm so sorry," she murmured, wishing she could find other words. Better words. "For your friends. For you."

His stride caught, hesitated, just a bit, just for a second, but he didn't turn to look at her. "The fire was not an accident, no matter what their authorities chose to reveal. Wardens can create fire, and they can extinguish fire. Such a thing as an uncontrollable blaze could never have occurred unless there was Dark magic deliberately fanning the flames."

Ella started, realization jolting through her. "You think the *nocturnis* caused the fire. You think they tried to wipe out the entire Guild?"

Finally he looked at her. Gone were the black eyes and pinprick flames she had grown accustomed to. In their place, the very fires of hell seemed to burn. Not even the fire at the Guild could have burned so hotly and so bright.

"I think that twenty-four Wardens are dead in three years," he snarled, fangs bared fully and fiercely. "I think such a thing has never occurred in all the ages that I have known. I think that such a thing feels to me like an act of war against those who oppose the Darkness. Do you think differently?"

"No. I—I—I don't know. I mean, I don't think I know enough to know." She wished idly for a jolt of caffeine.

Or maybe liquor. Something that would clear the confusion buzzing through it. A short pause let her try again. "I think it's really weird that we went to find our Warden, and he turned out to be dead without you getting a replacement like you expected. And I think it's even weirder that the people who were supposed to provide that replacement wound up dead, too. But I also think that the things you guys go up against, the things that killed Gregory and burned down the Guild house? Those things scare the crap out of me. And the thing they want to do? That scares me even more."

When Kees opened his mouth to roar at her, she held up a hand and pushed herself to her feet.

"I think there's something really big going on here," she continued, "bigger than just you and me. You're one Guardian, and I'm one human being. Whether or not I have the potential to be something more someday, I'm not even a Warden, and I so do not feel capable of rushing out of here and taking on an entire Order of magic-wielding sociopaths and their demon overlords. I don't have that kind of courage. Or that kind of stupidity."

She saw some new kind of emotion flash behind Kees's blazing eyes, but it was gone too fast for her to read. All she could do was read his expression, which at the moment was bad enough. He looked like he wanted to simultaneously howl at the moon, bench-press Mount Waddington, and rip the heads and limbs off every last living member of the Order of Eternal Darkness. And then he could really start to vent.

Her reptilian hindbrain had its suitcases in hand and was screaming at her that South America was really nice this time of year, but Ella didn't move. Whether that was because her legs were frozen in fear, or she knew Kees wouldn't hurt her was not a question she wanted to bet on right now.

She gathered her courage and reached out to lay a hand on his arm. She could almost feel the rage seething beneath his skin like flows of lava. Somehow, just touching all that anger and contained power filled her with strength and she felt her spine straighten.

"I think that if this is an act of war, you're going to need an army to take into battle," she said, marveling at the strength of her own voice. When had she become some kind of warrior woman?

"The Guild has been destroyed, human," he sneered. "What army would you have me gather?"

"The building was destroyed, and we know that Gregory is dead," Ella agreed, "but does that mean the Guild itself was wiped out? An organization that's been around, according to you, since practically the dawn of time? I'm pretty certain any group like that is going to be made up of more than twenty-four humans. There have to be survivors out there. Not to mention the other Guardians. If you're still around, shouldn't they be, too? If you're this anxious to kick demonic ass, imagine how your friends are going to feel."

Ella watched as his eyes narrowed and the harsh planes of his face shifted from frozen rage to bloodthirsty anticipation.

"You are right, little human," he rumbled, warmth returning to heat the gravel of his voice. "My brothers must hear of this. The must be woken as I was, and for that, we will need to find other members of the Guild." He bent his head to look down at her. "I still do not know how you woke me from my slumber, but I have never heard of it happening before, so we cannot rely on your ability to wake the others, even if I knew where all of them were located now."

"I agree. I don't even know what I did, let alone how I did it. We need to find surviving Wardens, and hopefully those with enough experience to know how to wake the other Guardians. They will at least know how to find them, won't they?"

"The Guild always knows where each of the Guardians lies at rest. If we find the Wardens, we can find my brothers."

"Okay." Ella's mind raced as she considered the possibilities. "With the headquarters of the Guild destroyed, and so publicly, we have to assume that any Wardens who survived also believe that every member of the organization is under attack. If I were in their shoes, I think I'd be keeping a pretty low profile at the moment, so I think we should move forward on the understanding that the remaining Wardens have gone underground. That means we won't be able to track them through their association."

She was mostly talking to herself, playing through the idea to see where it led, but she knew Kees had been listening. She had come to recognize the feel of his gaze on hers. She just knew when he was close by, and when he was paying close attention. It was a little weird and a little cool.

"I'm going to need some specific names to search for," she informed him. "That's the quickest way I can think of to track them down, especially if they're trying to escape notice. Do you remember any that you can give me?"

Kees grimaced. "I know the name of my own Warden, and the names of the three High Initiates of my last waking, but most of the others I would never have had reason to meet or to know. I cannot guarantee the names I give you are for Wardens still living."

"Crap." Ella chewed her lip as she considered what to do. She couldn't say she was surprised by what Kees told her. From everything she'd learned of the Guardians and the Guild of Wardens, it was a loosely banded confederation, to say the least. Now, with the central authority taken out with the fire, stringing the pieces back together would be a challenge.

An idea occurred to her, and she felt her lips curve at the edges.

"Wait a minute. You said that most of the time, Wardens pass on their duties to their kids, right? The sons and daughters of Wardens usually become Wardens in their own right and take over when the parent retires."

Kees nodded.

Ella flexed her fingers and plopped down in her computer chair. "Perfect. Give me those names you remember."

"You think you will be able to locate them after so many years? They were not young the last time I woke. I would be very surprised if they still lived."

She dismissed the concern, still smiling. "They don't need to be alive," she explained and pulled up the homepage for a huge genealogical database. "They just need to have offspring. Give me the names, big guy. If I can't find the people themselves, I'll bet you a toonie I can find their families. From there, it will be a. Piece. Of. Cake."

Chapter Seven

Okay, so "piece of cake" might have been a slight exaggeration. Ella worked the Web site for four more hours, but hit a wall sometime after midnight. Considering how little she'd slept the night before, it shocked her that she hadn't keeled over before the first of the prime-time TV lineup came on.

Damn, but she needed a nap.

Pushing away from the desk, she rose and stretched until every muscle in her body screamed a protest. The way they all fell back into place when she relaxed made her sigh. Better, but when this was all over, she needed to treat herself to a massage.

Of course, that idea raised the question of when all this *would* be over, and perhaps even more significantly, what all this was to begin with.

Somehow in the last twenty-four hours, Ella had gone from not knowing magic existed to working side by side with a living gargoyle to muster the forces of good and defeat the powers of evil. Along the way, she'd discovered that the thing she feared most about herself was of no concern to Kees, just magic she needed to learn to use, like somehow she'd gotten through school without learning how to read and now she was about to get a tutor to help with her ABC's.

She'd also found out that demons existed, on more than creepy-fun television programs, and that they had a hankering to destroy the world. More than that, she—Ella Marie Harrow—might just be able to help stop them.

And underneath it all, Ella had learned that something about the huge, mythological monster who was guiding her through this fun house of her new reality drew her like nothing else she'd ever experienced.

Ella sighed and wrapped her arms around herself to ward off a sudden chill. She glanced around the open living-dining area of the apartment and realized it lay empty. Frowning, she recalled—vaguely, as she had a tendency to get lost in her head when she was concentrating on something—that Kees had excused himself a while ago with a rumble about fresh air. She didn't, however, recall hearing the front door open or close, and she would swear in the Crown Court that he hadn't shifted forms before he left. The process was so compelling and fascinating to watch, there was no way she would have missed that.

Recalling the moment when he had first introduced himself, Ella padded on her stocking feet through the door into the bedroom. Sure enough, the window was open and she could see a dark shadow leaning against the high railing of her fire escape.

She stuck her head out the window and looked up at him. "Aren't you worried someone might walk by and see you out here?"

Kees snorted. "And what is a human more likely to think if they do see me? That a Guardian is hanging out on a human's fire escape? Or that the human in this apartment has a strange fixation with Gothic sculpture?"

"You're right. I suppose if you can refrain from singing

or tap dancing while you're out here, no one would think anything of it."

"I think I can contain myself."

The idea of the huge, muscular, fierce-looking creature beside her breaking into an old Fred Astaire routine made Ella grin. She could just imagine him in a top hat and tails.

She sobered as she caught him up on her efforts. "I didn't find anything yet, but I did make progress. I think I can track down at least one or two of the descendants of the names you gave me, but it might take me another day or two."

He grunted, but said nothing.

Kees and his enormous form filled every last square inch of space on Ella's tiny fire escape, so rather than trying to climb out and join him, she tugged a footstool over to the window and knelt on it, bracing her elbows on the sill and leaning her upper body out into the crisp night air.

She looked up and drew in the clear and cool. "I can't see very many stars tonight."

"One of the reasons I never understood the human impulse to cram themselves into cities and light lamps that never burn out. The first time I looked up at the night sky, I saw so many stars that if I had started counting that instant and never slept, I would still be counting right now."

The poetic words from the figure carved with fangs and wings and devil's horns only made them somehow more evocative. They made Ella long to see that same sky and count those same stars.

Lord, was this the exhaustion starting to get to her?

She and turned her gaze back to Kees. "Has the fresh air helped any?"

He glanced down at her. "I already told you how I feel about cities. Do you wish to discuss my opinion of the air in them as well?"

"Hey, I'm just trying to make conversation. You went from sticking to me like Velcro and insisting I couldn't be out of your sight for more than ten seconds at a time to brooding out on the fire escape in the space of a few hours. And let me just say, that asking personal questions of someone who could eat me with ketchup if I pissed him off is not the easiest thing in the world."

She huffed and looked away, staring toward the street at the end of the alley beside her building. "I wanted to know if you were okay."

She felt the air stir as his wings rustled and resettled behind him.

"I am fine."

Ella rolled her eyes and glanced back at him. "Fine? Wow, it really is true that all males are alike, no matter what their species. You don't look fine."

He didn't. In spite of his stony expressions, Ella had learned to read him in the short time she'd known him. She knew what it meant when he set his jaw at a certain angle, when his eyes glinted with a particular pattern of flame. Right now, those subtle little clues told her the Guardian was not fine at all. He was angry and frustrated and shocked and, unless she missed her guess, grieving, too.

"I really am sorry," she murmured, watching his profile as he gazed up at the sky. "No matter how few of them you'd met or how little you knew them, I know losing those Wardens upsets you. I know that the Guild was attacked while you were asleep bothers you, too. But I hope you realize that the fact that you didn't stop it doesn't make it your fault."

He stiffened, but he didn't look at her. "You make many presumptions about my feelings, human. Perhaps you would think again if I informed you that you may keep your concern and forget your soft heart. Guardians are sons of the stone. We do not experience human emotions."

Ella couldn't help it. She laughed.

Kees looked down at her and frowned. "What do you find amusing about that, little human? You laugh at hearing the truth?"

"I laugh at hearing bullshit," she countered. "And trust me, I spent six years in foster care. I know bullshit when I hear it."

"Foster care?"

She shrugged. "My parents died when I was twelve, and I didn't have any other close relatives. I lived in foster homes until I went to university." This wasn't where she'd pictured this conversation going, and she steered it right back onto a more comfortable track. "The point is, I've heard a lot of stupid stories, but the idea that you don't have emotions is about the dumbest one yet."

"I do not tell you stories. I speak only the truth. I was summoned to this plane for the sole purpose of battling the Seven. Why would I need to feel human emotion? I think you forget that I am not human."

"Forget you're not human? Don't make me laugh. I'm looking at you right now, Kees. You. With your wings and your tail and your horns and your fangs. Trust me, my vision is just fine, and there's no way that anyone seeing you like this could forget that you are something entirely different from human. But different doesn't mean diametrically opposed to. I know you're not human, and I also know that you feel emotions just like me. Whether you want to admit to it or not is an entirely different story."

Kees rounded on her and glared, temper lighting tiny little sparks that flitted through the blackness of his eyes. He crossed his arms over his chest and stared down at her as if he could intimidate her into changing her opinion.

"And how is it that you think you know what I feel or do not feel, little human? You have some other magical talent that is trained enough to allow you access into my mind? That would be quite a feat, considering that at this time last night, you did not even recognize magic when it was pouring through you like floodwaters."

"I don't need magic and I don't need to be psychic to know you feel emotion, big guy. You're feeling it right now. Admit it. At the moment you're feeling more than a little irritated with me."

His lip curled, baring a gleaming fang. "Irritation is not an emotion. An animal feels irritation when a thorn sticks in its fur. This is no different."

"First of all, let's not get into a debate about whether or not animals feel emotion, because I will have to kill you before it's over. Second, thanks for calling me a thorn in your side. I appreciate that. And third, irritation is totally an emotion. As is jealousy, which I know for sure you felt this morning when the police detective was flirting with me."

She mimicked his pose, crossing her arms over her chest and glaring at him. The fact that she was currently bent at the waist with her ass sticking up halfway into her bedroom maybe put her at a slight disadvantage, but she ignored it. Or pretended to.

"Do not be ridiculous, human," Kees scoffed, his brows drawing down so far, she worried he might blind himself. "That was not jealousy. It was merely another example of irritation. I found it irritating that the human male had interrupted our attempt to acquire information from the museum."

"Uh-huh. And that's why you made it a point to kiss me in front of him, right? To punish him for 'interrupting' us? 'Cause that makes a lot of sense. I know that my immediate thought when I try to come up with ways to punish people for interruptions, kissing someone is always the first thing I think of."

Her sarcasm lit more sparks in his eyes until the tiny pinpricks of flame joined together in a steady blaze.

"Would you prefer I had kissed you for another reason, little human?" Somehow his voice dropped even lower, until Ella could feel it vibrating through her, like the aftershocks of a major earthquake.

Faster than she had thought possible, he moved, his enormous hands wrapping around her arms until his claws overlapped onto the heels of his hands. He tugged and her lower body slid through the open window until he had her out on the fire escape with him, once more with her feet dangling inches and inches above the floor. But this time, he didn't pin her against a wall. This time he pinned her against his own body, her breasts flattened against his massive chest, her hips bumping against his, dangling boneless and helpless at his whim.

She had a fleeting, frantic thought about his size—my God, he was *huge*—before his head descended, and he sealed his mouth over hers for the second time that day.

There was no comparison to the first.

No matter what Kees claimed when she had taunted him a moment ago, Ella knew very well that the first kiss had been a show, deliberately staged and carefully gauged to stake a claim on her that Detective Mike McQuaid would have to be blind, deaf, and brain-dead not to recognize. The fact that Kees thought he could convince her there had been no emotion behind the act then by repeating it now—repeating it and outdoing it by a landslide, mind you—almost made Ella want to laugh.

Instead, she groaned.

She also squirmed against the body holding her, not because she felt the need to escape, but because she wanted to get closer.

Their earlier kiss had taken Ella by surprise. Despite his taking on the disguise of being her boyfriend in front of the museum staff and the police they had encountered this morning, until that moment, Kees had given no indication he thought of her in any intimate or sexual way. He'd never so much as hinted he wanted to put the moves on her.

This, however, this kiss was definitely a move.

His lips covered hers, warm and exciting, sealing her off from the cold night air. At first they settled, nudged, shifted, exploring the softness of her, the contrast of it against his own, more unforgiving planes. The teasing made her shiver, and his arms closed tighter around her. She pressed close, wanting more.

Her lips parted on a sigh of longing that she had never intended to let escape, but she couldn't regret it, not when it seemed to spur Kees on. His mouth opened, his tongue pressed forward, demanding entry she gladly gave him. Even this small part of him inside her made her body tighten, her hands shake, and she longed to steady them by pressing them against his skin, tangling them in his hair, touching him any way she could.

He seemed to hear her thoughts. A groan rumbled through his chest and his grip shifted. He released his hold on her upper arms, one hand drifting down to cup her bottom, supporting her weight on his palm and muscular forearm. She gasped and melted against him, feeling a surge of heat at the core of her. Kees slid his other hand up her back until she felt his fingers tangle in her hair, pulling her head gently but firmly to the perfect position, allowing him to dive even deeper into the kiss.

Now free to touch him, Ella took instant advantage. She wrapped her arms around his shoulders and clung, wanting to twine around him and climb toward the sun like a honeysuckle vine. The fact that it was after midnight didn't bother her in the least. She'd be more than happy to take her time and savor every minute.

She gasped when she felt the sharp edge of a fang against her tongue, but there was no fear in her. Her subconscious had stopped telling her to look at Kees as some sort of monster hours ago. Like she'd told him, she knew perfectly well he wasn't human, but that didn't matter to her.

When he touched her, nothing mattered but that he continue to touch her.

In fact, Ella found herself savoring his uniqueness. He kissed her as if he wanted to devour her, but he took care not to so much as prick her with a fang, and his claws never broke her skin where he touched her.

His skin fascinated her and she ran her fingers back and forth over the surface again and again until the tips tingled. When she smoothed her hands down, his skin felt silky smooth, no hair marring the lines and grooves of his extraordinarily developed musculature. But when she ran her fingers back up in the opposite direction, the sensation changed to something like unpolished stone, or a fine-grain emery board. The contrast had her nearly hypnotized, and the thought of that skin rubbing against hers made her shiver uncontrollably.

Kees felt the ripples and lifted his head, his dark eyes blazing down at her. "As you can see, instinct can be a powerful thing, little human."

She stared right back up at him. "My name is Ella. And you can hide behind instinct all you want, but we both know that's what you're doing, so let me point out: fear is just another kind of emotion."

Anger flashed in his expression, but she refrained from pointing that out as well. He didn't appear in the right frame of mind to hear it.

"You think this is an emotion?" He demanded, his hand clenching around the cheek of her ass and grinding her pelvis against a remarkably human-feeling erection.

Only, you know, ginormous. "It doesn't take emotion for me to want to fuck you, *human,* any more than it takes emotion for me to feel hunger. It is instinct. All animals have the instinct to rut."

Ella knew she certainly did. She wanted Kees with a surprising intensity, one she hadn't experienced before, but she knew what she felt was more than instinct. She felt something for this man, this myth, who held her so carnally yet so carefully against him. She just didn't think he was ready to hear that.

That fear thing again.

Instead of pushing him further, Ella backed off, at least emotionally. If Kees didn't want to discuss the idea of having feelings, maybe they should stop talking altogether.

She slid a hand up his back, briefly kneading the back of his neck before spearing her fingers into the surprisingly soft, dark hair that curled against his nape. Using her grip as leverage, she stretched up against him and pressed her lips back to his. "Well, if you're really driven by instinct," she breathed into his mouth, "maybe you should just give in."

He froze, momentarily going so still, Ella almost wondered if he'd turned back to stone. Then he let out a growl so deep and so long, she feared she might have pushed him too far.

She felt her head spin, saw the world tilt, and wondered if she was going to pass out. No, she'd just been readjusting to the change in altitude and position when Kees swept a hand under her legs and shifted her to a cradle hold against his chest. At the same moment, he had shifted back into his human form.

Confused, Ella frowned up at him. "What are you doing?"

"Giving in to instinct."

Without saying another word, he maneuvered her back

inside through the bedroom window and quickly climbed in behind her. Crowding against her, he cupped his hands around her hips and guided her relentlessly toward the bed. Ella didn't bother to protest.

Instead, she scooted backwards into the center of the mattress and continued to scowl at him. "Why did you change your form?"

He raised an eyebrow and stripped off the shirt that had appeared when he shifted. "You think you'd like being fucked by a monster?"

"You're not a monster," she said with a glare, trying not to be distracted by the smooth, bronzed expanse of his muscled chest. Lord, no matter what he looked like. "And either way, you're you. Did I give you any indication you creeped me out in your natural form?"

He stared at her through narrowed eyes, then shrugged. "No. But I can't take you in that body. I could hurt you too easily. As it is, I will have to take great care not to injure you. You are so small and delicate. So different from me."

Ella grinned. "Well, I hope so—otherwise, this would be an entirely different experience. One I'd not be so into."

Kees stalked closer and reached for the fly of his jeans. "Don't worry, little human. I will be gentle."

"Not too gentle, I hope. I'm tougher than I look." She rose to her knees as he approached, and ran a hand over the bare skin of his chest. In neither form had she seen him with body hair. She didn't mind a man with hair, but this allowed her to see every twitch and ripple of his delicious muscles. "And my name is Ella."

He growled and cupped the back of her head in one giant hand, yanking her forward for another devouring kiss.

Ella met him hunger for hunger. Her tongue tangled with his, briefly caressing, then sliding away to tease with fleeting touches to his lips. He gave chase, a born conqueror, and fisted his hand in her hair. Ella moaned at the slight pressure and dug her fingers into his shoulders.

God, how she wanted him.

The feeling—the *instinct*—appeared to be mutual.

His free hand ran down her arm, over her hip and back up, sliding over her ribs to cup her breast. Electricity jolted through her. She'd never thought of her breasts as particularly sensitive, but she could swear she felt every single nerve ending under her skin jump at his touch. His hand felt warm, a burning pressure even through the fabric of her blouse and bra.

The layers of cotton didn't seem to impress him. He grumbled something beneath his breath, drawing back from her mouth to scowl down at her still fully clothed form.

He released her and grasped the hem of her cotton top. "Off," he snarled, and yanked the offending garment up over her head.

She couldn't have cared less where it landed when he tossed it aside. All she wanted was to feel his hot, smooth skin against hers.

His hands came back around her, sliding along the indent of her waist, seeming to savor the softness of her skin and the warmth of her curves. Ella had what she considered an ordinary body, not fat and not thin, with breasts too big to go braless and too small to draw unwanted attention. She had always thought her stomach a little too soft, her waist and thighs a little too thick, but Kees seemed to savor the feel of her. The expression of intense admiration on his face made her even hotter, if that were possible. A minute ago, she would have argued no.

She would have been oh so wrong.

Dark eyes gleaming, Kees leaned forward and pressed his face against the curve of her shoulder. She felt his chest expand as he inhaled deeply, drawing in her scent.

She turned her head into him, feeling his dark hair brush like strands of satin against her cheek, and savored his own unique fragrance. He smelled of night and dark forests and clean burning flames. She wanted to warm herself against his skin.

Her head fell back, too heavy to support, when he closed his teeth gently on the vulnerable spot where her neck met her shoulder. The heat and pressure shot straight to her center and she could feel herself growing wet. Suddenly the comfortable trousers she wore felt anything but, and her bra seemed to cut into her skin, now three sizes too small. She whimpered and wriggled against him.

She felt a huff of air against her skin, like a silent chuckle, and Kees released the bite. His tongue smoothed over the spot, laving at the indentations left by his teeth, before he trailed a line of kisses over her skin, following the path left by the finger he used to push her bra strap off her shoulder and down her arm.

He repeated the action on the other side, first the bite, then the kisses, until both her bra straps drooped uselessly against her arms and she felt ready to scream with the frustration of still being mostly and irritatingly dressed.

"Kees," she moaned, digging her nails into his biceps, holding on for dear life while her world went up in flames.

He heard the plea in her voice, he must have, but he merely laughed again, softly, and let his hands go wandering, sliding up and down her already overly sensitive skin. He teased around the waistband of her trousers, then down the top of the material to knead the tense muscles of her thighs.

Who would have thought an emotionless stone warrior could be such a damned tease?

He pressed a kiss to the skin between her breasts just above the clasp of her bra. If he didn't flick the thing open and peel the damned bra off her in the next fifteen seconds, she swore to all that was holy, she would find a way to make him suffer. Just see if she didn't.

In fact, she should start now.

Releasing her grip on him, she opened the clasp herself and let the two halves peel away. Just before her nipples popped into sight, she used her hands to sweep the lacy fabric away and covered herself, deliberately denying him a glimpse.

He hissed a warning and his eyes narrowed, his hands abandoning their explorations to close over her own. He tugged gently, but his gaze remained on her face, not her breasts.

"Let me see," he demanded.

"Oh, so now you want to? A minute ago, you didn't seem like you were in any particular hurry."

He leaned in and set his teeth against the inner curve of her left breast where her small hands left too much skin exposed.

"A minute ago, the only thing standing in my way was a scrap of nothing. I could see your pink little nipples begging for me through the fabric. But these—" He tugged her hands again, more firmly. "—these have cut off my view. Let me see."

Ella's mouth curved, naughty impulses she'd never felt before urging her to tease and taunt him for every inch she surrendered. She parted the fingers of her right hand just enough for the tip of her tightly beaded nipple to poke through and nestle against his palm. "Let you see? You mean, like this?"

Kees made a low sound of arousal and let his hands fall. He gripped her hips and pulled her toward the edge of the mattress, imprisoning her between his muscled thighs. "The other."

"Oh, like this." Grinning even wider, Ella closed her right hand and parted the fingers on her left, concealing the first nipple even as she revealed the second.

Kees grumbled a warning, and Ella giggled softly, feeling like a temptress for the first time in her life. She could sense the desire pouring off the man in front of her, and to be wanted so obviously, so fiercely, went to her head like moonshine. He made her feel like a goddess.

Provided goddesses got this horny.

Before she could think of another way to taunt him, his head swooped down, and she felt the hot swipe of his tongue against her nipple. She nearly collapsed into a heap of boneless lust.

Suddenly she went from teasing to begging, moving her hands from concealing her breasts to cupping and raising them to his mouth like an offering. He took immediate advantage, closing his lips around one firm peak and drawing on it with fierce intensity. Ella moaned and arched to encourage him in taking even more. Whatever he could take, she burned to give.

He used his teeth and tongue on her, scraping over the peaks, then swirling around and tugging her deeper for another bout of strong suction. She could feel her bones melting and reached out to brace herself against his shoulders, struggling to stay upright where he could feast on her forever.

Kees, though, had other ideas. His hands tightened around her hips, lifting her easily and settling her in the middle of the wide mattress. He came down over her, releasing her nipple only to move to its twin to repeat the torture nibble for nibble. His hands finally—finally—went to her trousers and stripped the garment from her, taking her panties along with it. She stretched beneath him, bare and aching, held captive by an entirely new form of magic, one she'd thought existed only in books and movies.

And porn. Only in porn did people appear to need sex as badly as she needed it right that minute. If Kees didn't fuck her soon, she was going to die. Literally. She could spontaneously combust at any minute now.

Ella bent her knees, drawing her legs up to wrap them around his waist, only to encounter the thick, rough fabric of his jeans. She whined in protest and immediately reached for the offending denim, intent on sending it wherever her own clothes had disappeared to.

To her surprise and pleasure, instead of finding a buttoned fly, she found an open vee of hot skin and rough hair that began on his lower belly and traced a happy path down to his groin. She recalled briefly that he'd opened his jeans earlier, but she distracted him before he'd gotten them off. Now she was distracted, her attention immediately wandering when she realized she could slip her hand into that opening and curl her fingers tightly around his erect shaft.

He felt huge and hot and hard, velvety skin over red-hot iron. He was thick enough that her fingers didn't close around his girth, and as she stroked slowly from tip to root, she realized he boasted impressive length as well. Her pussy clenched in anticipation. She hadn't had a lover in a long time, and never one like Kees. The idea of taking him inside her both aroused and intimidated her. She knew her body was designed to stretch, but she didn't think it had ever stretched quite so far before.

Ella squeezed, wringing a groan from his throat that echoed the torments of the damned. Usually, though, the damned didn't lean into the torment in a silent entreaty for more. Or so she assumed. She didn't think hell was likely to be kinky.

She repeated the motion and could almost hear the snap of the thread that had held Kees back until now. Abandoning her nipple with a pop of released suction, he swooped down for a ravenous kiss before levering himself off the bed and to his feet.

Momentarily dazed, she reached out for him, but by the time she raised her heavy limbs, he had stripped off the last barrier between them. His eyes glowed, almost more flame than black, as he turned to climb back into the bed above her.

Another kiss had her moaning and gasping for air, her arms wrapping around him, hands clutching as she tried to bring him down over her. She felt desperate to experience his weight, the sheer bulk of him pressing her against the mattress, pinning her in place with his hands and his body as he drove into her softness.

Kees had other plans, apparently. Instead of settling over her and bringing their bodies together the way she needed, he dragged his mouth from hers and drew it over her chin and down her throat, nipping and scraping and licking as he went. It felt as if he mapped her body, tracing every curve from the soft angle of her collarbone, over the slope of her breast.

Her nipples received special attention, enough to make her pant and plead, but then he moved on, nuzzling the heavy undersides of her breasts, drawing in her scent. He moved slowly, almost reverently, down her rib cage and over the soft curve of her belly until she felt his breath stir the short, dense curls over her mound.

He was trying to kill her, she decided, struggling for air or sanity, already convinced she could forget having both. When his big, rough hands slid down her legs to grasp her just above the knees, her heart nearly did give out. Her muscles definitely did. They yielded at his slightest touch, parting at his urging, giving to the pressure until he had spread her obscenely wide before him.

Ella quivered, as tense as a drawn bow. She felt the cold air against her most tender flesh, her own dampness chilling her when the faintest draft feathered over her. Then she felt a grazing warmth puff of air, and she tucked her head back hard against the mattress and prayed for him to touch her.

He didn't disappoint.

She heard a low rumble of pleasure and felt his fingers tighten on her inner thighs as he dipped his head and set the flat of his tongue firmly against her damp folds. A cry escaped her, thin and high, but she was too far gone to care. It caught and stuttered in her throat when he dragged through the softness, swirling slowly around her clit before finishing the swipe with a flick to the sensitive nub. Ella whimpered.

When he did it again, she shuddered.

The tenth time, she screamed as her body unraveled in a rush of ecstasy.

She heard his rumble of amusement under the strangled rasp of her own panting. She felt limp and wrung out and hoped he could take care of the rest of this without a lot of help from her. She figured it would be Thursday before she regained control of her own limbs.

Thursday at the earliest.

Kees gave no indication that he noticed her lack of energy. He simply eased his way up her body until he pressed against her side from the top of her tousled hair to the tip of her limp toes. He held himself half over her, braced on one arm and the knee he tucked between her thighs, and when he bent toward her, he blocked out all the light in the room.

He stole all the oxygen, too. As if she wasn't having enough trouble breathing.

She felt his lips brush against hers, and a small tingle of electricity took her by surprise. She hadn't thought she had it in her. Then his tongue teased between, and she sighed. He kissed her deeply, intently, but slowly, and Ella did her best to respond. The man deserved that much, even if she doubted she could offer much more than limp compliance. At least, not until after she'd had a nap. Give her a couple of hours of sleep, and she'd rock his Rip Van Winkled little world.

Her throat caught when his hand stroked over her slowly cooling skin, cupping her breast and giving a fond squeeze before sliding down over her belly to ruffle her curls. The man was trying to get milk from a boar hog at this point, but his touch felt so good, she made no move to warn him. Not even to apologize. After all, if she was too tired to fuck him now, whose fault was that?

His fingers delved further, sliding over her clit firmly enough to make her twitch. There must have been one last synapse holding out on her, but now she was definitely down for the count. Still, her hips arched just a bit into his touch as he parted her folds and traced the seam of her sex down to her tender opening. A long, lean finger circled, teased, then pressed inside and her muscles clamped instinctively around him.

Something else she hadn't thought she had the energy for.

Opening her eyes, she gazed blearily up into a face drawn taut and fierce with passion. Still, even now his mouth curved slightly at the corners and his eyes glowed bright and dark as he gazed down at her. He kept his gaze trained on her face even as he began to stroke in and out of her body, his callused finger gliding easily through her abundant wetness.

Ella opened her mouth to apologize, to confess that he'd wrung her out, but a small quiver deep in her womb stopped her. Her heart stuttered, and she looked down at his palm pressed tightly against her mound as if she couldn't figure out what it was doing there.

Well, sure, she knew what it was doing; she just couldn't

figure out how it was doing it. Was part of Kees's Guardian magic the ability to wring blood from a stone? Or, in this case, orgasms from an exhausted pussy?

His teeth flashed in a feral grin, and Ella almost missed the glint of fang that usually accompanied his smiles. The finger inside her curled and pressed against her inner walls, rubbing firmly on a spot that made her eyes cross and her legs tremble. And just like that, desire flooded through her, bringing every last nerve ending back to life and filling her with renewed energy.

Dear sweet heaven, how did he *do* that?

He laughed dark and low and leaned closer, letting his exhalation stir the damp, silky strands of hair at her ear.

"I feel an instinctive need to make you come again, little human," he purred, shifting his hand and pressing a second finger inside her. "Let's see if I can manage that, hmmm?"

His fingers hooked and rubbed, and Ella gasped and arched and begged for more. He gave her more pleasure than she had ever imagined and simultaneously stripped away every last impulse she might have to resist him. She had propositioned Kees thinking to prove to him that he did feel emotion, that what was between them was more than just instinct, more than just the animal urge to mate, and here he had reduced her to little more than a female in heat. She would have done almost anything in that moment just for the pleasure of feeling his body joined to hers.

"Please," she half sobbed, unsure if she wanted him to stop or give her more, unsure if she could take it either way.

He made the decision for her, adding a third finger, stretching her, preparing her, even as he pressed the heel of his hand hard against her swollen clit. The sensations quickly overwhelmed her, and she came again with a scream, hoarser this time, her throat already roughened by the first time.

Her body clamped down around his fingers, but he stroked through her grip for several long seconds, prolonging the orgasm, keeping the sharp sensations rolling over her in wave after wave. But this time, he moved before the pleasure could drag her under.

His hand slid away, leaving her empty and still reeling, but not for long. In the space between heartbeats, he moved over her, overwhelming her, bracing his hands beside her shoulders and using his knees to spread her legs even wider until she felt the burning stretch high in her inner thighs.

Her hands came up, damp and shaking, and she gripped his shoulders desperately, her gaze locking with his as he settled himself in the cradle of her hips.

She felt the head of his cock, wide and damp with his own desire, pressing urgently against her. She couldn't speak, couldn't move, couldn't moan, but she could shift her hips just a little, just enough to tilt them to a more welcoming angle. Just enough to lure him inside her, into the place that ached and burned to feel him.

His lips parted, and she thought he meant to speak, but he only groaned and eased forward, breaching the tight ring of muscle at her entrance and feeding her the head of his cock.

She felt the burn, the stretching, but it wasn't enough. He had made her so hungry, she didn't know if there was such a thing anymore. All she knew was that she ached, deep inside, and he was the only thing that could ease her.

Her lips parted as his gaze slid down, watching as she licked the dry, cracked skin before returning to lock with hers. She could see no blackness now, only fire. Flames leapt and danced in his eyes, a million shades of red and gold, orange and amber, blue and white at the center, where he burned the hottest.

The heat threatened to sear her, to leave scars like a permanent brand on her flesh. Instead of fearing it, Ella longed for it. She wanted to throw herself into those flames and emerge new, like a phoenix taking flight.

She lifted her head from the mattress, straining toward him. She didn't know what she thought, if she honestly believed she could walk into the fire of his eyes. She just knew she needed to be closer, to be one, to feel him with every inch of her body and every fiber of her soul.

And oh, he gave her inches.

With a muffled roar, his restraint shattered. Gone was the slow, measured torment. Kees thrust inside her with the impact of a battering ram, forcing her tight channel to part around his invading shaft. She felt him so deep inside her, she pictured him bumping up against her heart. She felt him nudge her cervix, but the slight instant of discomfort only seemed to make her hotter.

After pulling back, he thrust again, this time causing nothing but wild, unspeakable pleasure. He settled into a fast, pounding rhythm, and all Ella could do was hold on and hope she made it through in one piece.

Her hands gripped him hard, her nails digging in when sweat made his skin slick and slippery. She felt her toes curl and drew her legs up to wrap around his pistoning hips.

Kees rode her like a madman. He seemed utterly lost in the moment, his breath billowing in and out like steam from a mighty engine, but his eyes never left her face.

He stared at her like she held the secrets of the universe, but the only truth she had to offer was the one he had already discovered: that they fit together like pieces of a puzzle, two halves of a whole. One being, separated by time, by space, by species and experience, yet united by magic and passion.

Despite the pleasure he poured on her like hot summer rain, Ella had thought she was finished. She hadn't expected the second climax, but when a third threatened to gather deep in her womb, she wanted to scream for mercy. Another explosion like that might just rip her apart.

Kees didn't seem to care. He continued to ride her, hard and desperate. His hands dropped to close about her hips. Shifting his weight backwards, he slid his palms beneath her and curled his fingers around her ass cheeks to yank her firmly into his increasingly wild thrusts.

In and out he thrust, but his rhythm started to break down. Now he just moved according to the force of his lust. Ella felt her body tighten, felt her clit draw up, felt her heart leap into her throat as sensation blew over her, rushing in like a tidal wave and sweeping everything but her and Kees away in its path.

Even as her pussy clenched tight, she heard his sharp curse and felt his hips jerk convulsively. His cock twitched inside her, and he came with a roar, bellowing her name as he released a torrent of heat deep inside her.

Still shuddering, he collapsed atop her on a long, strangled groan. It sounded as if someone had just wrung out his soul.

Ella knew precisely how he felt.

Chapter Eight

Kees felt nothing.

He reminded himself of that, over and over, but doubt continued to claw at his gut, unsettling him. He had intended to demonstrate to Ella that a Guardian was ruled by logic and instinct. He wanted her to realize that no emotion polluted his thoughts or actions. Sex, after all, was the most fundamentally instinctive of acts, an action ruled by hormones and the most primal and reptilian areas of the brain.

Instead, he had ended up making love to her, showering her with pleasure as if she were the most precious thing in his universe. And he'd done it all for the simple joy of hearing her sigh.

What in the name of the Light was the matter with him?

Kees lay in the dark of the bedroom and stared at the ceiling. Sometime ago, he had rolled off his human lover for fear of crushing her and settled onto his back. She had followed, soft and sleepy, and curled against his side like a contented kitten. She'd nestled her cheek into the hollow of his shoulder, draped an arm across his chest, and promptly drifted into sleep. So, at least one of them was getting some rest.

Not that he really needed any. He'd been resting for centuries, after all, and could go for days at a time before adjusting to the pace of the waking world. Even then, he'd need no more than three or four hours of rest a night to remain at full energy. His problem, then, wasn't lack of sleep; it was the thoughts keeping him awake.

Thoughts, he told himself firmly. Not emotions.

Just the idea that he might be experiencing human emotion for the first time in his long existence filled Kees with unease. He'd battled and slept through ages of men without ever suffering such an affliction. He hadn't thought it was possible.

It shouldn't be. The Guardians had been formed from stone, carved by the powers of the Light, and summoned from the ether into bodies as hard and enduring as their mission. They needed to be tough, strong, impervious to all but the fiercest attacks; otherwise, they could never succeed in keeping the demons of the Darkness at bay. Like mountains of rock, he and his brothers withstood the forces of evil that buffeted them, wearing down the opposition until it could be banished into the prisons of the barren planes.

Never had he heard of a Guardian who felt as the humans felt. Guardians experienced rage and frustration at the continued existence of the Seven. Those glimpses of feeling fueled their warfare, made them stronger and deadlier, but beyond that, they existed in an eternal state of cool detachment.

Even for the Wardens who served them, no Guardian ever developed feelings of caring or love. Kees still raged over Gregory's death, but not because he cared about the mage; he raged because the *nocturnis* had dared to strike against him while he slept. Part of his task was to protect the Wardens of the Guild so that their mission continued for as long as the Seven continued to exist. Failing at that task angered Kees, and he had to remind himself not to clench his hand around the soft human female beside him. He had no desire to injure her, and less to wake her.

He still needed to think.

How could an emotionless Guardian define what he experienced around his small human? The lust was easy. Lust was simple, as he'd told Ella, animal and instinctive. Kees had known lust before, mostly after battle, when the hot tide of fury still coursed through him. In those times, he and his brothers had taken women, some human, some mages. Occasionally a minor guard who had joined in the fight. Sex acted as a release and a pressure valve, allowing the Guardians to let go of the intensity of the fight so that they could settle once more to sleep. That made it even harder for him to understand why sex with the human beside him didn't make him feel relaxed and ready to slumber, but awake and electric and hungry to taste her again.

Was this some sort of magic she possessed that he had never encountered before?

Kees had a feeling such an explanation was much too easy.

In actuality it didn't matter how or why he experienced these unfamiliar sensations around Ella. What mattered was that such a thing could not be allowed. Lust he could tolerate, but from now on, Kees would ensure that no more than lust would color his view of the small human. He would not allow it.

When dawn broke, he would make certain that the woman knew exactly where she stood. There would be no more tenderness, no more of her attempting to probe his soul and convince him of impossible ideas.

Kees was a Guardian, and while the loss of so many members of the Guild of Wardens made finding someone with Ella's magical talent critical to their future, he must make her understand what the future would hold.

Stone and magic, not sweetness and love.

Resolved on his next moves, Kees closed his eyes. He would need his rest if he intended to follow through with his plan, and Kees always followed through.

"Today we must begin your training."

Ella stepped out of the bathroom wearing a stretchy tank top and baggy pajama pants, holding a towel to her still dripping hair. She froze at the bark in Kees's voice. Why did he sound angry?

"What?"

Kees stood in the doorway to the bedroom, his natural form filling the doorway, his wings actually rising above the lintel on either side of the opening. He appeared even more enormous that usual. And more intimidating. His harsh features were drawn tight into a fearsome scowl, and he glared at her as if he found her a particularly bothersome irritation.

What the hell was going on?

"You need to learn to control your magic, then you need to learn to use it," he snapped, his expression never changing. "I had hoped Gregory would take on the responsibility, or at least contact the Guild and ask them to assign you a proper mentor, but neither of those options is available to us any longer. Until we locate another Warden and discover the current state of the Guild, I will have to do it myself."

Ella had been a little surprised to wake in her bed alone an hour earlier, but she hadn't worried. Maybe she should have. The Guardian currently staring at her like something nasty on the sole of his shoe—you know, if he had worn shoes—bore absolutely no resemblance to her lover from the night before. All she could remember were stunning mutual orgasms and the sense of peace that filled her as she had fallen asleep in his arms. Had she slapped his face in her sleep or something?

Clearly something had gone on that Ella wasn't aware of, because this was not how she'd been expecting things to go between them this morning. Awkwardness she could have dealt with. Hell, everyone felt a little off the first time they woke up next to a new person, but she did not appreciate being treated like a mistake.

A mistake. That was exactly how Kees was looking at her, and Ella felt her spine stiffen in response. Gathering up the resulting anger made it easier to ignore the hurt.

And there was a lot of hurt.

"Don't do me any favors," she bit out, squaring her shoulders and meeting him glare for glare. "Frankly, I'm not sure I'm up for any lessons at the moment. Particularly not if you're teaching them."

"We don't have a choice." His words stopped her as she made to turn back to the bathroom. Right now, she wanted to slam the door and get a bit of space to regroup, but Kees didn't appear inclined to cooperate. "It doesn't matter what either of us would prefer. Your magic is out of control, and that makes you vulnerable. The *nocturnis* have clearly made Wardens a target of attack for whatever reason, but we can't assume that they wouldn't also go after latent talents like you. You need to learn control, so that you can then learn to defend."

Ella gritted her teeth. "Trust me, big guy, if I weren't in control of my magic, you wouldn't still be standing. Right now, I wouldn't let you teach me to finger paint, much less cast spells or some shit. I think a better idea would be for you to get the hell out of my apartment and come back about half past kiss-my-ass, okay?"

He ignored her. "Finish dressing. I will wait in the other room."

"Yeah, well, you can wait until hell freezes over."

Ella swept around and stalked back into the bathroom, slamming the door hard behind her. No sound from Kees seeped through from the other side.

Sagging against the wooden panels, Ella let herself sink to the floor. What the hell had just happened? she asked herself, drawing her knees up to her chest and cupping her head in her hands. How the hell had they gone from lovers to opposing sides in a new cold war without her even being conscious for the opening skirmish?

Sometime while she slept, a bug of gigantic proportions had crawled up Kees Livingston's ass. (Yeah, don't think she'd forgotten about that little pun of his, but him having a last name—even one as obvious as that—made being mad at him a lot more comfortable. It was easier to mentally yell at someone with two names than with just one. Better scansion.) Ella really couldn't think of a better explanation. After all, the last time they'd interacted with each other, she'd been too busy coming to somehow piss him off. And considering that he'd made her do it three times, somehow she didn't think her orgasms were the root of his issues.

And boy, did that gargoyle have 'sues. Big floppy clown 'sues, as a matter of fact, but that didn't give him the right to take those out on Ella. She was the only one helping him at the moment. The least he could do was treat her with a little human decency.

Of course, Kees wasn't human, so what would he know about that? Maybe gargoyle decency was an entirely different sort of thing. Or maybe gargoyles didn't have any decency to begin with.

She wanted to stick with that explanation, just to make it easier to hate the big, winged jerk, but she couldn't do it. Kees had proved to be remarkably decent in the short—ridiculously short, considering what they'd done last night—time that she'd known him. He'd never hurt her, he'd defended her, tried to protect her from the police, and shown her appreciation for the help she'd given him, even if his impatience simmered at the lack of immediate answers to all his questions.

No, Kees was a decent guy, for a gargoyle.

Sighing, Ella pushed to her feet and reached for the hair dryer. Sitting on the bathroom floor brooding wasn't going to get her anywhere. Whatever Kees's problem was, she couldn't figure it out from behind a closed door. For that, she'd need to be with him.

Which, on the bright side, would also give her the opportunity to gift him with a good, solid kick to the nuts, if he continued to act like an asshole.

Feeling the tiniest bit better, Ella turned on the noisy machine and set about preparing for the day. Whatever it turned out to hold, she would deal with it, even if that meant voluntarily taking instructions from the grumpy, bug-up-his-ass gargoyle in the other room. On top of everything else, Ella was just too damned proud to hide away just because the jerk had hurt her feelings. Oh, no, she was way better than that.

When she stepped out of the bedroom fifteen minutes later, she had her hair pulled back in a loose braid and her armor on, in the form of comfortable black yoga pants and a slim-fitting T-shirt in soft pink. She didn't see any reason to dress up for magic lessons, and the yoga pants gave her lots of freedom of movement.

You know, for ball-kicking.

Drawing back her shoulders, she spoke clearly and without expression. "I'm ready."

Kees looked up from where he'd been moving her furniture out of the center of the room and nodded. His face remained carved in harsh lines, but Ella ignored it. Let him enjoy his bad mood. She had better things to do than worry about him.

"Fine. Come here and sit."

He pointed to a spot on the carpet, roughly in the center of the room. Ella walked forward and sank to the floor, folding her legs in front of her tailor-fashion.

"So, what now?" she asked flatly.

"Now we get to work."

Two hours later, Ella appreciated why Kees called it work. A fine sheen of sweat covered her forehead, and she felt as if she'd just run a half marathon in really old sneakers.

The first thing he made her do was open the door, and frankly, it had been the hardest. She still cringed at the memories, expecting to lose all control and hear the screaming and the grinding and the explosive crash of metal on metal. She knew Kees must have seen her expression, but he said nothing, only told her to let the magic through until she gave in and allowed it to escape.

It rushed through her with force and momentum just as it had the other night when she tried to use it to drive away the monster at the museum, but just like last time, Kees stood firm and let the power flow around him. He might actually have been made of stone, standing like a boulder in the path of a rushing river. He remained solid and untouched by the current.

That helped to reassure Ella. For several minutes, he instructed her to do nothing, to just let the magic go and give up trying to hold it back. Keeping it all pent up just made it harder to handle, he told her, and she found that his words almost made sense. For instance, the flood didn't last as long this time as it had the other night, when it had been years and years since she allowed much of the energy to escape. This time, it burst out at first, but then settled into a strong, steady but bearable stream.

Before the power could begin to thin and drain her as it had the last time, Kees's voice cut through the electric hum and told her to ground the magic. She didn't understand what he meant at first, but he talked her through it, his voice remarkably patient if still devoid of any emotion. He told her to picture her spine growing downward like the root of a great tree. He told her how it sank through the floor, through the building beneath her until it tapped into the rock and soil below.

His voice guided her as she imagined the root branching, spreading, burrowing through the earth until she felt truly anchored, more settled than she'd ever been in her life. It was glorious.

Ella could feel the power of the earth all around her. It all but vibrated with untapped energy of life. The potential in it shook her. Here, she realized, was a natural resource she'd never know existed, more infinite than any water or mineral known to man. Magic, she now knew, was what really powered the earth.

She gasped softly as she learned to hear the power, like a sweet song sung by a billion voices.

"That's the Source." She heard Kees's voice, a low rumble that somehow provided the perfect bass note to the music filling her soul. "You can always draw on the Source for power, but right now you're going to give power back. You have too much built up inside you, and it's time to restore the balance."

Ella could think of nothing she wanted more.

She listened intently and followed his instructions to the letter. Holding herself still, she just waited, listening to the earth's song and feeling her own magic flowing through her. Slowly, she felt understanding flower, felt the rhythms whispering to her, and when Kees spoke again, she understood instinctively how to follow his commands.

Carefully, she reached out to gather the magic to her, not so much interrupting the flow as redirecting it. Rather than overwhelming her, this time the magic enveloped her and started to sing its own song. It shifted and formed until she could perceive it with her artist's eye, now perceiving the layers and layers of color in the stream that had previously appeared an even bluish white. Now she could see red and orange and yellow and green and purple and brown and every color she could imagine all twining and blending together in masterful brushstrokes of power.

She wanted to weep at the beauty of it.

Instead, she followed Kees's instructions, forming the magic to her will and directing it to the center of her, to the root she now had planted deep in the earth. The magic cooperated eagerly, feeling joyous as it anticipated returning to the Source of everything. Ella felt a sense of joy herself, knowing that for the first time, she could nourish the earth that had nourished mankind for so many hundreds of thousands of years.

When the stream of magic inside her ebbed, the last trickles sliding down into the earth, Ella realized she didn't feel drained, but exhilarated. Somehow she knew that with her newfound connection to the earth, she could call upon the magic at any time and it would answer, because the magic was part of her.

God, she felt like dancing for joy.

"Open your eyes," Kees said.

Ella obeyed and took a second to focus. Kees sat across from her, crouched as if on his pedestal, which considering his tail was probably the most comfortable position for him. It took her a minute to realize that he was glowing, and another minute to realize that the glow wasn't actually coming from him. It encompassed the entire room, a warm white light sparkling with all the colors Ella had just seen. The beauty of it made her smile in wonder.

"What do you see?"

She described the radiance of the light covering almost every surface of her apartment, floor to ceiling, end to end, and Kees nodded.

"Good," he grunted. "That's what you're supposed to see. All of that is magic that's been leaking out of you for years. You might think you've been in control because it didn't escape in a huge rush most of the time, but it has been escaping. It had to, or you would have exploded. There's only so much power a human can contain at any one time without going insane. You've been lucky so far, but luck will last only so long. Now you have to learn to be good. Control the magic, or eventually it will take control of you."

Ella nodded, her smile fading until she faced him with a look of pure determination. "Okay. So what do I need to learn?"

"Everything."

Chapter Nine

From that moment on, Ella spent every spare second learning to control and use her magic. She practiced for hours a day, coming home from the museum and heading right into her training until she didn't even have to think to ground herself, and she could call the magic forth as easily as she could sink it into the earth.

Gradually, Kees changed the focus of her lessons from simply learning to control the magic and see it in the space around her, to manipulating it into actual spells. Too bad he seemed so determined to stick with defensive magic to start with, because she had an intense desire to learn how to change him into a banana slug.

He hadn't touched her in the four days since their one night together. Most of the time, he went out of his way not to look at her, and Ella had run the gauntlet of emotion from anger to hurt to confusion and back to anger. Usually, thinking about the dumb-ass gargoyle made her blood boil, but that didn't make it any easier to ignore the way he turned her on just by existing, or the way he could make her laugh out of nowhere with one jab of his dry, sly wit. It would be so much easier if she could just settle into a nice consistent hate-on, but no—Kees had to go ruin it by being . . . Kees.

Ella hadn't repeated her attempts to get the gargoyle to acknowledge his feelings, or the fact that he had feelings. Frankly, she was no longer certain he did. He treated her like a piece of furniture, or maybe more like a valuable vase, or something. He took care not to hurt her, physically, but he spent absolutely no time or attention on her that wasn't required by their daily lessons.

Well, okay, that wasn't quite true. He did exert himself enough to ask her each day how her search for the descendants of the Wardens he had named for her was going. Unfortunately, she hadn't found much worth telling him.

As it turned out, two of the five men—all the Wardens Kees named had been male, and she was starting to detect a certain amount of sexism among the Guardians and their ancient Guild, which she should address later, if she ever became a member—had never had children at all. Of the other three, one had fathered a single son, but another had clearly had too much time of his hands, because the records Ella found listed eight sons, five daughters, and a total of five wives during his lifetime. Busy little beaver.

The fifth name was the one currently giving Ella fits. She'd uncovered the names of three daughters of a Warden called Josiah Jameson, who had lived in Brighton in the south of England during Kees's escapade of 1703. Unfortunately, the parish records of the time had not all been uploaded onto the Internet, and what information she managed to dig up offered a far from complete picture of the Jameson family. Add to that the fact that a woman's name changed when she married, and changed again if she was widowed or divorced and subsequently remarried, and the hours spent poring over Web pages had given Ella more than one vicious headache.

And that was in addition to the seven-foot headache

who alternated between pacing her apartment and decorating the fire escape and roof of her building.

She'd given up worrying that someone would see him and cause trouble. As he'd pointed out on the night-that-was-not-to-be-mentioned, most humans would look at him and see the statue he had been, not the living creature of myth and legend. While Ella had learned over the course of her lessons that gargoyles could not cast spells the way he was teaching her, as a mage-in-training, to do, the magic that had created them offered them certain advantages, and the ability to go mostly unnoticed in the human world was one of those.

With a noisy exhalation—she was much too mature to consider blowing a raspberry at the world, no matter how much it sucked right now—Ella dragged her attention back to her computer screen and continued reading. A couple of paragraphs later her gaze caught on a juicy tidbit, and within minutes her fingers were flying over the keyboard and scrolling through links and pages with the speed of a hyped-up greyhound.

Hot damn! She was finally on to something.

A little over an hour later she picked up a pen and scribbled down a few lines on the back of a torn envelope. She was too excited to look for the notebook she had supposedly been using to organize her information, organization not being her strong suit.

Grabbing the envelope, she raced through the bedroom, scrambled through the open window with more urgency than grace, and dashed up the last level of fire stairs to the roof of the old building. She found Kees right where she'd expected him to be, crouched on the elevated roof edge, staring out into the night like an unblinking sentry in the darkness.

"Kees."

Her voice remained quiet, but carried a low note of

urgency that actually caught the Guardian's attention. He turned to look at her, but his face remained expressionless. It always did these days.

Ella bit back a sigh. "I found something. There's a man in Seattle, Washington. His name is Alan Parsons, and he's the bunch-of-times-great-grandson of Josiah Jameson. The Internet doesn't tell me if he or his parents and grandparents were Wardens, of course, but he's the most direct descendant of any of those five men that I was able to find. I think he's worth checking out."

Kees rose to his feet and stepped away from the edge of the roof, his tail twitching restlessly behind him. "How far are we from Seattle?"

"Well, it's like a two-and-a-half-, maybe three-hour drive," she noted, wrinkling her nose, "but we have to cross the border. That usually adds a few minutes these days."

"We should leave immediately."

Ella raised an eyebrow. "Hold your horses, big guy. It's not quite that easy. First of all, showing up on a stranger's doorstep at—" She checked her watch. "—one o'clock in the morning is not normally the best way to endear yourself to him. Second, we can't go until I have a day off, because the last thing I can manage right now is time off, not with the museum still buzzing over your disappearance. And lastly, we have to rent another car, and my bank account is not going to like that."

Kees scowled. "You are worried about money? That is no problem. Once we make contact with the Guild, they will reimburse you for any expense."

She goggled. "The Guild has money? I didn't know the magic business paid well."

"No organization remains alive and active for hundreds upon hundreds of years without funds. The notion that money makes the world go round is not a modern invention."

"Huh, good to know. But that's still not the big problem."

"Then what is the problem?"

"The border." When he continued to frown at her, Ella sighed. "Right, sometimes I forget you've missed some stuff about the modern world. To get to Seattle, which is in the State of Washington, we have to cross the Canada–U.S. border. That would be a bigger deal if the countries weren't longtime allies, but it still requires a passport be shown at the entry point.

"Paperwork that proves what country you have citizenship with," she explained when he remained silent.

"Do you not have this passport?"

"Of course I have a passport," she said, pursing her lips. "But somehow I doubt you've got one stashed in that skirt of yours."

Kees didn't react to the taunt about his clothing, but he looked thoughtful. "So you believe I will not be allowed to cross the border unless I have one of these passports you speak of."

"I know you won't be allowed to."

The gargoyle shrugged and started to walk toward the fire escape stairs. "Then I will just have to make certain these border officials do not see me cross."

Ella glared at his back. "What? You think you have the ability to make yourself invisible while we drive into the U.S.?"

"Of course not. But I do think that I have wings. If I cannot go through the border, I will simply go over it."

The gargoyle had no intention of listening to reason. He insisted that they could not afford to waste more time in reaching the possible Warden in Seattle. Since Ella had absolutely no notion of how a person went about obtaining a fake passport, she didn't fight too hard on how he planned to get over the border, but she did fight him about almost everything else.

Kees originally proposed that he go to Seattle alone, just fly there immediately and return with whatever information he could gather before dawn. Ella called that idea idiotic. First she reminded him that the middle of the night was not the best time to ring a human's doorbell, Warden or not, and second, she told him it was stupid to risk the sun rising before he made it back, since it increased his chances of being spotted by humans. As likely as the average person might be to chalk up seeing a huge gargoyle-shaped thing sitting on a roof to someone's weird taste in statuary, it would be a lot more difficult for one to ignore seeing that same gargoyle flying through the sky on enormous bat wings. It just wasn't worth the risk.

Besides, though Ella didn't point this out, now that she'd invested so much time into this whole experience, she had absolutely no intention of being left behind.

Ella countered with an alternate proposal. Since the chances of a man deciding to move in the next twenty-four hours seemed small, the two of them would wait until tomorrow afternoon. She was already scheduled to have the next two days off, so she could spare the time. They would rent a car and begin the drive to Seattle with the intention of hitting the border shortly after dark. If they timed matters properly, Ella could stop a few miles north of the border in an unpopulated area and let Kees out of the car. He could then fly across the border and meet Ella, who would drive through the checkpoint normally. Once they rendezvoused in Washington, Kees would return to the car, and they would complete the drive to Parsons's house together, arriving late, but still at a reasonable hour of the night.

And just to be sure Kees didn't decide to forget waiting for her and fly straight to Parsons's house without her, Ella made certain he didn't catch so much as a glimpse of the man's address. So there, Mr. Take-Charge-Alpha-Gargoyle-Man.

Kees agreed bad-naturedly, but for the first time in days, Ella went to bed with a sense of anticipation that actually outweighed the heaviness of her heart. Her bed might still be big and lonely and too filled with recent memories of the best sex of her life, but at least tonight she had something to look forward to that wasn't seeing her Guardian's grumpy, beloved face.

In the end, getting a few minutes in the car without Kees turned out to be a positive thing. First off, she didn't have to worry about anyone questioning the guy's species and thus winding up in Guantánamo Bay for the next eighty years; and second, the break allowed her to calm down after the steady buildup of irritation caused by the first forty minutes of the trip. Sure, Kees had been avoiding her for the past five days, but she didn't know he would manage to continue that little feat while trapped inside a car with her. Talk about hidden talents; the man was full of them.

Well, he was full of something.

Ella passed through the Peace Arch border crossing without incident and continued south along I-5 to the designated meeting point at the rest area in Custer, just south of Blaine. By the time Kees emerged—in human form— from the tree-lined darkness to the west of the parking area, she had schooled herself to appear just as detached and remote as her traveling companion. It would serve him right.

They completed the rest of the trip in silence, Ella using the rental car's built-in GPS to navigate around the unfamiliar city. Alan Parsons, it turned out, lived in an outlying suburb of a city called Newcastle, and Ella had to maneuver off the busy highway and onto I-90 to reach the smaller community.

By the time the computerized voice of the GPS advised her to turn onto Parsons's street, Ella felt stiff and weary from the stress of driving. She'd done more of the miserable task in the week since she met Kees than she had in the last year, and she hated every second of it. Maybe next time he pestered her, she'd actually let him get behind the wheel.

As she slowed the car close to their destination, Ella risked a glance at her silent, brooding companion. "So. Do we have a plan?"

Kees actually looked at her for a change, though she wouldn't call his expression exactly encouraging. More like, "dour."

"Why would we need a plan? We meet this Warden and gather what information we can."

Ella parked the car at the curb, across the street and about fifty yards down from their target address. Trees lined the road here, but she preferred not to pull into the man's drive or park right out front. No other cars lined the street here, and she got the feeling that if she parked in front of a house, every neighbor in the area would be peering out their windows wondering what was going on. An audience was the last thing they needed.

"But we're only hoping the guy is a Warden," she said, stilling the engine. "They don't exactly publish a roster on Facebook, you know. I can tell you his buttload-of-greats-granddad was a Warden, but that's hardly conclusive proof that he's one, too."

"Then the best way to find out is to ask." He stepped out of the car and slammed the door without another word.

"Wow, he's a charmer," Ella muttered under her breath,

hurrying to follow. God only knew what he would do when he got to the guy's house. She wouldn't put it past him to just kick down the door and invite himself the hell inside.

Not that she could stop him, physically or magically, but she could at least keep a wary eye out for the cops.

His long strides ate up the distance from the curb to Alan Parsons's front door. It was a little after nine thirty at this point, but the lights at the front of the house burned brightly, and Ella could see evidence of more glowing through and around the curtains on several windows. At least at this hour she could reasonably hope they weren't about to drag some poor soul out of his comfy bed.

The house where Parsons lived couldn't compete with Gregory Lascaux's mountaintop estate, but Ella couldn't immediately bring to mind a house that could. Versailles, maybe. With that said, the potential Warden appeared to live a very comfortable life.

The house occupied an enormous lot at the dead end of a street filled with other enormous lots. It rose two stories amid a semicircle of tall pines and leafy trees with the carefully manicured appearance of wealth. Judging by a quick once-over, the occupant of the building, which had to measure a minimum of five thousand square feet, wasn't hurting for money. Maybe this Warden gig paid better than Ella had assumed.

A neat brick pathway curved gracefully from the sidewalk to the house's front door. It seemed to demand better than the awkward scurry Ella had to use not to be left in Kees's dust, but the gargoyle moved with the speed and determination of a bull toward a red cape. It was all she could do to keep up.

She actually found herself panting when they finally stepped onto the small front porch—more of a portico, really. She reached for Kees's arm, hoping to stall him long enough to ask that he let her do the talking, but he'd already banged his big fist on the slate blue door.

Ella sighed and dropped her hand. "You realize there's a doorbell, right?"

He ignored her.

The sound of movement inside the house distracted her, pulling her attention away from the uncooperative gargoyle. She could hear footsteps pause on the other side of the entry, and a moment passed before the knob began a slow turn.

Ella fixed a smile on her face, aiming for harmless and pleasant. Maybe it would counteract Kees's look of menace and power.

The door opened, and a man stood in the entry. Of average height and build, he possessed a thick head of gray hair and bright blue eyes framed by *GQ*-fashionable glasses. He looked to be in his late sixties, still fit but beginning to show the signs of his age in his softening jawline and liver-spotted hands.

"Can I help you?" he asked, his voice calm and polite.

Giving herself a little test, Ella allowed her vision to blur and then refocus on an entirely different level. Her heart jumped and raced when the bright blue-white of strong magical wards appeared around the door of the home.

She turned to tell Kees, which was why she witnessed the split second of power and shimmer that accompanied not a shift, but a momentary glimpse of the true shape behind his human disguise.

Ella heard the old man gasp and quickly glanced his way, hoping she hadn't misjudged him. She opened her mouth, reassurances dancing on the tip of her tongue, but she never spoke them. She didn't get the chance.

The man closed his eyes and seemed to sag in the open doorway. "You've come," he nearly sobbed, the words filled with relief and joy and fear and frustration. "Thank the Fates. You've finally come."

Chapter Ten

Fifteen minutes later, Ella found herself seated at a rustic wooden table in an enormous gourmet kitchen with her hands curled gratefully around a mug of steaming English tea. Alan Parsons, she had discovered, had been born in Kent, southeast of London. And yes, he was a Warden. For what that was now worth.

"It's bad. I can't pretty it up for you. Things look very bleak." Alan frowned across the table, the steam from his tea briefly fogging his glasses. "We knew the *nocturnis* had been stirring, and we'd lost a handful of Wardens, but the attack in Paris took us all by surprise. We weren't even close to prepared."

Kees had refused the tea but accepted a large snifter of brandy. The delicate glass balloon looked almost comical cupped in his huge clawed hand. He had taken Alan seriously when their host had instructed them to "be comfortable." He had shifted immediately.

"Tell us," the Guardian ordered, using the same flat, commanding voice Ella had learned to recognize during her lessons. "Everything. From the beginning. How did it start?"

Alan glanced at Ella and frowned. "How much does she know?"

"Just the basics. I found her less than a week ago, but she has potential. There's magic in her, but the only training she's had is what I've had time to give her in the last few days. I had hoped the Guild could take that over."

"Her name is Ella," she reminded them with a snap, "and she doesn't appreciate being talked around like a frog on a dissection table. I know about the Guild and obviously about the Guardians and the Wardens. I'm the one who tracked you down, so I think I can sit up here at the big people's table and hear what's what."

Alan's mouth quirked and his eyes sparkled with humor. "Feisty. You'll need to be."

He turned back to Kees and sobered. "There's barely a Guild left to speak of, but let me go back further for you. About five years ago, the Guild began to make note of an increasing level of minor fiend activity. The guards seemed to be handling it, but it made some of us curious, especially since we first picked up on it in England, but quickly discovered it was not an isolated incident. It seemed to be happening all over the globe. That raised some eyebrows."

Kees nodded over his snifter, encouraging the Warden to continue.

"We began to monitor the situation closely. It didn't take long to trace the outbreaks of activity back to the Order."

Ella frowned, and then realized he must be talking about the *nocturnis'* more formal name, the Order of Eternal Darkness.

"New sects were discovered in England, Brussels, Slovenia, Brazil, and the United States. Brand-new cells, not replacing the ones we already knew existed in those areas, but augmenting them. The stones know where they got all those new recruits, but they found them somewhere. Before the fire, we estimated that their numbers had potentially doubled. Maybe more."

Kees cursed, and Ella felt a rush of unease. She might be new at all this, but that did not sound like good news.

"Clearly, we knew something was going on, but we didn't know what. And we were too slow in figuring it out. When the first Warden was killed, the death was made to look accidental, and no one took much notice, except to shake their heads at the unfortunate fact that he had had no children and his last apprentice had recently left to work in Paris. No one was immediately available to replace him. It didn't cause too much worry, because he didn't serve directly under a Guardian, so the need to replace him didn't seem urgent.

"The second and third death caused more concern. Again, those Wardens had no obvious successors in place, so that now left three positions in need of filling. That finally rattled some chains. Then Gregory died."

Ella saw Kees stiffen out of the corner of her eye. He'd told Alan the name of his former Warden, and she had noticed the fleeting look of sadness cross the old man's face when he heard. Now she understood that he'd known about the death, but hadn't realized Kees was Gregory's Guardian until he heard it from Kees.

A welling of sympathy made Ella soften. She reached out to place a hand over Kees's, but he pulled away. Hiding the sting, she pulled back to lift her mug to her lips with both hands. Only sheer stubbornness kept them from shaking. The gargoyle didn't want her sympathy. After all, it was a worthless human emotion. Fine. Next time, she'd remember.

If Alan noticed the exchange, he didn't comment. He merely continued with his tale.

"Gregory was the first of the Guardian Wardens to die. The mundane officials ruled it a natural death, but we knew better by that point, and we definitely didn't want to leave a Guardian unwarded. We never intended for you to be abandoned, Guardian. Please believe that."

Kees nodded, but his jaw flexed with tension.

"We immediately sent a replacement to wake you and officially commit to your service. He never made it to you. His plane mysteriously crashed just after takeoff outside Prague. He and fifty other humans were killed."

"Nocturnis," Kees hissed.

"We have little proof, but it had to be. They picked off the Guardians' Wardens one by one, and every time we tried to replace one, the replacement died as well. We had determined that only drastic action, a decisive counter-strike, could halt the killings, and plans were under way, but we were naïve. We didn't believe they would dare to attack the Guild headquarters itself. Our pride and arrogance wiped out all of our eldest and most powerful members in one blow."

The agony in his voice pulled at Ella's heart. She could hear the grief over all the friends and coworkers he had lost. He sounded like the victim of a terrorist attack. And he had been, she realized. Terror was exactly what the *nocturnis* had accomplished.

"How many are left?"

Ella turned and looked at Kees, startled. She'd never heard him sound like that before. His voice had deepened to a register like approaching thunder and carried the dark promise of blood and retribution. If she had met him for the first time at this moment, she would have run screaming. Right after she finished peeing her pants and passing out. He set his glass carefully away from him, which she figured was a good idea, considering he then clenched his fists so tight, she could see blood welling up around the tips of his claws. She also noted the signs of the war he waged to keep his expression stony. The tiny muscles around his lips and jaw twitched and quivered with the need to draw back, to bare his fangs in a roaring snarl of rage. Ella could almost hear it, like a distant echo in the back of her mind.

This time, she didn't allow him to brush her off. She grounded herself and laid her hand against the hot flesh of the gargoyle's forearm. The muscles jumped under her touch, and he immediately tried to pull away. Stubbornly, she hung on. If she could ground magic, maybe she could ground other things as well. She could at least try. A deep breath filled her chest, and as she exhaled she cautiously worked to siphon the excess rage from Kees's vibrating form.

He froze, his gaze jumping to her face with obvious reluctance. As if she needed the reminder of how little he wanted her near him lately. Ignoring the heat of his regard, she continued to breathe in and out in a deliberately meditative rhythm. Within minutes, she felt the easing of his tension. He still felt rage—heck, he was filled with it—but Ella had lowered the heat from a rolling, bubbling, spewing boil to a low, intense simmer.

Opening her eyes, Ella removed her hand and felt herself flush. She had realized she'd shut her eyes, but she knew she had a tendency to do so when she was concentrating hard on something magical. Kees had already warned her she would have to break the habit. She braced herself for another lecture.

"That was remarkable," Alan breathed, shattering the tense silence and drawing Ella's gaze back to his weathered face. "I've never seen anything like that. Where did you learn such a thing, child?"

Child?

Ella tried not to take offense. She shrugged. "Kees taught me to ground. I loved it from the first minute. Things inside me got pretty chaotic before that. Grounding helps." She glanced sideways at Kees and colored further. "I thought it might help him, too."

The gargoyle shook his head. "I taught her to ground the magic. This is something new."

Alan marveled. "I've never seen the like before. One being should not be able to ground for another. It just doesn't happen that way. Grounding requires intense focus, for all its simplicity, and it is intensely personal. Each creature must learn to do it for himself. That was . . . extraordinary."

Ella shifted uncomfortably. "Sorry."

Kees shot her one last, intent look, then turned back to Alan. "We can worry about such things later. Tell me now, how many Wardens are left?"

Still clearly surprised, Alan seemed to sink into his chair. All at once, he looked every minute of his age and older. Grief and worry sat heavy on his shoulders. "I wish I could tell you, but the truth is, I have no idea. After Paris, there was panic. With our center of operations wiped out, many of us lost touch with each other. Wardens talked about moving underground, going into hiding. No one wanted to be the next target, but I know the murders haven't stopped. Our membership in the Guild and our magic have become the very things that make us vulnerable. The *nocturnis* can identify us too easily, and rumors are they get more names by torturing each victim before moving on to the next. None of us wants to give up our brothers, but we're only human. We can be broken."

Ella shuddered and rapidly revised her opinion of the benefits of life as a Warden. Maybe she should stick to museum work.

"Can you estimate?" Kees pressed. "You survived. Others must have done the same."

"I'm sure some did, but we don't dare communicate.

Every time we speak to each other is another opportunity for the *nocturnis* to find us."

"But how do you plan to regroup and rebuild if you cannot ever muster the courage to join together again? It will take the strength of many to bring the Guild back to life."

"There are too few of us overcome by too much fear. To fight this battle we need the Guardians. That's why I gave thanks when I saw you on my doorstep. The only hope we have is for the Guardians to wake and go to battle. If you lead the troops, I know I will follow, and I believe others will as well, but at the moment, we are too vastly outnumbered. Only with you seven to champion us do we have any hope of success."

"Then the Guardians survive? The *nocturnis* have not destroyed them?"

Alan sighed. "We don't think so. As I said, none of them have Wardens any longer, but Guardians are extraordinarily hard to kill. That's why you were summoned to battle the Seven. I'm certain that the ultimate goal of the Order is to destroy all of you, because then there would be nothing to stop them from freeing the Seven and unleashing the Darkness on the world. But for the moment, we think all the Guardians remain."

Ella finished her tea and pushed away her mug. "If you know you need the Guardians to fight off the *nocturnis,* why haven't you guys gone and woken them all up? Kees tells me that's part of the job description."

"It is, but things haven't been so simple. The *nocturnis* clearly have a strategy. It took us a while, but we eventually realized that the first Wardens to die all came from areas where the new cells first formed. They would have been our early warning system. If they had survived, they would have reported on the upsurge in *nocturnis* activity, and the Guild might have taken steps, but they died before they were able to. After that, the Order went straight for the Wardens assigned to Guardians. Take them out, and the Guardians cannot be woken until they're replaced. Kill the replacements, and they buy themselves more time without interference by the only force they truly fear."

It was a crazy line of logic: ruthless, brutal, and frighteningly effective. Ella grimaced.

"I can say again that every time we've tried to replace a Guardian's Warden, the Warden has not survived," Alan said wearily. "Even now I hear rumors now and again of another of us emerging from hiding just to make the attempt, but every one ends in death. Plus, killing off the Wardens created logistical problems as well."

"Logistical problems?"

"Take Kees here." Alan nodded at the gargoyle. "When we last had access to our records, he was safely housed at Gregory's home in British Columbia, miles from any major areas of Order activity. Where did you find him?"

"In Vancouver," Ella admitted. "I work at a museum there, and they purchased him—er, they purchased the statue of a gargoyle from the estate of Gregory Lascaux about two years ago."

Alan nodded. "Exactly. As I said, the *nocturnis* strategized over this. They had elaborate plans that involved more than just killing Wardens. In every case, they either created some kind of legal gray areas around ownership or provenance of the Guardians' stone forms, or they arranged for the statues to be moved or sold or lost once the Wardens were no longer there to guard their sleeping forms. We've lost track of them, though a few of us have been working on fixing that. None of them are where we last knew them to be. We have to find them before we can wake them, and once we find them, we have to reach them alive. Neither has been possible. Until now."

The Warden looked from Ella to Kees and frowned. "How were you woken, Guardian? Do you recall?"

Kees barked out a humorless laugh. "One of the reasons we sought you out was so that you could explain it to us, Warden. All I remember was sleeping on the museum terrace until she walked by and got herself into trouble."

He pointed at Ella, who wanted to disappear under the table. Why did he make the story sound like an arrest report, damn it? From what she could tell, if she'd had any hand in waking Kees from his magical slumber, she'd done the world a pretty damned big—if unintentional—favor. The least the jerk could do was say thank you.

Kees watched as the little human's cheeks flushed, then went pale, and then flushed again. The fact that she continued to fascinate him both angered and worried him. He had spent the past few days doing everything he could to erect barriers between them, but somehow she managed to bring them down without the slightest bit of force.

Frankly, Ella almost scared him. And that slippery hint of emotion made him want to turn tail and run, something a Guardian could never do. So he continued to push her away at every turn, even as her importance to him and his mission continued to grow.

When he was quiet, he swore he could hear Fate laughing at him.

"Hey, I didn't do anything," she protested, glaring at him. He was growing used to the expression. "I was minding my own business when you jumped off a pedestal, scared the ever-living crap out of me, then grabbed me, flew me twenty blocks without so much as a seatbelt, and broke into my damned apartment. None of this was my fault."

She crossed her arms over her chest, managing to look both sullen and adorable. Also amusing, if the cough Parsons used to disguise a laugh was anything to go by.

"I see," the Warden managed after clearing his throat. "I mean, I think I understand the facts as you've explained them, but I'm not sure I can offer any explanation of them. As far as I am aware, only a Warden has ever been able to wake a Guardian, and it's been that way since the first summoning. I seem to recall tales of one or two instances when extreme emergency caused a Guardian to awake, but those were times when one of the Seven escaped its prison without warning. The echo of the tear caused in this reality woke them. I didn't think anything less than that could manage it."

Kees frowned. He had thought the same, but here he was, walking, talking, breathing. And lusting after a human woman. Clearly, something odd was going on here.

"I looked for evidence of amdemon after I woke," he said. "I found nothing. Not one of the Seven, not even a powerful fiend. I would never have abandoned duty if I had. Even now, I would be locked in battle."

"Of course," Parsons acknowledged. "I never thought otherwise, but still I cannot account for your awakening."

Not precisely what Kees wanted to hear. He gestured toward Ella. "My instincts tell me it has to do with the woman, but I cannot pinpoint why, or how. All I know is that she was present when I woke. Her distress at being attacked penetrated my slumber, and when she drew close, I could sense the magic in her. Ella must be the key."

His key bared her even little teeth at him. "Like I said, I don't appreciate you talking about me like I'm not here, big guy, so cut it out."

He ignored her, or pretended to, which was the best he'd been able to manage since she fell asleep in his arms. "Could it have something to do with her untapped potential as a Warden?"

Parsons pursed his lips and stared at her. "I don't think so. It is not the first time an uneducated recruit has been discovered under a Guardian's nose. Certainly such things are rare, but they are not unprecedented. Are you certain you do not come from a Warden family, Ella?"

She denied that firmly. "No way. My parents were both scientists, my mom a teacher and my dad a university researcher. They didn't even believe magic existed." Her expression took on a wry cast. "Neither did I, until Kees explained it to me. I didn't know what that stuff was inside me, but magic wasn't one of my three guesses."

"Hm. And you never had any training? How old are you, if you don't mind a truly old man asking."

"I don't mind. I'm twenty-seven. And no, no training. Can't train in something you think is entirely fictional, right? Well, unless you count memorizing lines out of Harry Potter."

Parsons chuckled. "Unfortunately not, though I always fancied trying to duplicate that Puking Pastilles recipe for real." He looked back at Kees. "I'm sorry, but I don't have any answers. Perhaps if I had time to get to know both of you, something might pop out at me, but currently, I'm as baffled as either of you."

"That makes things more difficult. If we don't know how I was woken, we can't replicate the process to wake the others, which means we need to find more Wardens to do the deed."

"If they even agree," Parsons said. "I would be willing to try, especially knowing one of you is already awake, but the deaths have shaken most of the survivors to the core. Many begin to give up hope, and without the protection of a Guardian, the idea of approaching a Guardian has become unthinkable."

"Catch-22," Ella murmured.

"Exactly."

Kees snarled his displeasure. "We have no choice. If what you said is true, then all of this has merely been a way of setting the stage so that the *nocturnis* can unleash the Seven uncontested. That cannot happen. The Guardians must prevent it; therefore, the Guardians must rise."

"No one is saying anything different," Ella said, "but we still have to locate the six sleeping Guardians, and then we have to locate enough Wardens to set their alarm clocks."

His jaw clenched as Kees considered the problem. He had hoped that finding this Warden would lead him to a Guild already gathered and moving toward rebuilding. He had never considered the mages might be hiding, running scared from the very threat they had been founded to help work against. He had trouble grasping the idea of it. Guardians never ran. They fought until they won, and if someone fell in battle, his comrades took over until a new Guardian was summoned. They never considered anything less than meeting the enemy head-on and battling to the bitter end.

He had to remind himself once again that talented mages or no, in the end, the Wardens were only human. They could be killed, like his Ella.

The thought cut him short and he shoved it roughly aside. He could protect his little human. Even if he needed her to help him continue the search for more Wardens and more Guardians, she could come to little harm sitting before her computer machine. He would just have to ensure that she stayed there, safely out of danger, while he destroyed any and every threat to her and the world she lived in. Even if he had to do it alone, so be it. A motivated Guardian could accomplish impressive things.

"Do you think I might be able to wake another Guardian, even though I'm not a Warden?"

Ella's voice came out hesitant but strong, and it chilled Kees straight to the bone.

"I mean, I'm not saying that I know for sure I had anything to do with Kees waking up, because I have no idea if I did," she continued, "but I'd be willing to try again. I mean, this is some serious sh—er, stuff going on, and I don't think I can just sit by and watch some psychos try to end the world if I could help stop them."

"Absolutely not," Kees bellowed.

"That's an interesting question," Parsons said, eyeing her with consideration. "Since we don't know for certain what happened to wake him, I don't know if it would be wise to rely on lightning striking twice, if you take my meaning. As I said, I'm willing to make the attempt myself."

Relief coursed through Kees. No, not relief. Of course not relief. He merely wanted to rely on known rather than unknown methods of waking his brothers. His feel—his *thoughts* had nothing to do with the little human's safety or lack thereof. Nothing.

"We still need to locate a Guardian to wake," Kees said, trying to draw the attention away from Ella. "Even if we have a Warden who can perform the call."

"I might have an encouraging bit of news there," Alan said. "I don't want anyone getting too excited, because nothing is certain yet, but I've been following a particular line of inquiry, and I think it might be leading me back to Canada, but the other side of the country. There's a *chance,*" he stressed the uncertain word, "that another Guardian might have been acquired by a museum in or around Montreal. I don't have the details yet, but it's still a place to begin looking."

"But that's great!"

Kees heard the excitement in Ella's voice and paused. Somehow it appeared that his small human had taken his mission to heart as her own. When had that happened? And why had it happened? After the distance he'd tried over and over to create between them, she should want nothing to do with helping him. Actually, he wouldn't have been surprised if she'd relished his pain. Would she never stop surprising him?

"No, it's awesome," she continued when neither man spoke. "I have a friend—well, an acquaintance really—from college who works in Montreal. We weren't terribly close, but we worked together on a couple of projects and we always got along. I'm sure I could call her and get her help. If we think a Guardian could be in a museum around there, Fil would be the perfect person to find out."

"Why is that?" Parsons asked. "Is she magically talented as well?"

"No." Ella frowned. "I don't think so. Not that I know of, anyway, but I know she didn't freak out at finding out I might be . . . I dunno, psychic or something, which is what I settled on as the best explanation before I met Kees." She didn't bother to glance at him. "Either way, she's at least open-minded. And better than that, she's in the arts community in Montreal, so they know her name at all the museums. She's an art restorer."

"A human female art restorer named Phil," Kees repeated flatly. "And she can help us."

"*A*, I don't see what her sex has to do with anything. I'm female, and I'm helping," she snapped. "*B*, Fil is a nickname. Her real name is Felicity Shaltis, and she's one of the top restorers in Eastern Canada, so she not only knows the museums and visits regularly, she has access behind the scenes, too. That's important, because if for some reason the Guardian was there but not on display, she could still find out by checking the storage and prep areas that are off-limits to regular visitors."

Parsons looked across the table at Kees and raised his brows. "That does sound promising, Guardian."

Reluctantly, Kees had to agree. "You can contact her when we return to Vancouver, but tell her only what we are looking for—a statue similar in look to mine. She does not need to know why."

Ella rolled her eyes. "Trust me, I wouldn't even begin to try telling her more than that. I want her to help us, not call the police and report that I need to be taken in for a mental health check. I've been living with all this for a week now, and I still have moments where I doubt my own sanity."

Parsons cleared his throat. "Guardian, are you certain it's wise for Ella to return to Vancouver with you? I know you want to be in the city in case your waking did have something to do with a threat to that area, but Ella clearly requires further training in the use of her magic. I would be glad to offer that to her and watch out for her safety while she was here."

The idea froze Kees in place. It had merit. After all, just moments ago he had been thinking up ways to keep her safe and out of the way of the upcoming battle. Not only would leaving her with Parsons accomplish the goal of keeping her out of the line of fire should the *nocturnis* attempt to harm him, but further training would improve her abilities to defend herself. It would also make her another Warden in the end, and if what Parsons had told them was true, they would need all the Wardens they could find, even if they had to train new ones to increase their ranks. Yes, such training would take time, but if all-out war with the Order did erupt, every Warden would have a role to play.

So why did every fiber of his being protest the idea of Ella leaving his side for so much as an instant?

"I don't think that's a good idea," Ella protested even as Kees opened his mouth, unsure exactly what he would say. "I might be lacking in training, but I had none of it when I woke Kees, if that's what happened, so I don't think that has anything to do with it. Also, sorry to disappoint everyone who does the demon-fighting thing for a living, but I still have a job that expects me to show up the day after tomorrow. Not being independently wealthy, I need to do that if I want to keep getting paychecks. And believe me, I do."

Parsons immediately looked contrite. "I'm sorry, I should have thought, especially since you drove all the way down here, and gas prices are so high. For a recruit, which I think we can safely say you are, since your talent is obvious, the Guild would normally provide a stipend for your living expenses. Full Wardens draw salaries. Now, though"—he made a face—"the accounts remain and are set up to be managed automatically by accountants, but adding your name would only draw you to the attention of the Order. It wouldn't be wise."

"No, anonymity is her greatest protection at the moment." The last thing Kees wanted was the *nocturnis* to turn their attention to his human. "You may continue your work for the time being, maintain your normal routine. Once the Order is defeated and the Guild is back on its feet, we can take care of any financial issues."

"Um, hello." The little female punched him in the shoulder. It didn't hurt, of course, but the violence surprised him. "Stop making decisions for me, you big jerk. I'll work because I want to work, I'll return to Vancouver because that's where I live, and if you think that just because you're used to Wardens being your servants I'm going to lean over and kiss your ass, I'll drop trou right now and you can kiss mine."

That time, Parsons could not contain his laughter. It burst out like pellets from a BB gun. Kees glared until the old man got himself under control, but Parsons couldn't completely suppress his grin.

"Like I said." The Warden shrugged, his lips twitching. "She's feisty."

Kees snarled an insult in the old language of his kind. Parsons just laughed.

"If you can't stay here, there are some things I would like to give you," the older man told his guests. "Independent study is not a route the Guild normally encourages recruits to take, but these are special circumstances, and you already have a Guardian who can help with your training. I have some volumes I can give you to teach you the fundamentals of spellcasting, including some rudimentary spells you might find useful. Basic wards, protection spells, things like that. You can take them with you to Vancouver and practice what and when you can."

"Thank you," Ella said, her tone conveying both surprise and pleasure. "That would be hugely helpful, I'm sure. Kees has been a good teacher, but there are times I think it would help if he'd had personal experience with spells."

Kees snorted. He'd had plenty of experience with spells over the course of his long life. He simply couldn't cast any of them. But apparently his little human wanted to be fussy.

"One is a grimoire, so you should find that particularly valuable. It's an individual mage's collection of the spells he found most useful during his life, and he's annotated them with notes and commentary. Very enlightening."

Ella nodded, her excitement beginning to show through.

"There's also a spell I would like to cast for you. With your permission, Guardian."

Kees stiffened. The Warden had proved helpful, but this was not a request he had ever heard before. "What sort of spell?"

"A specialized kind of binding. On the two of you." Parsons hurried to explain, spreading his hands on the table and leaning forward as if to impress his point upon them. "For a recruit who knew nothing of her own magic a mere week ago, Ella's grounding and control are re-markable. Part of that might be due to receiving her train-ing directly from a Guardian, since magic is part of the very fiber of your being, but I believe that part of it is simply because one day, Ella will be a very, very power-ful Warden."

Parsons caught Ella's gaze and held it, speaking di-rectly to her. "I can sense the strength of your magic, Ella. It's a peculiar talent of mine, and I've never encountered anything quite like you. Your raw potential for magic is . . . simply breathtaking. I believe that you are going to do great things for the Guild and for humanity."

Kees heard his female catch her breath as the Warden turned his attention back to him.

"That power comes with some risk," the old man con-tinued. "The Light forbid that you should directly encoun-ter the *nocturnis* before we have woken the Guardians, but if such a thing were to happen, there is a chance that at-tempting a spell just a little too advanced, or even pouring too much raw magic into a simple spell, something like that could cause a dangerous backlash. Ella could be hurt. Perhaps gravely. The spell I'm proposing could prevent that."

"How?" Kees demanded.

"By binding the two of you together, Ella, you would be able to draw on Kees's energy and control. In essence, his magic would keep your power from getting out of hand. It would be a second, more powerful method of grounding. A fail-safe, if you will."

Ella swallowed and edged her chair farther from Kees's. He had to exert his supposed control not to reach out and yank her back. Even closer this time.

"I don't know if that's a good idea," she told the War-den. "That seems like a big burden to put on Kees. I mean, what if I ended up draining too much energy from him? I could end up leaving him vulnerable to an attack. He's a lot more important to this whole thing than I am. That feels like an unacceptable risk to me."

He heard her words, but Kees also knew she had other concerns. He could sense that she held something back. "If I feel the risk is acceptable, then it is. I'm not afraid you would drain me."

"She couldn't. It doesn't work like that," Parsons said. "When I said you'd draw on his energy, Ella, I didn't mean it in the same sense that you draw on the earth for power and magic when in need. The binding is deeper than that."

He paused and looked uncomfortable, which made Kees suspicious. "Just spit it out, old man. What are you trying not to tell us?"

Parsons sighed. "The binding joins your souls together. Ella couldn't drain your energy, because it would be her energy as well. And whatever power she pulled from the earth, you would share as well."

"That sounds risky," Ella said, already shaking her head in refusal. "And permanent. In fact, it just sounds like a really bad idea."

"It wouldn't have to be permanent. I could remove it when it became unnecessary, but there is some risk," Parsons admitted. "All spells take as well as give. If I performed the binding, your survival would become linked, as well as your energies. If one of you died while the binding was in place, the other would perish as well."

Ella jumped out of her chair, the wood scraping and squeaking against the tile floor. "No way. That's crazy. You want to take the chance that some *nocturnis* bumps me off while I'm not looking, and Kees winds up dead? That's just stupid. Or even worse, I forget to look both ways before I cross the street, and—*wham!*—I get hit by a damned car. Now not only does someone have to scrape me up off the pavement, but you've lost a Guardian just as war is about to break out. I've never heard anything so dumb! Kees is immortal. He told me so himself. If you link his life to mine, all you do is make him vulnerable at a time when no one can afford for that to happen. I won't do it."

She turned, whether to emphasize her point or to stalk from the room, Kees didn't know. Frankly, he didn't care. She was not getting away from him. All she had heard when Parsons proposed his plan was that the spell would make him closer to mortal, easier to kill. What Kees had heard was the opposite. If Parsons cast this spell, Ella would have all his strength and power to draw on. With her magic, that would make her a very dangerous opponent. In essence, it would make his little human much harder to kill.

Kees pulled Ella to his side and nodded at the Warden. "Do it."

She promptly kicked him in the shin.

Once again, he felt no pain, but his female's growing penchant for violence was something he thought they should maybe discuss. "What was that for?"

"Excuse me?" Her glare could have flayed the flesh from his bones. "What was that for? I don't know, do you think it could maybe have had something to do with the fact that you don't make decisions for me, you giant bat-winged jerk? Or how about that I just got finished saying no to something, and the last time I checked, I was the only person allowed to change that to a yes? Which there is no way I'm doing, by the way. You think I want to be bound to an arrogant, high-handed, dictatorial asshole who can't even admit when something makes him feel good? Fat frickin' chance, big guy. You can just bite me."

Kees looked from his red-faced, narrow-eyed human to the Warden on the other side of the table, who had begun to appear very uncomfortable. "Leave us."

"You know what, I'll just pop upstairs and put some towels in the guest rooms," Parsons babbled, already edging toward the door. "It's too late for you to drive back to Vancouver before sunrise, so you'll need to spend the night. I'll just, ah, go get things ready. You two, um, make yourselves at home."

He made his escape while Ella tried to stop him with empty words about there not being a problem and Parsons not putting himself to any trouble because she'd sooner spend the night in the rental car than under the same roof with Kees.

Not, of course, that she used his name. No, she made up some new ones for him. Some of which even took him by surprise. He hadn't known his little human had such an extensive vocabulary. It was really quite impressive.

Once Parsons had disappeared, Kees gripped the still-ranting woman by the shoulders and shook her gently. "Quiet."

She kicked his other shin. "Stop trying to dictate to me."

"Very well. Will you please be quiet so that we may discuss this rationally?"

Surprisingly, Ella closed her mouth, though she continued to eye him with irritation and no small amount of suspicion. "If by discuss, you mean you're going to order me to do whatever you say, then no. If you intend to treat me like a thinking, feeling, and logical human being, then feel free to try. I'll let you know how you're doing."

By kicking him, presumably, but Kees knew better than to say that aloud.

Kees gathered his temper. Asking for a human to do as he wished was not an exercise he was accustomed to. It made him uncomfortable, but he'd seen Ella's reaction to his usual tactics, and clearly he needed a new strategy.

"I would like for us to consider the Warden's proposal," he said, making an attempt to keep his voice calm and even. "Perhaps if we reviewed its advantages and disadvantages, we could come to some kind of an agreement that would satisfy us both."

"I don't see how." She frowned up at him. "As far as I can tell, the risks just vastly outweigh the benefits. I get a little more juju, but you potentially get dead. That's not a fair trade. I've been doing fine with what you've taught me. I don't need this binding thing, and I'm not willing to put you at risk 'just in case' things go wrong and we end up facing the *nocturnis* before we're ready. At that point, the last thing you're going to need or want is me as a walking, talking Achilles' heel."

"I think the benefits are worth the risks. You have looked at this only in terms of what could go wrong, but consider the advantages that Parsons has offered us."

"What, that I'd be less likely to blow myself up accidentally? I'm not worried. I've been doing fine so far."

"No, that you would be able to draw on my power if the need arose. If we did face the *nocturnis,* you would need every bit of that power. They fill their order with magic-users in their own right, and the spells needed to defend against them require large amounts of energy. You might need more than you can access from the earth with the necessary speed. If the binding makes my power your power, it would be at your fingertips with no need to call it up from the Source."

He had decided to focus on the easily imagined benefits the Warden had mentioned. At the moment, he didn't think Ella would appreciate his argument that he needed to keep her safe almost as much as he needed to defeat the Order. Or worse, she might misinterpret the statement as a revelation of emotion. He felt no emotion to reveal.

Ella adopted a mulish expression and shrugged out of his grip. She crossed her arms over her chest and stepped back to put additional space between them. "I still don't think that's worth risking your life."

"Not even if I am willing to take the risk? It is my life, after all. You should not make decisions about it anymore than I should make decisions about yours, correct?"

"Don't try to throw my own words back at me, you jackass. That is so not the way to woo me over to the dark side."

Kees sighed. "I simply wish to point out that if I am aware of the risks and I do not mind them, then they should not matter so much to you. I do not understand why you would object to any chances I might take with my own safety."

She looked uncomfortable, and the index finger of her right hand tapped a restless rhythm where it was tucked snugly against her left bicep. "Oh, don't you? Then you don't mind if I take charge of my own safety and refuse to allow the spell."

The thought made Kees's gut tighten and he bit back a growl. Right. That had gotten him nowhere.

"I do not wish to see you hurt, of course," he began again, "and knowing you are better able to defend yourself will make both of us safer, because I will not be distracted from a foe if I do not have to concern myself with you first. But more than that," he plowed on, seeing her about to object, "the spell Parsons proposes is reciprocal. It will allow you to draw on my power, but it will also allow me to draw on yours."

Ella's mouth snapped shut, and she eyed him with obvious suspicion. "What do you mean?"

Her tone sounded sullen and hostile, but at least she had asked the question and not simply shot him down without thought. That was progress. Wasn't it?

He hurried to explain. "I can allow you to draw on my power, but the bond will work both ways. You will also be able to augment my power with your own. I cannot describe to you how useful such a boon could be in the heat of battle. My kind relies on our strength and size to fight the enemy. Our magical blood offers us immunity to many of the *nocturnis* spells, but we cannot perform magic ourselves, so our ability to tap into the Source as you have learned to do is very limited. If we were bonded, you could send that energy to me if I began to tire. Far from costing me my life, a bond with you could save it, little human. You could save all of us."

She let out a huff and turned away from him to pace toward the darkened windows. "Nice strategy, big guy, but you almost went right over the edge there. I'm not the kind of girl who goes around saving the world. That's taking the melodrama just a footstep too far."

Kees frowned. He could no longer see her face, which made him realize how accustomed he'd become to reading her thoughts and emotions in those gray eyes and soft, pink lips. He could always tell when he had angered her, even before she started kicking, just as he knew he had hurt her when she stepped from the bathroom after their night together only to find him cold and distant toward her. Now she was hiding from him, and he found he disliked the reaction that caused. It made his chest tighten and his palms itch.

"I did not mean to speak dramatically," he said after a long stretch of silence. "I said only what was true. I do not expect you to save the world; I only point out that you can influence the coming battle more than I think you realize."

He heard her sigh and saw her head drop, her chin tucking into her chest and her shoulders rolling forward. She looked sad and vulnerable, and the sight made him tense further. He wanted to wipe the image away. He wanted to wipe the sadness away and protect her from whatever harmed her, except an uneasy feeling told him that he might be the cause of her pain.

"Well, I'm glad we agree on that, at least." She spoke softly, her voice tinged with an odd note, a sort of sad humor, woven through the rich tones. She turned back to him. "If I agree to this, I have one condition."

He gave a short nod and waited, his heart beginning to gain speed.

"Before Parsons casts the spell, he has to give *me* a way to remove it." Her voice grew strong as she presented her demand, and she lifted her head to look him determinedly square in the eye. "I won't agree otherwise. I'm not going to put up with years and years of being tied to someone who comes to resent me. You already made it clear that you don't want to be tied to me by anything other than the task at hand, and that's fine. It works for me, but the spell doesn't. Not unless I know for certain that I can get out of it when I nee—when I think it's time."

Kees stared at her pale little face. Her jaw was set, as stubborn as her heart, and her lips had compressed into a firm line, but her brow was furrowed and dark circles shadowed the tender skin beneath her eyes. She looked set and fierce and heartbreakingly fragile. He wanted to go to her, to touch her, but the minute his weight shifted forward, she drew back, pulling herself even farther away from him.

The itching in his palms intensified, and Kees wanted to roar his irritation. He just didn't know whom he wanted to roar at.

He nodded. "Agreed. We will do this as you desire. Shall we go find Parsons and tell him to proceed?"

"Might as well." Ella nodded briskly and turned to leave the room by the exit the Warden had used earlier. He followed close behind and thought he heard her words drift back to him as they entered the hall.

"Before I change my mind."

Chapter Eleven

The binding spell had been brief, simple, and disarmingly anticlimactic, especially since when it was over, Ella felt absolutely no different. She even asked Alan if he'd done things properly, and he laughed as he assured her he had. She and Kees had been well and truly bound.

She supposed the short, simple nature of the spell should be counted as a plus. After all, being new at this whole magic thing, she wouldn't have wanted the unbinding Alan had taught her—and included in her textbooks, as she called them, just in case—to be something long and complicated that had to be recited in ancient Sumerian under the light of a gibbous moon and over the body of a sacrificial salamander, but still. She'd expected something a little more impressive. Would one tiny whiff of frankincense have hurt anybody? A tingle in her right big toe? Something.

But no, Ella had felt nothing.

Kees had wanted to wait for morning to do the spell. By the time they found Parsons and made their request, it was nearly three in the morning, and Ella was swaying on her feet—but no, she'd wanted to get it over with before she lost her nerve. Sleep, she figured, would come the instant her head touched the pillow, so better to have it done now, when she wouldn't have time to lie around and brood over it.

Famous last words.

Turning her head, she glanced at the small alarm clock that sat on the bedside table in Alan's comfortable guest room. The Rose Room, he called it, not because it was pink, but because a beautiful climbing rose twined around a trellis just outside the bedroom window. Ella had cracked it open before she climbed into bed, and the sweet scent of cool and fading roses soothed her into sleep.

Or it would have. If she hadn't been lying here wide awake, trying to count sheep and force herself into dreamland. At this point, she thought she had enough of the woolly little beggars to start her own ranch in New Zealand.

She knew exactly what her problem was, of course. It was hard to miss, considering it stood over seven feet tall, growled like a grizzly bear, and currently slept in the room beside hers.

Ella tugged at the covers and twisted onto her side to stare out the rose-bordered window. Every time she thought she'd adjusted to the Guardian, regained her equilibrium and had her feet back on solid ground, he went and jerked the rug out from under her. Did he realize how maddening that was?

It had started That Night, which now glowed in capital neon letters in Ella's confused mind. He had spent all that time telling her that he experienced as little emotion as the stone he appeared to be carved from, yet all the while he treated her with a tenderness she had never expected. He had touched her as if he cared for her, and when he emptied himself inside her, he'd done it with her name on his lips like a prayer.

And yet, the next morning, he treated her like a disease. The shock had almost knocked her down, but Ella considered herself stronger than that, and smarter. She'd taken the hint, and she'd given him what he seemed to want: space, distance, and chilly formality. Of course, she'd continued to argue with him, because the gargoyle operated under the vastly mistaken assumption that he was always right, and Ella felt she had a duty to point out how misguided such a belief really was. But she'd stopped trying to show him that for a cold, emotionless, warrior monster, the man showed an awful lot of heart.

Take their earlier argument, for example. She had to wonder if he'd actually heard himself speaking. She had, and she saw right through his bellows to the meaning behind it. He worried for her. Worry. That human emotion. And he felt the need to protect her, almost as if he cared (another emotion) about what happened to her. He also hadn't liked the idea of her staying in Seattle while he returned to Vancouver one little bit. He'd sounded darn close to possessive to her.

Did she sense a theme developing?

She really had to wonder if all gargoyles were so stupid, or was it just Kees? The man honestly appeared to believe his own nonsense about lacking emotion, as if by pretending the feelings weren't there, he could make them go away. He reminded her of a toddler playing peek-a-boo; just cover his eyes and no one else would be able to see him.

Ella could definitely see him, crystal clear and in living color. Now, she just had to decide if she should continue trying to make him open his own eyes, or just let the whole thing go. Would the chance that she could convince Kees to recognize and acknowledge his own emotions be worth the effort—the supreme effort—it would take her to accomplish the seemingly Herculean task?

She had no trouble recognizing her own emotions. Ella was falling in love with the gargoyle, as strange and ridiculous as that sounded. A week ago, she hadn't even known he existed, hadn't known a creature like him *could* exist, and yet here she lay, staring out into the night and trying to reconcile her increasingly hard-to-ignore feelings for a man who wasn't even of her same species.

Who'da thunk, right?

Maybe she would understand the emotions tormenting her more easily if she felt them for a different man. You know, a nicer one. Kees, she admitted, was a grumpy, grouchy, dictatorial, annoying, and often thoroughly unpleasant individual. But he was also protective, patient, intelligent, and fiercely loyal.

His commitment to what he called his mission never wavered. He never questioned the long, lonely period he spent trapped in sleep waiting to be released for the sole purpose of fighting. He believed absolutely in the need to defend the world against the forces of evil, and he would do whatever he deemed necessary to emerge victorious. Ella could admire all of that. God knew she'd met more than enough human men in her life who could barely commit to what they wanted for dinner, let alone to the sacrifice required of a Guardian. His strength, both physical and mental, left her slightly in awe.

He had also demonstrated often that he had the ability to be gentle and supportive. Not just when he touched her, although her body heated and softened every time she remembered That Night, but when he taught her. She would have expected him to be a stern, unforgiving teacher, but while he demanded a lot from her, he never failed to offer encouragement when she needed it, or praise for a job well done. She knew that he had grown to respect her magical abilities and her mind, if not her ability to protect herself from the enemies they were likely to face. And soon. He showed that respect in the way he spoke of her to Alan, and the way he never hesitated to offer her a new challenge when she had demonstrated mastery over an earlier skill.

There was a lot to love about the ornery, stubborn, closed-minded jerk. And unfortunately, her heart seemed determined to ferret out all of it.

In a way, her own uncontrollable feelings for Kees made it easier for her to understand why he seemed so determined to deny his every emotion. Life would be a lot easier if she didn't have feelings. Then, she wouldn't experience the hurt that sliced her every time the gargoyle pushed her away. She wouldn't be lying in bed wishing for something she could never have. And she probably wouldn't be having any trouble sleeping.

Kees, she thought bitterly, was probably snoozing like a baby next door. The jerk.

With a groan, Ella flopped onto her back again and stared up at the ceiling. Maybe she should just give up on sleep. Trying to force it had gotten her nowhere. She'd noticed a small stack of books—non-magical ones—arranged artistically on the dainty writing desk under the window. Maybe one of them would be boring enough to numb her overactive brain into submission. The last thing she needed was to be too sleepy to drive home tomorrow.

She threw the covers back and swung her legs over the side of the mattress. Through the small opening in the window, she could hear the quiet sounds of the night, wind rustling leaves, a few remaining insects, something small scampering through the undergrowth. The scent of faded roses and pine needles drifted in on a soft breeze, carrying with them the sharp, incongruous smells of gasoline and magic.

Shit.

Ella jumped to her feet even as her door burst open and thudded hard against the bedroom wall.

"Hurry." Kees's voice remained low, but carried a hard note of urgency. "*Nocturnis* are here. I can feel them."

"I know. I recognized the smell of that nasty Dark magic, and I can smell gas," she said, grabbing her jeans from the back of a chair along with the knapsack of training texts Alan had given her. She padded quickly and quietly to his side, the bag slug over her shoulder. She sniffed the air again. "And smoke. Kees, this is bad."

"I know. Hurry," he repeated, and stepped back into the hall.

Ella tugged on the denim and rushed after him.

The air around them appeared hazy, the scent of burning intensifying rapidly. Before they had reached the top of the stairway, the thickening smoke was making it uncomfortable to breathe. Ella pulled the collar of the T-shirt she'd gone to bed in up over her nose and mouth and peered through the fumes.

She spotted flickering light at the bottom of the stairs, and tugged the edge of Kees's wing. "We can't go that way. The fire's on the ground floor. I can see the glow from here. We need to go out a window or something. I think this is spreading fast. And what about Alan?"

Kees set his jaw. "He sleeps down there. He will have to get himself out. We will make our way out of the building and regroup outside."

"Which is where the *nocturnis* will be," she guessed. "They're trying to flush us out."

He nodded grimly. "It will work, but not, I think, as they imagined."

Ella followed as the gargoyle turned away from the stairs and headed down the hall in the direction of the clearer air. Smoke was everywhere now, but it was thicker near the opening to the lower level, thinning as they approached the end of the hall. Throwing open a door, Kees strode inside to peer out the window. She noticed that he remained to the side of the glass and used the curtains to conceal his presence from the outside.

"I see one of them near the tree line and two more closer to the house," he said, his voice beginning to take on that gravelly rumble that indicated he wasn't a happy gargoyle. "They are bold. There are too many humans in this neighborhood for them to make such a brazen move. Even with the covering of the trees, they could be spotted at any moment."

Ella chewed the inside of her lip. "It sounds almost like they don't care who sees them."

"That's what I'm afraid of. If that is true, the situation may be even more dire than Parsons indicated. No fear of discovery means they do not worry about the human authorities."

"And we already know they've made a serious dent in the magical kind of authority."

Oh, wow, Ella thought. Bad just kept getting worse.

"We can't go out this way. Exiting by a window in sight of three Dark magic users would make us easy targets."

Kees stepped away from the window and left the room, crossing the hall to a door on the opposite side, overlooking the street at the front of the house. Ella knew just from his expression that *nocturnis* lurked there as well.

Still, she couldn't hold back her incredulous murmur. "In the middle of the street?"

"In plain view," he answered grimly. "They show no fear."

Fear rushed through Ella, tightening her chest even more than the smoke had done. She pushed it back and shrugged into the second knapsack strap. With the bag more secure now, she was ready to move. She looked at Kees. "Okay. So what do we do now?"

He headed for the door before she could finish speaking and stepped back out into the hall. Peering into the progressively thickening smoke above the two-story entry hall beside the stairs, he grunted.

"We go up."

Reaching back, he grabbed Ella hand and towed her after him. She used her other hand to press her shirt more firmly over her mouth. The smoke was so dense now, she could barely see a foot in front of her, a task made even more difficult by the way her eyes stung and watered from the vapor. She wanted to ask Kees what he meant, but the air had gone too warm and thick to talk. She hadn't noticed an attic entrance earlier, but maybe the gargoyle was more observant than she was.

He stopped abruptly at the edge of the banister, and Ella humphed as she collided with his back. She would have stepped away, but he turned and hooked a large, powerful arm around her waist beneath the backpack.

"Hold on," he growled, and then the world dropped away beneath her feet.

She heard the heavy beat of enormous wings and felt the rush of air against her skin as they rose toward the cathedral ceiling of the house's entry hall. With the smoke thickening the higher they went, she had no way to protest, and once the realization that they were flying hit her, the last thing she wanted to do was distract the gargoyle and get dropped to the tiles for her trouble. If the fire didn't kill her, she didn't want a thirty-foot fall to do it either.

For an instant, it felt as if they hovered just beneath the peaked roof, and the change in the light levels finally clued Ella in to what was happening. Kees had remembered the enormous skylight in the ceiling and had flown them right up to it.

"Put your face against my shoulder," he commanded, giving her a split second to comply before he hauled his free arm back and then threw it at the thick, tempered glass so hard, Ella felt the impact jar through his body and into hers. She gritted her teeth, held her breath and felt shards rain down onto her hair and shoulders. Then the smoke and air seemed to rush up around her and Kees followed them through the opening and into the night sky.

She half expected him to land on the roof and set her down so they could regroup and decide the safest route out of the house, but the gargoyle didn't pause. He shot straight for the trees, moving toward cover faster than Ella imagined possible.

A chill of foul Dark magic arching past them told her why. The *nocturnis* who waited outside had seen them on the roof and wanted to ensure no survivors escaped from their fiery trap.

Tugging her shirt back into place, Ella adjusted her grip on Kees's shoulders and squeezed. "What about Alan? We can't just abandon him to the *nocturnis*."

"It's too late," he bit out, sinking lower to hug the treetops. "I saw the lower floor. They had the doors and windows sealed with magic. He never made it outside."

Ella choked back a protest and pressed her face against his shoulder again as he halted their momentum and dropped to land softly on the forest floor. Her eyes filled, and she knew she couldn't even blame the lingering effects of the smoke. Alan was dead.

Suddenly the abstract danger she had heard about over and over during the last week felt very real. Her work with Kees had just morphed from an entertaining diversion—an intriguing puzzle to solve with missing persons and magic and adventure—into a war with blood and casualties and the very real possibility of death and defeat. Only Ella couldn't just decide to stop playing. She was part of this now and she had to see that part through, for her own sake as well as for those who had already sacrificed themselves to the cause. Like Alan.

Unlocking his arm from around her waist, Kees reached

for her shoulders to steady her. "We have to keep moving. They're searching for us. We need to leave."

Dragging the back of her hand across her eyes, Ella sniffled briefly and nodded. "I know. Let's go."

"We're behind the end of the road. I would fly us farther, but it's nearly dawn, and I don't want to be trapped in the air when the sun comes up. We'll have to go on foot."

"If we can double back on the other side of the road and get to the car, I can drive us out of here. Will the *nocturnis* recognize you in your human form?"

"If they look closely enough, yes, but there's a chance they'll be too distracted to pay enough attention."

Ella figured a chance was better than nothing. "Shift, then. We can use the woods for cover until we get close to the car. It's right up against them, so if we're lucky, we could climb in from the passenger side before they see us. But you're right; it's not long till sunrise. We'll have to move fast."

Kees looked down at her with a faint expression of surprise, as if he'd expected her to protest the danger or whine about having to move quickly and quietly while psycho killer magicians searched the woods for them. She supposed she could do that, but what was the point? They needed to move, and so they'd move.

Finally, he nodded and shifted, appearing a second later in dark pattered trousers and a matching shirt. It took a second for her eyes to adjust in the darkness; then she almost grinned. Maybe it was the adrenaline making her punchy, but it struck her funny that he'd dressed in camo. Too bad she hadn't been prepared to run for her life, or she'd have chosen a top that wasn't pink. Oh well, there was always next time.

He didn't waste time, just began moving swiftly and silently through the trees. Ella followed as best she could, but she knew her footsteps practically echoed compared to his. Having never practiced at being stealthy, she kind of sucked at it.

Kees didn't comment, just led the way through the trees and presumably back toward the rental car. He hadn't actually told her to stick close, but then, he hadn't really needed to. She had no intention of getting farther than an arm's length behind him, and given his wings weren't in the way at the moment, closer, if she could manage it.

Hell, if his pockets had been bigger, she'd have climbed inside one.

With the weight of the books in her backpack, she had to work even harder than usual to keep up with the gargoyle's long strides. The panting didn't help her stay any quieter, but with luck anyone hearing would assume someone in the neighborhood had a big dog they let wander around. It made more sense than a fleeing mage-in-training and her gargoyle protector, right?

A flash of movement caught her attention as Kees held up a hand in a signal for her to stop. She froze and peered into the slowly lifting darkness around them. She couldn't see anything in the gloom, but she knew by now that Kees could see in the dark better than a cat. Creature of the night, and all that.

Her gaze remained glued to his profile as he scanned the area between the trees. She held herself perfectly still, waiting, nerves all but vibrating from the adrenaline coursing through her. At the most instinctive level, she wanted to turn tail and run—somewhere, anywhere—as fast as her legs could carry her, but she knew she was better off sticking with Kees.

She was certainly learning a lot tonight, though. For instance, apparently the "fight" portion of her fight-or-flight instinct was defective. Her fists hadn't clenched, but her stomach sure had. Into knots.

The attack came with no warning—at least, none Ella

could see. One moment she balanced on the balls of her feet, waiting for Kees to tell her to move or to drop to the ground, and the next she went flying into a tree trunk when a huge palm pressed against her sternum and pushed.

Damn, she thought as she lay half-dazed at the base of the tree and struggled to clear her head. If this was what happened when a friend hit her, she'd better hope one of the *nocturnis* never got their hands on her.

Kees, she knew, had shoved her to get her out of the line of fire, and immediately moved in front of her. Anyone attempting to harm her would have to get through him first. His roar of fury echoed in the woods, accompanied by the shimmer of magic that signaled his change, and Ella had a hard time imagining anyone trying.

She didn't wait for instructions. She might be new to this, but after she'd learned how to ground, one of her earliest lessons covered the most basic of wards—personal shielding. At the time she'd begun practicing, Ella giggled to herself, chanting the old "I'm rubber / you're glue" rhyme in her head as she built a magical wall around herself and tried to make it impervious to attack. It looked like she was about to take her first and final exam.

Two figures emerged simultaneously from the trees ahead of them. They appeared to be human men in their twenties or thirties, which Ella should have anticipated, but apparently part of her had assumed the evil they served would show in hideous faces or monstrous deformities. She saw neither.

She did get a bit of a charge, though, from their outfits. The long, dark hooded robes covered them from the tops of their heads to the soles of their feet, with wide, billowing sleeves to give them the appropriate air of otherworldly and sinister intent.

She appreciated when folks paid homage to tradition.

Fear of dying also made her a little punch drunk, apparently.

Shield in place, she scrambled to her feet and braced her back against the tree trunk. A brief pause helped her gather herself, and then she opened her eyes to that other type of vision. The blue-white of her shields glowed at the edge of her vision, but in front of her, Kees raged with magical energy. It swirled around him like storm winds, all of it restlessly eager for release.

Beyond him, the *nocturnis* stepped forward, the dark tendrils of their magic oozing and twining, making it appear as if they were wrapped in black, greasy brambles. They left trails of it behind them where they stepped, and Ella almost thought she could hear the trees in the copse of woods shudder in revulsion. She knew she would, if any of that nasty stuff touched her.

One of the figures, the one on the right, slightly shorter than his fellow sociopath, halted no more than fifteen feet from where Kees stood his ground and raised a hand. His companion stopped as well.

"You can't win this war, Guardian," the *nocturnis* said, his voice high and hissing, like a snake. "We are too many, and our masters grow restless. They have been denied too long their rightful due."

Kees didn't bother answering. He simply sprang forward like a tiger, all coiled and lethal power. His arms stretched out, claws exposed, one hand raking hard against each opponent as he landed. Ella heard one of them scream and winced, but she felt no sympathy. After seeing the evil that surrounded these men, she knew they had to be stopped.

She stayed pressed against the tree and watched. Two mostly human mages didn't seem like unfair odds against a seriously pissed-off gargoyle, and she knew Kees would not appreciate her jumping into the fray. As long as he could handle things, he would want her out of the way and not distracting him.

At the moment, she felt fine with that.

A low, guttural chant built, coming from the taller of the *nocturnis*. He had stepped backwards after the claws hit, leaving the one who had spoken to take the brunt of Kees's attack. One more quick strike and the speaker lay dead, blood pouring almost black in the dim light from the gashes in his throat.

The gargoyle turned to the other enemy and bared his teeth just as the man's voice rose sharply and his hands thrust forward. Bursts of black energy emerged from his palms like concentrated flares of darkness and slammed hard against Kees's chest, hard enough to stop him and rock him slightly on his heels.

Ella gasped and instinctively took a step forward. A hand in her hair jerked her back hard enough to make her scream.

"Well, well, what have we here?" A voice cackled in her ear, sharp and grating as broken glass. She could hear the malice in it and knew she wasn't cut out for this business. She should have been watching her back—their backs—while Kees forged ahead into battle. Next time, she would know better.

"A little human, following like a puppy at the monster's heels. How precious."

Ella threw back an elbow, but the man holding her merely twisted away and yanked hard enough to bring tears to her eyes. Asshole.

She heard another laugh, then felt his hot, nasty breath as he leaned in close and—*ew*—sniffed at her skin.

"Ooh, I smell magic," the *nocturnis* purred, sounding way too interested for Ella's peace of mind. "She's a little mageling, isn't she? No wonder the Guardian leaps to your defense. Not a Warden, though. Not . . . ripe enough. Too bad they didn't have time to train you up, puppy. Maybe if they had, you'd have made for an amusing few minutes of diversion before you died. Not that many of the others did, but a man can hope."

Ella made a low sound of fury and reached up to dig her nails into the hand holding her hair, but the *nocturnis* just hissed and shook her. "No. No scratching, naughty little puppy. Someone needs to teach you some manners."

Okay, maybe she should get to work on those offensive spells everyone said she could worry about later. She planned to start worrying now.

"And someone needs to teach you to lay off the frickin' metaphors, dick lick."

With a savage growl, Ella gripped the man's hand tightly and gave him all her weight, leaving her legs free to kick up and outward. It wasn't the most graceful backflip she'd ever performed—God knew her third-grade gymnastics teacher would roll over in his grave if he could see it—but it worked. At least partly.

The man's grip on her hair tightened for an instant, which hurt like hell on fire, but then dropped away as Ella tumbled backwards over his shoulder to land inelegantly on her ass behind him. He spun around, but Ella had her shoulders out of her backpack and the straps in her hands. The second he leaned toward her, she swung with all her might and clapped him a solid blow to the side of the head with the book-weighted knapsack.

Thank God for old-fashioned hardcovers. The e-book reader she had at home wouldn't have packed nearly the same punch.

The man staggered sideways, cursing. His black robe twirled around him, parting slightly to reveal a very ordinary pair of blue jeans and beat-up tennis shoes. Somehow the sight reminded her that *nocturnis* or not, this man was just a man, a human, and like all of them, vulnerable to injury and entirely mortal. Evil itself did not make him better than her.

She could do this, damn it.

At least, she thought she could until he righted himself and shouted something foreign and nasty sounding that caused a bolt of black light to come shooting at her head. That kind of thing could pose a problem.

Even as she ducked, she knew she'd be too late, but it turned out not to matter. The bolt made it three inches from the side of her head before abruptly stopping, drawing one last inch closer, then springing back toward her attacker like a stone from a slingshot. When it hit him, he cried out and shook like a dog coming out of the rain.

Hey, maybe she *was* rubber!

It didn't appear that the reflected magic had done him any harm—maybe because it was his magic to begin with, and therefore not a foreign invader—but it did surprise the hell out of him.

He stared at Ella with bloodshot dark eyes and snarled. "Who are you, insolent puppy? I want your name before I end you."

Ella stared straight at him and flipped him the bird. "End this, asshole."

And then Kees landed on his head like a ton of stone.

Literally.

Chapter Twelve

They got the hell out of Dodge.

Ella spared not a thought to the three bodies lying in the woods until about halfway through Seattle. When she mentioned something, Kees grunted not to worry. Apparently, one of the prices paid by users of Dark magic was that once their life force flickered out, the magic devoured whatever was left over in order to sustain itself.

Gross in theory, but highly practical in action.

At least no one would be collecting hair and fiber sample and knocking on Ella's apartment door. She figured she had enough to worry about.

Making the return trip to Vancouver in broad daylight had not factored into their original plans, and the border continued to present a problem. In the end, they had no choice but to split up. Kees would have to wait for darkness to fly, unless he could find an isolated spot to sneak across on foot. While intellectually Ella knew the Guardian could take care of himself—and her and half the population of BC single-handedly—she knew she wouldn't really relax until they reunited at her apartment.

Even then, it might take a bottle of tequila and a very long bath.

Somehow, the silence of the lonely return trip bothered her more than Kees's antisocial silence on the trip down. She must have it bad if sitting next to a surly gargoyle, being pointedly ignored, made her happier than a little bit of solo peace and quiet.

God, she was hopeless.

She was also stiff and sore by the time she returned the rental car and arrived back at her apartment a little after 11 A.M. A particularly achy butt reminded her that landing on said spot with all her weight and a considerable amount of force, followed by four hours sitting in a car had not added up to her finest moment.

Taking the bath she had fantasized about helped a little, but she decided against the tequila. She wanted her wits about her. Odd how being attacked and threatened with death could change a girl's priorities like that.

In the end, she whiled away the time with a clever combination of chewing on her knuckles, paging through the books Alan had given her, and checking the clock every five minutes until dusk. Then she checked it every two.

Because she'd been listening so closely—not to say obsessively—she heard the faint metallic squeak from the fire escape when Kees landed. Before it had even stopped, she'd made it off the sofa, across the bedroom, and had her hands on the window sash. She shoved it high and stepped back as Kees eased carefully into the room.

"This window is too small for you. You're going to end up tearing a wing, or something. I think you should start planning to shift and use the door. You know you're welcome to."

Okay, so she was babbling—and inanely, at that—so sue her. She'd had a rough day. Night. Whatever.

Kees didn't comment, just pulled his tail inside, and

then slid the window mostly shut. He looked perfectly normal. No oozing holes or bloody slashes, and nothing on fire, which Ella decided to take as a good sign.

"How was the trip back? Did you have any trouble? Did you run into any more *nocturnis*? What did—?"

He held up a hand. "Everything is fine, but you appear nervous. Has something happened?"

Ella wrapped her arms around her chest. She wanted to wrap them around him, but the risk of being pushed away held her back. "No, it's been quiet. I just wasn't sure when you'd be able to cross the border, so I guess I had a hard time relaxing. I'm new at this whole sneaking and running thing."

And the unrequited love thing, too.

"I encountered no difficulties, but I had to wait until dusk to make my way into Canada. The wasted time annoyed me, but my journey was uneventful."

She nodded awkwardly. "Good. Good. Um, are you hungry? Do you need something to eat?"

He shrugged and padded through into the kitchen. "I can take care of myself, little human. Do not bother yourself. I have become quite familiar with your kitchen and cooking appliances, remember?"

Ella did. She'd had to teach him to use the microwave and the electric range, but he caught on quickly. Probably because he'd been trying to ignore her by that point, and his lessons to her on magic ate up his daily allotment of acknowledging her presence.

"Right. Okay, then. I'll just . . . go back to my book."

He nodded and turned away to fix himself a snack. Ella suited actions to words, picking up the book she'd been staring at for most of the day and settling into the corner of the sofa. Drawing her legs up, she balanced the book on her knees and focused on the open pages.

She still had no idea what they said.

Her incomprehension had nothing to do with obscure spells being recorded in archaic languages. That would have been too simple. No, the truth was that Ella had no idea what she was reading, because for the last eleven hours, she hadn't been able to focus enough to decipher a bloody word. And now that the source of her confusion was back, things just seemed worse. Having him in the room played just as much havoc with her concentration as wondering when he'd arrive.

Hopeless. She was utterly hopeless.

Sighing, she let her head thump against the back of the sofa and closed her eyes. She had to find a way to get over these feelings for Kees. Not only did they have no future, but if she slipped and let him know what he meant to her, it would only make him angrier. Colder. As it was, the only time he voluntarily got anywhere near her was when their working together required it. Otherwise, he went out of his way to avoid her.

Ella could take a hint, and she did have some pride left. She would find a way to get over this. She had no other choice.

Surprise had her eyelids popping open when she felt the sofa cushions sink beside her. Kees settled on the other end of the seat with a huge sandwich on a plate in one hand and a bottle of beer in the other. Placing his dish on the coffee table, he raised the drink to his lips, pointing it at her book on the way.

"What are you reading?"

Ella blinked. Had Kees just spoken to her? Voluntarily? She wanted to pinch herself, just to make sure it wasn't a hallucination.

"Uh, me?" she squeaked, and then fought back the urge to smack herself. Who else would he be talking to? He knew the people on the TV screen weren't actually in the room, and she didn't even have the set on in the first place.

"Um, it's one of the books Alan loaned me. Gave me, I guess." She stroked her hand over the paper and tilted her head into her shoulders. "I feel guilty that he's gone, like I should have done more. Somehow knowing he died in the house when we made it out . . . I don't know. It kinda makes me feel like I stole these. Like I shouldn't have taken them."

Kees swallowed a mouthful of sandwich. "No. He wanted you to have them. That's why he gave them to you. You would have returned them if circumstances were different, but keeping them doesn't shame you. It honors him."

She peered at him suspiciously. "You really think so?"

"I do. Alan Parsons was a Warden. Part of his duty was to pass his knowledge on to others, for the good of the Guild and the good of humanity. You should have the books. You may need them now more than ever."

"I guess."

"Do not guess. Know. Alan died honorably, but his death is on the hands of the *nocturnis,* not yours."

He waited until she nodded before returning to his meal.

Ella sat silently while he finished his sandwich and settled back with his beer. If it weren't for the wings folded behind his shoulders and the tail wrapped around his lower leg, he'd look like a pretty normal guy enjoying a brew at the end of a long day. You know, almost.

The silence between them tonight felt easier somehow, less tense, less full of unspoken words and hurt and anger. Ella wondered if it had to do with having worked together against the enemy—a kind of battlefield camaraderie—or if the spell Alan had cast was responsible. Either way, she had no reason to complain. Comfortable silence beat armed détente with a baseball bat, but it might take some getting used to.

Hey, she'd gotten used to his unprecedented ability to

sit in front of a television without turning it on, not to mention the fact that he could watch a program all the way through and without a remote control in his hand, but these things took time.

Sighing, Ella looked back down at the book while Kees sat and sipped his beer. Weren't they just the picture of an old married couple? Minus the TV, the remote, and the species barrier, of course.

Maybe that little exchange had been the olive branch she'd been waiting for. She just had to decide if it was enough.

This time, the words on the page cooperated and aligned themselves into neat lines made up of phrases and sentences. Interesting ones, too. Hallelujah.

The page Ella had randomly opened to appeared to describe a spell that would detect the presence of deceptive magic. Not knowing such a thing existed, Ella read on and learned that while certain magics could be seen by viewing them with the mage's eye—the trick Ella had learned that allowed her to see the broken wards at Gregory's and the Dark magic that swirled around the *nocturnis* back in the woods outside Seattle, there were ways to hide magic from that sort of generalized perusal.

For instance, the mage who had authored this book mentioned that some *nocturnis,* particularly those used to recruit new servants for the darkness or who infiltrated and corrupted mundane organizations, would cast spells that could make another mage overlook that they even possessed magic, let alone its type or intent. The mage's eye would not see through those spells. Instead a suspicious mage would have to focus his own magic and speak an unmasking spell. That definitely sounded useful.

Turning the page, Ella found something even more useful—an absorption spell. At first, the name made her think of sponges and water retention, but she kept reading and discovered that this particular bit of magic built on the defensive skills she had already learned and turned them into a combination of offense and defense. The casting mage could create an energy shield that not only protected from a magical attack, but actually absorbed the energy of the incoming spell and then sent it back to the original caster. Sort of like what Ella had accidentally done in the woods. Only because the magic in this spell became encapsulated in the magic of the intended target, it could actually damage the person it rebounded on.

She liked the justice inherent in that technique. It harmed an enemy no more and no less than he had intended to harm you. It was almost elegant.

Ella read the words, mouthing them silently as she committed the information to memory. She had expected the spell thing to be a lot more complicated than this— frankincense and tingles again—but she was learning quickly that the key to the magic practiced by the Wardens was its intent. What a Warden intended to create, he created; what he intended to affect, he affected.

She, Ella reminded herself. Enough with the male-centrism. She would be a Warden one of these days, and she was very definitely not male. Down with the patriarchy, and all that crap. Time for the Guild to wake up and smell the twenty-first century.

Provided any of them were still alive.

"Oh, that reminds me." Ella looked up from her book and leaned over to snag a piece of paper from the coffee table. "I looked up Fil's phone number earlier. First time I've ever gotten a use for those alumni directories the university keeps sending me. Anyway, if you still want me to, I can call her in the morning. That sound okay?"

Kees nodded, and Ella realized he hadn't turned to look at her when she spoke. He hadn't needed to. His gaze had already been trained on her.

"That would be helpful," he murmured, and even low and soft, his voice retained the quality of gravel and dark molasses. "Before I woke, I would not have expected to rely on a female art restorer I had never met with no talent for magic to help me bring together my Guild and my brethren. But then again, before now, I would not have expected a human woman to have called me from my sleep, nor that she would be so clever and so talented."

Ella shivered, his words sliding over her skin like the memory of his callused fingers. Her head spun, confusion and longing butting heads and struggling for control of her mind and heart. If she didn't know better, if he hadn't spent the past week and more trying to convince her of his indifference toward her, Ella would have thought that the gargoyle was trying to seduce her.

Ha! Even if he wanted to, it would be a wasted effort. In spite of her hurt and anger and fear, Ella knew that all he had to do was crook a finger, and she would go to him, the consequences be damned.

In the end, she'd be the one in hell, but for another taste of him, she might be willing to risk it.

With shaking hands, Ella closed her book and clasped the heavy volume against her chest. Maybe it would keep her heart from pounding straight through her rib cage.

She opened her mouth to say something, then shut it. She had no words. As much as she wanted him, she still couldn't bring herself to say it out loud. She'd been burned badly, so this time the fire would have to come to her.

It did. Slowly, deliberately, Kees set aside his empty bottle and wrapped a huge clawed hand around her ankle. With a gentle tug he pulled her leg out straight and tugged her slowly toward him across the cushions.

The sight of his dark, gray-toned skin and heavy, lethal talons neither frightened nor disgusted her. They belonged to Kees, and in a very quiet, very secret corner of herself, Ella admitted that she did as well. Whether he wanted her or not, she was his.

While she studied the contrast between his gargoyle's hand and her pale human skin, she saw his flesh shimmer and his human hand appeared instead. The flash of disappointment surprised her, but her gaze flew up to his.

"You don't have to do that," she whispered. "I told you before, your natural form doesn't frighten me. It doesn't disgust me. It doesn't bother me. It's just you."

He flashed her a slow smile that made her stomach turn somersaults, and her thighs clench like a pair of Vise-Grips. "I like the way this me fits against you."

He tugged again, pulling her close enough to grab her hips and haul her into his lap, the book dropping to the rug with a muffled thump. Her heart jumped and her pussy clenched as he arranged her the way her wanted her, spreading her thighs with his until her knees hugged his hips, and wrapping her arms around his neck in a loose embrace. Then, he pulled her flush against him so that she could feel the heat of his erection pressing her core through the layers of their clothes, and her nipples poked against his chest in firm, eager points.

Ella watched the building fire in his dark eyes and realized that as long as she could look into those eyes, his never-changing, always hypnotizing eyes, it didn't matter if he looked like a man or a gargoyle or a Muppet. He was Kees, and she loved it.

He continued to smile, pressing the curve of his lips against hers in a closed-mouth, teasing caress. She felt the rasp of his chin against her as he trailed those lips across her cheek until they teased her ear and his voice whispered through her like another set of hands, these ones able to reach inside her and stroke her very heart.

"Also, I have a confession to make," he murmured, teasing the shell of her ear with gentle nips. "In this form, I'm more sensitive. I can feel everywhere you touch me. I can feel your breath, your warmth, your smooth, soft skin."

Another nip, this one less gentle.

"Your hot, silky pussy."

Ella melted and gasped, wondering when all the oxygen had been sucked from the room.

"I am greedy, little human. I don't want to sacrifice a single, glorious touch. With this body, I can wallow in sensation. With these hands, I can feel every last inch of you."

He pulled back and grinned into her panting, wide-eyed face. "So, little human, do you still object that I shift my forms to make love to you?"

Ella offered a fervent denial and gripped the back of his neck in an attempt to draw him forward into the kiss she needed more than food and water.

He resisted, his hands sliding up and down her sides in teasing strokes. "Then you have nothing else to say, sweet girl?"

She nodded, and he raised an eyebrow.

"What do you need to say, Ella?"

"Touch me."

As if Kees could do anything else.

He started with her lips, pressing his to the plump, rosy pillows, loving the way they immediately softened as they parted under his. He moved into her mouth slowly, confidently, accepting her instinctive offer of surrender. For every surrender she offered him, he wanted more. The urgency of his own need unsettled him, but he felt helpless against it. Having this woman had become more important than the rest of existence.

He touched her back next, pressed his hands against the long line of her spine and wondered at the idea that a body so small and fragile could contain a spirit so strong and resilient. Her bones felt like they would grind to powder if he so much as embraced her too tightly. Yet he remembered having her beneath him the last time, remembered how she had met every thrust, taken every thoughtless, passion-roughened caress and pleaded for more.

She amazed him, more and more every moment. He wanted to touch all that ferocity, all that strength, to wallow in it, to mark it and claim it and keep it beside him forever.

The thought made him shudder. How had he gotten to this point? He'd been made a warrior, summoned from the ether fully formed and fully trained, with no other purpose than to fight or die in defense of the human world, but he'd known from the very beginning that that world held no place for him. Guardians were not meant to mingle with humans, other than the Wardens who kept their secrets and aided in their mission. They were not meant to feel, to want, or to have.

Guardians, their stories told, had no hearts apart from rough-hewn stone. They felt no emotion, formed no bonds, took no mates. They did not breed to replenish their ranks. When one fell, another would be summoned from the ether. Like the carved images of gargoyles that decorated abbeys and castles in the Old World, the Guardians existed to drive off evil and nothing else.

So why did Kees now feel that touching Ella was the only purpose in his cold and solitary life? What was the stirring he felt in his chest every time he turned his gaze upon her? Why did he nearly give thanks that the Darkness was stirring once more, if only because he had woken and found her in his path? Was this what the humans called emotion?

Love?

"Kees."

Her voice washed over him like a full-body caress. He loved the sound of his name on her lips. Especially when she struggled for sanity, overwhelmed with wanting.

Especially when her body clasped around him, hot and wet and feeling like heaven.

Abandoning his thoughts, Kees stroked his hands down and pulled the hem of her shirt up and away from her curving hips. He wanted no fabric between them. He needed to see her, to watch her skin turn rosy under his hands, his mouth.

She raised her arms over her head and helped him strip the garment off her. Her fingers went straight to her bra, releasing the clasp and shrugging out of the confining garment before letting it fall unheeded to the floor. Her eyes remained on his, her gaze heated but uncertain. He had caused that, he knew, with his coldness. He'd pushed her away until she couldn't understand why he pulled her closer.

Regret filled him. He had never wanted to cause his little human pain. He had thought he had no choice but to pull back from her. He'd thought he needed to remain cold and alone, untouched and separate. Maybe he did, but even if that were true, he no longer had the strength to do it. She had robbed him of it with her sweet and stubborn and sassy nature. If Fate wanted to punish him, let Her. He would worry about that later.

Now, all he could think of was Ella.

He continued to watch her, holding her gaze with his even as his hands shifted to cup her breasts. The warm weights nestled against his palms as if they had been designed for his touch. Her pink nipples tightened the moment of contact and pressed into his skin in a silent plea for torment.

Kees gave it to her, first with his fingers, stroking and rolling and pinching the little peaks into ever harder points. Her breathing grew more and more ragged, faster and shallower until a moan broke from her lips and she raised her hands to cover his, tugging futilely.

"Please," she whimpered. "Don't tease. Give me more."

How could he refuse?

She cried out when he abruptly stood, lifting her from him, as if she expected him to set her aside and walk away again. He could never do that. He was too far gone, but he knew he would have to prove it to Ella. Actions, after all, spoke louder than words.

Instead of pushing her away, something he intended never to do again, he lifted her easily by the hips and set her down atop the low coffee table. She shot him a look of surprised confusion, but said nothing, just stood there looking soft and vulnerable and filled with anticipation.

Kees liked that. He paused just to look at her. He would never get over the pale cream of her skin, the way it seemed to glow in the lamplight. It looked as soft as he knew it felt, like warm satin laid over soft flesh.

Trailing a finger down her throat, he felt it tighten as she swallowed, felt the soft whimper bubble up an instant before it broke from her lips. He continued his path downward, over her collarbone, down between her beautiful breasts, over her quivering belly until he hooked his finger in the waistband of her snug black trousers. Then he leaned forward, taking advantage of the added height standing on the table lent her to press his lips hard against her.

He plundered, savoring the taste of her, sweet and spicy and deeply rich, before he pulled back and smiled. "I want you bare, little human. Every pretty inch of you. Take these off for me."

The flash of heat in her gaze was all he'd waited for. Dropping his hands to his sides, he stepped back and resumed his seat on the sofa.

She hesitated when he first pulled back, but he nodded in encouragement and settled in, parting his legs. When she looked down, she would see the hard bulge at the front of his jeans. He had no reason to hide it.

Ella nibbled her lip uncertainly, then released it to take a deep breath. Her thumbs hooked in her waistband, and she yanked the covering off with the quick, awkward motions of someone pulling off an adhesive bandage. A quick kick sent it sliding to the floor and left his little human totally, gloriously nude.

He'd never seen anything as seductive as her shy, inelegant striptease. He wondered if she knew that her courage and uncertainty made him a thousand times hotter than the most practiced teasing or the most intense comehither glance. To know that she had deliberately exposed herself to him, showed him her vulnerabilities, made him want to simultaneously wrap her up in the safety of his embrace and throw her to the floor to claim her quickly and savagely. But for the moment, Kees had other plans.

He leaned forward just in time to catch her hands and stop them from covering herself. With her position atop the low table, the juncture of her thighs sat in perfect position just level with his hungry gaze. It made her look like an offering, and he knew of no way on earth to refuse.

Her voice shuddered out in a hoarse cry at the first brush of his lips on her sex. Kees leaned in and breathed deeply, taking in the warm, intoxicating scent of her as if he could imprint it on his memory. As if it weren't already embedded there.

His hands gripped her thighs just above the knees and pulled gently. Uneasily, she shifted her feet, spreading her legs to give him access to the treasure he wanted most. The light glistened on her wet folds, partially exposed behind the tiny mat of neatly trimmed curls. The sight made his mouth go dry and thirst rise up, fierce and urgent, so he pressed his lips against her and drank.

Her folds parted against the intrusion of his tongue, and he lapped at her wetness, letting the hot, sweet liquid coat his tongue until he couldn't hold back his groan of pleasure. She tasted like ambrosia, as thick and sweet as honey, as rich and tangy as the finest brandy. Her flavor both quenched his thirst and heightened it. The way her hips jerked when his tongue found her sensitive clit already peeking out of its protective hood made hunger dig its claws deep into his flesh.

Small hands settled on his head, combed through his hair and then fisted. The sting made him growl, urged him on like spurs to his side. His tongue stroked again and again, gathering up her cream and demanding more. It no longer satisfied him to make her tremble. He needed to hear her scream.

Long fingers pushed inside her, relished the tight clasp of her internal muscles. He gave her no time to catch her breath but began an immediate driving rhythm. He wanted her to climb fast and fall far.

He searched for her G-spot and worked it ruthlessly. When her legs gave out, no longer able to support her weight, he wrapped an arm around her hips to pin her in place. And still he feasted.

Her pleasure became his own. Every time he heard her gasp or whimper, every echoing cry and breathless plea shot heat straight to his cock. He felt his balls drawing up tight to his body and knew he had to get inside her soon. Now. Before he exploded.

But first, he needed to feel her come apart for him.

A third finger slid inside her, stretching her tight passage, making her hips jerk and her hands yank hard against his scalp. The pain only drove him on.

He pumped hard and fast inside her and showed her clit no mercy. His tongue circled and teased and flicked before he closed his lips about the bud and drew with a firm, intense suction.

Ella's high-pitched scream made him feel like a god.

He worked her through the orgasm, his fingers stroking through her spasming internal muscles, marveling at the strength of her pleasure. His tongue rubbed firmly against her clit until she let out a whine that shivered through the air and pushed weakly against his shoulders.

"No more," she panted, every beautiful inch of her shaking and glowing with perspiration. "Too much. Too sensitive."

Reluctantly he lifted his head, licking the last traces of her from his lips and gazing up into her heavy-lidded eyes. He noted her flushed cheeks and the way the rosy color spread down her chest almost to her dusky-rose nipples. They were beginning to soften after her climax. Kees grunted. He liked them better firm and pointy with arousal.

Good thing he had no intention of letting her rest before he drove her right back up into mindless need.

His arm around her waist dragged her forward as he shifted back to settle deeper into the couch. Her body followed naturally, limp and boneless from pleasure and settled back into position on his lap, her thighs spread wide by his, her knees hugging his hips.

One hand rose to cup the back of her head, his fingers tangling in her silky brown hair, as soft and sleek as mink. He used the grip to drag her mouth down to his, consuming her with a kiss filled with gnawing hunger.

His cock throbbed in the prison of his human clothing until he could no longer stand it. The clothes that he had materialized with his shift disappeared just as quickly, melting away with a thought. Even if Guardians couldn't cast spells like Wardens, being made of magic still had its benefits.

Ella gasped and squirmed in his lap, aware of the sudden press of his thick erection against the soft pillow of her belly. He loved the way her body seemed to curve just where he craved softness, and he pressed up, grinding himself against her. The sensation made him groan deep in his throat. He fed her the sound, his tongue tangled with hers, and heard her echo it in her own softer tones.

She pulled away from him and gasped hard, as if she couldn't draw in enough air. Her hands came up to his shoulders and pushed weakly even as she tried to arch away.

"Wait. Wait. I can't—"

"And I need, little human. Now."

A cry broke on her lips, sweet and shaking, but her body melted against him. She would deny him nothing. Her generosity only fueled his craving for her.

Her hands slid from the front of his shoulders to the back and drew him against her. Kees gave a rumbling purr of satisfaction and pressed grateful lips to first one nipple, then the other, drawing each into his mouth for a reverent moment before he caught her gaze and held it.

A hand at her hip urged her to rise. She did so instantly, gracefully, though her thighs trembled as if she didn't know how long they could support her. She wouldn't need to worry for long.

With his free hand, Kees reached between them and took his cock in his fist, guiding it to her entrance. Then, eyes still locked with hers, he pulled her down to him, impaling her on the thick shaft.

He'd meant it to be slow, a gradual, incremental joining of flesh to flesh. Something to be savored and lingered over. He wanted to embed this memory in his brain for all time, something he could call up and relive over and over through all the centuries of eternity. This alone could sustain him.

But Ella didn't cooperate. Her legs gave out, the trembling bleeding into total collapse, the weight of her body driving him into her with one brutal stroke.

He heard her scream, but it echoed in the distance, drowned out by his own bellow of ecstasy. He'd forgotten how perfect she felt around him. Or maybe he just hadn't believed his own memory. Nothing, he'd believed, could really be that good.

It was better.

She fit around him as if her body had been designed to take his. Her muscles clamped tight, squeezing until he had to struggle to draw back, resisting as he pushed forward. He'd have worried that he hurt her, except that she cried out with every stroke, her body aching to meet him, her pussy already quivering with impending climax.

Kees grunted and jerked her head down for a kiss. His mouth claimed her, conquered her, devoured her. And she surrendered so beautifully, giving him everything he asked, meeting every demand with a generous spirit and a whimper of pleasure. Stones, she was perfect.

Starving and desperate, he released her hair to grasp her hips and began to move her up and down over his shaft, thrusting up into every stroke. Her head fell back against her shoulders, exposing her throat, and his mouth began to water. He wanted to sink his teeth into the soft, white flesh, to mark her like an animal. To show the world she was his.

But first, he needed her to come again.

His fingers tightened until he knew they would leave round, purple bruises in her delicate flesh, but Kees couldn't bring himself to care. They only represented more proof of his possession. Increasing the speed of his thrusts, he hammered into her. Her body arched back and her hands braced against his thighs, offering her the leverage to give as good as she got.

He knew he wouldn't last much longer.

A snarl broke from his lips and he shoved a hand down to where their bodies joined, finding her swollen clit and closing her fingers around the little peak. Her body jerked against his, and her breath froze as he pinched the nub with quick, hard pressure, sending her screaming into climax.

He loved the way she came. Her eyes went blank and hazy; then they snapped shut and her mouth opened as her body struggled to vocalize her pleasure and draw in oxygen at the same time. Her nipples drew up so tightly, they looked almost red, and just the stirring of his breath over them made her hips jerk against him. Every muscle in her body clenched under his hands and around his cock and he knew he would never see a more beautiful sight if he lived until the ending of the world.

His thrusts never paused as he rode her through the crisis. He continued to drive hard and deep into her core until he felt her soft around him and her body melted against his chest. She pillowed her head on his shoulder and mumbled something in a voice slurred with exhaustion.

She thought she was finished, he knew, but he had other plans.

Holding back his own climax had taken every ounce of determination, but the struggle had been worth it—he'd gotten to watch her some as well as feel it, and now he wanted to feel it again when he finally loosened his reins and emptied himself inside her.

He let her rest for a moment, and then slid his hands around to cup her ass, his fingers teasing the shadowy valley between the rounded cheeks. Her still-sensitized skin heated immediately and he felt her jerk against him, her pussy clenching.

Murmuring wordless encouragement, he let his hands squeeze, then stroke upward, over her hips and back. His arms wrapped around her, holding her tight against him as he altered the rhythm of his thrusts, moving slower now, but more intently. Every thrust carried force, and he changed the angle to rub against her most sensitive spot on every stroke. The head of his cock teased her cervix on this deepest entries and he heard the way her breath caught in her throat.

Her fingers clenched against his skin and he felt her arousal returning quickly. She began to whimper again, her hips rocking against his almost involuntarily. He felt his mouth curve and reached up to cup her cheeks in his hands. He wanted to look into her eyes while he came, wanted her to see what she did to him.

What they did to each other.

Ella's whimpers turned into breathless pleas and her body began to tighten once more. The intensity of their passion remained, but it had shifted gears into something quieter, something deeper. It wrapped around them like an intimate cocoon, until the world fell away and nothing existed but the two of them, moving together as one.

Kees felt his balls tighten. He knew he couldn't hold out much longer. Shifting forward, he changed his angle again until the base of his cock rode against her slit with every thrust. He laid his forehead against hers and breathed her in as he strained toward climax.

In the end she pushed him over, not with a touch but with a word. Three words. They trembled on her lips even as he felt the pleasure roll through her, her third climax like a building wave. It began with tiny little flutters of her pussy and slowly gained strength until she clamped around him like a fist, milking him of pleasure.

"I love you," she breathed, and he exploded. One hand jerked her head to the side as his human teeth gave way to

Guardian fangs. He sank them into her shoulder with fierce pleasure and a primitive thought of, *Mine*. His vision went not dark but bright, a blinding flash of light like fireworks behind his eyelids.

He came forever, shooting burst after burst of fluid into her tight heat. He felt as if a piece of his soul was ripped out with every pulse, and it felt glorious. The little human was his now. His Ella.

And he never wanted to let her go.

Chapter Thirteen

The irony of being the one to wake alone was not lost on Kees. He knew almost before he regained consciousness that Ella no longer lay in the bed beside him, and before he opened his eyes he sensed she was not in the room.

He sighed and gazed up at the ceiling. He probably deserved this.

A glance to the right showed him an empty bathroom, the lights extinguished. Looking to the opposite side of the room, he saw sunlight flooding in through the bedroom window and frowned. It appeared to be later than he'd expected.

The clock told him he'd slept until almost 10 A.M.

Kees cursed and sat up, throwing back the covers. He remembered exhaustion weighing down on him when he carried Ella to bed in the middle of the night. They had both dozed off on the sofa after that amazing bout of lovemaking, but he'd woken after a few minutes and realized they would both be more comfortable in her bedroom. He recalled settling her gently onto the mattress before crawling in beside her. The last image in his mind was the sight of her hair spread over the pillow as he curled himself around her and drifted into sleep.

Why hadn't she woken him?

He didn't find her in the rest of the apartment, but he did find a note. Not propped on the pillow, the way a lover might leave it, but stuck to the door of the microwave.

Kees frowned as he reached for it. True, it was a good place to catch his attention, since even Guardians ate during their waking cycles, but it struck him as a little cold. As if she was trying to put distance between them.

The tone of what she'd written offered little reassurance.

> *Kees,*
> *I had to be back at work before 9:00. I plan to call Fil from there and let her know what we need. I don't imagine she'll say no, but I'll catch you up tonight.*
> *Also, I think it would be a good idea for me to learn some more useful spells in case we run into more* nocturnis. *Maybe we could work on that during our lesson tonight. I marked a couple in Alan's books I thought looked interesting.*
> *—E.*

What the hell?

Kees snarled and crumpled the paper in his hand. That was all she had to say to him? Last night she had told him she loved him, and this morning all she wrote about what their mission. As if they had nothing more between them.

His first instinct urged him to head right over to the museum, drag her into the nearest dark corner he could find, and demonstrate for her with brutal clarity exactly what they had between them. She was his, damn it, and she needed to understand that.

Sanity held him back.

He knew his little human well enough to realize that interrupting her at work and exposing her private relationship to public scrutiny wouldn't win him any points. Ella held herself a little apart from most people, and he had learned that she valued her privacy. As much as he wanted to demand she explain herself to him immediately, waiting for her return and discussing the matter here would probably get him an answer faster.

And without feeling her shoes against his shins.

The thought was almost enough to make him smile. His anger still simmered at the idea of her sneaking out while he slept and leaving him with no more than a terse, impersonal note, but he could bide his time for a few hours. Paging through the books she had left him might help.

Besides, he thought, shifting back to his natural form and smiling until the tip of a fang peeked out from between his lips, if they resolved their differences here, maybe Ella could help him understand something. There was a term humans used that had always made him curious. Tonight, maybe Kees would finally discover the definition of something called "make-up sex."

Ella pinched together a bite of bread and rolled it between her fingers while the phone rang in her ear. She'd like to blame her lack of appetite on nerves over calling someone she hadn't talked to in more than five years in order to ask for a favor, but not even at her most delusional would she ever buy that lameness. The knots in her stomach had nothing to do with her college classmate and everything to do with the monster she'd left in her bed.

And she wasn't referring just to his penis.

"Bonjour."

Distracted by her own thoughts, Ella hadn't even noticed that the phone had stopped ringing. She almost choked getting out a hasty reply.

"Uh, hi. Is this Fil? Er, Felicity?"

She knew that English was the woman's first language, but living and working in Montreal would make a French greeting pretty normal.

"Yeah, who's this?"

"Um, hi," Ella repeated nervously, wondering how she was going to explain things to her old friend, or if they ever were friends. Would friends have lost touch for so long? "I know this is totally out of the blue, and you might not even remember me, which would be really embarrassing, but you and I went to school together, and I—"

"Oh my God. Ella Harrow, is that you?"

Oh, wow. Maybe Fil did remember her.

Ella let out a relieved laugh. "Yeah, it's me."

"El, this is awesome. I haven't heard from you in, like, forever. How are you?"

The warmth in Felicity's voice made Ella's heart swell. She'd liked the other woman from the first moment they met in a Renaissance art class during their sophomore year, but she'd never been very good at making friends. Since she'd gone into foster care, she learned that losing people hurt too much, and keeping them at arm's distance was just easier. She and Fil had worked together on several projects and occasionally grabbed coffee or a snack together, but they hadn't maintained contact after graduation.

Ella had to admit that was probably her fault.

She knew her own weaknesses, and she remembered how Fil had dealt with them—mainly by ignoring their existence. As far as Ella could remember, all of the time they had spent together outside of their assigned class projects had been at Fil's instigation. For some reason, Fil had never taken offense at Ella's quiet reserve. Most other people thought it meant she was a snob or cold or unfriendly, but Fil had just acted as if the distance wasn't even there.

Nothing Ella had done—or more precisely, not done—had managed to push the other woman away. Fil had dug in her heels and decided the two of them were friends, so friends they were. Even the accidental revelation of Ella's magical secret hadn't frightened her off. Since the magic terrified Ella back then, back before she'd known what it was, that had left her speechless.

The girls had worked late—until well after midnight—on a project at the university library. By the time they left the building to return to their respective dorms, it had been pitch black and silent in the wooded section of campus that separated student housing from the library. Fil—practical, rational Fil—had seemed unfazed by the creepy atmosphere, but something had set Ella's nerves on edge.

She'd felt eyes on her from the moment they first left the library, but seen no hint of any other people along the trail. Telling herself it must be her imagination, she had tried to push aside the feeling, but her skin continued to crawl as they walked through the quiet night.

When one of the overhead lamps that illuminated their path blinked out without warning, Ella had jumped out of her skin. Whirling around, she peered into the trees at the side of the path and saw something move. Then she lost it.

The door walling off her magic had sprung open and the force of the power breaking through had tossed both women onto their asses. Maybe Ella's scream had scared away the figure in the trees, but by the time Fil had leapt to her feet and shouted for whoever was scaring her friend to show himself, the odd menacing feeling had disappeared. The night air felt entirely normal, and Ella felt like an idiot.

Fil had just grabbed her hand and helped her to her feet, given her a hug, and told her it was fine. There had been curiosity in the other woman's eyes when she stepped back, but she hadn't said a thing about what knocked her down, and she never brought up the incident again. Still, Ella always remembered it, and it had made her even more self-conscious when they saw each other. When graduation separated them, she felt something almost like relief.

"I'm good, Fil," she responded, her mouth relaxing into a smile as she focused again on the present. "How are you?"

"Oh, you know. I'm still waiting for fame, fortune, and Chris Hemsworth to show up on my doorstep, but other than that, things are pretty good." There was a slight pause, and the woman sighed. It was a good sound, relaxed and mellow. "It's good to hear from you, Ella. I'm really glad you called."

Once again, Ella felt a surge of pleasure. She got along well with people, and she knew she could probably call Bea a friend, but the easy acceptance of the woman on the other end of the phone warmed her. It also made her a little sad when she realized that she still didn't let many people get close to her. Maybe she needed to change that.

You know, once the fate of the world no longer hung in the balance.

"I hope you still think that once I tell you while I called," she said, trying to inject some levity into her voice.

"Totally. If you called to ask me a favor, I'll just make another call specifically so we can catch up and gab part of my price." The comment was so typically Fil that Ella grinned into the phone. "Whatcha need, sweetie?"

"Nothing too crazy," Ella assured her. "I'm trying to get some information, actually, on a piece of statuary I heard might be in one of the museums out near you."

"In Montreal, you mean?"

"Yes."

"You still in BC?"

"Vancouver," she confirmed. "Hence the need for the favor."

"Sure. Tell me more."

And here's where things got tricky. Ella called up the story she'd rehearsed in her head earlier and tried to keep her voice casual.

"I'm at Vancouver Art and History now, and—"

"Whoa, isn't that the place that just got robbed?"

Crap. Ella had been hoping the news hadn't spread all the way across Canada yet. She'd have to regroup fast.

"Um, yes. Actually, that's part of this whole thing. I think the piece we lost might have a companion out there in Montreal. Something with a similar theme and style."

Ella heard the rustle of paper on the other end of the line before Fil said, "Something in a twelfth-century limestone grotesque, perhaps?"

Her snooty French auctioneer impression made Ella laugh. "Exactly."

"I can't say I've seen anything like that around, but there's always the chance someone has it tucked away out of sight. Or, if the two pieces are related, they may be tucking it out of sight right now. Although, how someone steals a half-ton statue without leaving a single clue makes me think I'm reading one of those locked-room mysteries."

"You and me both." Ella didn't mention that it made a

lot more sense when you knew the statue was alive and those wings really worked.

"What do you need me to find out?"

"Just if someone's got it and where it's at. Can you do that?"

"Does a bear shit in the woods? What's going on? Does your director want to buy a replacement for the one you lost?"

Ella forced a laugh. " 'Lost' makes it sound like someone dropped it behind the sofa."

"Semantics. So?"

"Um, I'm not sure," Ella hedged. "I'm just gathering info. I don't know if it's for insurance or replacement or what. But if you can let me know, it would be a help."

"You got it, sweets. Want to hear about today's special pricing plan?"

This time a genuine laugh escaped her. "Sure, Fil. Just remember I'm a poor, underpaid art historian, though."

"Well, right now we're running a one-for-two offer," the other woman teased. "I do you this one favor and you promise me two things."

"Shoot."

"Okay, first, you give me your number, address, and e-mail right this very minute and promise me never to let it go this long before we talk again."

Ella's throat tightened. She had figured Fil remembered her warmly enough to agree to do her this favor, but she had never expected to be embraced like a long-lost friend. She hadn't thought she was anyone's long-lost friend. It felt good to be wrong.

"I promise," she managed after a short pause, then recited the information while Fil scratched it down.

"Perfect. Now, for number two."

"Lay it on me."

"Promise you'll come visit."

Ella froze. Go to Montreal on a friendly visit? In between being targeted for fricassee by minions of evil and learning how to cast magical spells against said evil minions. Sure, no problem.

"Uh, things are a little . . . crazy right now, Fil."

"What's the matter? You got a new guy you can't climb off of?"

Her choked gasp spoke for her.

"Holy hell, you do!" Fil roared with laughter. "Way to go, little Miss Retiring Flower. Is he hawt?"

Fil's outrageous mouth had always been able to make Ella smile. This time, it also made her cheeks flame. "Yes, not that it's any of your business."

"Well, then bring him along. But, seriously, I didn't mean right now. We're not college students anymore, right? We have to worry about things like jobs and vacation time and airline prices and all that crap. Just tell me you'll come see me." Her voice softened. "I miss you, El. I really am glad you called. Even if it was to ask for a favor."

"I am, too. Thanks, Fil."

"No worries. I'm delivering a finished portrait to the Heath Gallery tomorrow, so I should have time in the next couple of days to check out the big boys." Montreal had several museums with collections that could include a statue the size of a Guardian. "As soon as I find something, or decide there's nothing to find, I'll give you call."

"You're the greatest."

"I know," Fil replied matter-of-factly. "And now I know how to find you, so don't think you can hide from me, Ella Marie."

"No, ma'am."

Fil laughed and hung up with a cheerful good-bye. Ella turned off her cell phone and stared at the blank screen for a few minutes. Her old friend's warm greeting and enthusiastic conversation had taken her completely by surprise.

She hadn't expected a reaction like that, not after all these years.

Lately, it seemed like nothing turned out quite the way she expected it would, from phone calls to mind-blowing sex.

Which circled her mind right back to Kees.

Not that he was often far from her thoughts these days. In fact, he seemed to occupy a part of her brain that was large and growing.

Not to mention very, very confused.

What was she going to do about him? Every time she thought she had the gargoyle figured out, he changed the rules on her. First he told her he felt nothing for her, then he proceeded to devour her like a starving man, and then he spent the next week treating her with as much warmth and attention as a piece of furniture. That hurt her, a lot, but she'd seen the writing on the wall, and she had backed off. She hadn't pushed him, hadn't demanded to know how he could fuck her one minute and ignore her the next. She had just bitten back the pain and moved on.

Until last night, when the rules had changed again. Even after they'd talked in Alan's kitchen, even after their souls had been magically bound together, she hadn't pressed him. She'd thought she knew where things stood, and she'd been prepared to live with that. And then he touched her, seduced her, made her world tilt and her heart slam in her chest. He made her fall in love with him all over again.

The Guardian blew hot and cold, and Ella just couldn't keep up.

She'd known she was acting like a coward when she sneaked out of bed this morning. The instant she opened her eyes, she'd felt Kees's arms around her, his long, hard body snuggled up against her back, heating her more thoroughly than an electric blanket. Every moment of the night before had come flooding back to her, and she remembered the way he had taken her apart, inch by inch, touch by touch.

She remembered saying, "I love you."

Her stomach had clenched, and she felt panic well up inside her. She had told him, hadn't been able to hold it back, and in speaking, she handed him the only weapon he needed to destroy her. She heard her words again, and heard his answering silence.

She couldn't stay there. She couldn't remain in that bed, feeling his arms around her, feeling him hold her as if she were precious to him. She couldn't lie there and wait for him to wake up and see her next to him, then watch him turn right back to stone.

She wouldn't survive it again.

Like a coward, she'd peeled herself out of his arms and fled to the bathroom. Getting ready for work had been her excuse, her shield against him, but he remained sleeping while she took the world's fastest shower and dressed like fugitive. Or a ninja. Never in her life had she managed to move so silently, and she doubted it would ever happen again.

In the end, it was two hours too early when she'd left the apartment. She didn't need to be at work until nine, so she made the trip on foot, taking her time, even stopping on the way for a cup of coffee and a pastry. The coffee at least had warmed her cold hands, but she'd picked at the pastry with disinterest and ended up feeding most of it to the pigeons in the little park down the street from the museum.

A glance down at her desk told her the overindulged bird would have made better use of her lunch as well. She'd taken one bite of a sandwich and managed a couple of pieces of fruit, but her appetite remained elusive. At this rate, she'd be able to market the latest diet craze—the Gargoyle Gut-Buster! Guaranteed to shave inches off your hips in as few as seven days!

With a muttered word to herself, Ella tossed the remnants of her food in the trash can and pushed out of her chair. It was time to get back to work. Her next tour group was due in a few minutes. She only hoped that a class full of nine-year-olds would provide enough of a distraction to let her spend at least an hour or two of her day not brooding over the man waiting for her at home.

A girl could dream, right?

By seven o'clock that evening, Kees had made a list of the spells he thought Ella should concentrate on, eaten two meals, tidied the kitchen, made the bed, indulged in a shower—though he'd needed to be in his human form to squeeze into her small tub for that—and watched a fascinatingly horrible television program about vampires who attended high school and appeared to have remarkable amounts of sex. He shook his head over the idea that the myth he remembered being used to frighten villages earlier in his existence now appeared primarily aimed at selling automobiles and alcohol.

After turning off the television, Kees rose and stalked over to the window that looked out onto the street. He expected Ella home any minute now, and he had plans for his little human's return. At some point they might even make time for those magic lessons, but first he intended to take her again and demonstrate in no uncertain terms that sneaking away and leaving terse notes was not acceptable morning behavior.

The patience that came so easily during Kees's long periods of slumber eluded him now, and it took a concerted amount of effort to keep from leaving the apartment and going after his tardy human. He knew she must be getting close to the apartment, since he'd witnessed her schedule through all of last week, but logic offered him little comfort. Instead, he had to rely on sheer determination to get him through the waiting. He propped his shoulder against the window frame and settled down to watch for her.

Ten minutes later her familiar petite form stepped into view and moved toward the apartment. She wore a long coat and a hat against the slight chill, but he recognized her shape and the way she moved. Of course, if he'd doubted the accuracy of his eyes, the squeezing of his chest would have told him exactly who approached. Only Ella made him feel like this—alive, aware, with a heart of beating flesh, not cold, ragged stone.

Ella disappeared beneath the awning that sheltered the windows of the small boutique on the ground floor, as well as the door to the interior tenant stairs. Despite himself, he began ticking off the minutes it would take her to unlock the outer door, climb the two flights of stairs, and reach the apartment where he waited.

Impatience sent him striding across the room. If he met her at the door, he could open it for her and save the precious seconds it would take her to fit her key in the lock and send the tumblers into action.

He nearly had his hand on the knob when the sound of voices stopped him. Frowning, he heard Ella's feminine tones, then something lower. A man. His little human wasn't alone.

When he pulled the door open, he wore his human body and a penetrating stare. The stare became a glare when he recognized one of the figures that accompanied his female. Detective McQuaid looked just as happy to see him as Kees was to see the detective.

"Kees." Ella smiled at him, the expression slightly

strained at the edges, but then, he knew what her genuine smile looked like. He doubted the humans would notice.

"Welcome home, sweetheart," he said, deliberately leaning down to brush his lips over hers, staking a visual claim in front of the flirtatious policeman. "You're late. I was starting to worry."

"Buses," she explained, shrugging out of her coat and hanging it on the old-fashioned tree behind the door. "You remember Detective McQuaid, don't you? He was at the museum last week about the missing statue."

"I remember." Kees nodded at the human. He didn't offer to shake hands, having no desire to make the visitor appear welcome. "Detective."

"Mr. Livingston, wasn't it?" McQuaid nodded curtly in reply and gestured to the shorter, stockier man behind him. "This is my partner, Detective Harker."

Again, Kees jerked his chin, but he said nothing more.

Ella stepped close to him and leaned into his side. His arm immediately came around her.

She looked up with another of those not-quite smiles. "The detectives were waiting for me downstairs. I think they have a few more questions about the museum theft." She turned back to the intruders. "I'm happy to tell you whatever I can, but I think we covered most of it already. Can I, uh, offer the two of you coffee? That's what people always do on TV, right? Offer coffee to the police."

"Thanks, but we're good," McQuaid said with one of his pretty boy smiles. "This won't take long."

Kees lifted an eyebrow and didn't move. He stood just feet from the front door, blocking the police from moving any farther into the apartment. If this wouldn't take long, they didn't need to get comfortable. Besides, he could feel Ella's tension as she pressed up against him. She was nervous for some reason, and the only reason he could think of was because the detectives made her uncomfortable. That did little to endear them to him.

"Fire away," she said, her voice falsely cheerful.

McQuaid reached into his coat pocket and drew out a small pad and a pen. His eyes swept a casual glance around the apartment—or what he could see of it around Kees's physical wall—before they turned back to Ella.

"Can you describe for me again exactly what you saw as you were leaving the museum gardens last Friday night?"

Ella frowned, her lips pursing as she called up the memory. Kees looked from her face to McQuaid's, then over to the partner's. Harker's. The partner wasn't watching Ella. He wasn't even watching McQuaid. No, Detective Harker appeared to be taking an avid interest in Ella's interior decorating scheme.

His gaze drifted over the framed art on the walls and the bookcases that overflowed with both fiction and nonfiction titles. He looked briefly toward the open bedroom door, but Kees had left the lights off, so there wasn't much to see there. He appeared to note the alcove that was meant to contain a dining set and instead held Ella's desk and computer, along with a multifunction printer. He circled around to the small kitchen, separated from the main space by a peninsula counter, then turned back to the main living area.

Kees saw Harker's gaze skim the comfortable sofa and the overstuffed armchair that sat beside it. In the periphery of his awareness he heard McQuaid ask another question, then a third, and heard Ella's calm replies. What he didn't hear was her relaxing. Normally, when a person repeated a familiar story multiple times, they relaxed into the telling, because telling the truth was easy. Only liars stayed alert and on edge.

Liars, and people who sensed something wasn't right.

Even as the thought occurred to him, Kees saw Harker's gaze stop on the edge of his field of vision just where Kees's big frame created a blank space. He knew what was back there, the center of the sofa and most of the coffee table. And on the coffee table sat a stack of very old books with unique bindings and memorable titles.

Books of Warden magic.

He acted even before he thought. Using his arm around Ella's shoulder, he yanked her with him as he jumped backwards, using his Guardian athleticism to launch them over the table and sofa, putting the furniture between him and the men he no longer believed to be detectives. He twisted to put Ella behind him and faced off against two men who now wore expressions of open menace, one of whom had a very large gun pointed at his chest.

"You're a Warden?" McQuaid demanded, his mouth curling into a sneer as his finger tightened on the trigger of his weapon. "I knew there was something not right about you, Livingston. I knew it right from the beginning. And here it was the girl's magic I sensed. Are you supposed to be girl's mentor? I didn't think there were enough of you left to take on new projects. But don't worry, I'm happy to take her off your hands. We think she'll make a valuable member of *our* team. After a little persuasion, of course."

Kees felt Ella shift behind him and heard her angry shout. He braced his arm out to keep her from stepping forward.

"Who are you really, *Detective* McQuaid?" she demanded. "Do you even work for the police department?"

"Of course I do, but that's only part-time. You see, my real boss doesn't mind me doing a little moonlighting. In fact, he encourages it. Nothing like having the cops in your pocket when you rise up to destroy the world."

His laugh sounded like a donkey braying, and Kees

felt disgust welling within him. "You'll never get to meet your master, *nocturnis*," he growled. "If he puts one slimy tentacle out of the prison I made for him, I'll cut it off and send him right back to the abyss where he belongs."

McQuaid's gaze widened and his mouth fell open as Kees shifted and unfolded his enormous wings.

"Guardian!" The man shouted and pulled the trigger on his weapon.

Ella screamed, but Kees ignored the burn as the bullet scraped over his stony skin and tumbled to the ground. When he was in his natural form, bullets couldn't penetrate his tough hide, and only enchanted blades had the chance to cut through to actual flesh. That's what made the Guardians effective warriors. They were invulnerable to almost all human weapons, resistant to magic, and only a powerful demon could cause them serious harm. The close-range shot from McQuaid's service revolver had stung and left a small burn, but Kees barely noticed.

For the first time since entering the apartment, McQuaid's supposed partner spoke, and Kees did not like the sound of what he had to say. The words weren't English, but Sulaal, an ancient demonic tongue, one used only by demons themselves and their *nocturnis* servants, and exclusively used for worship and Dark magic.

Kees turned to bare his fangs at Harker, intending to silence him quickly before he could complete his spell, but a motion on his other side distracted him.

McQuaid tossed aside his gun and reached down to grab a knife from a concealed sheath in his boot. From the way the metal shone dull and dark in the lamplight, Kees knew the blade had been dipped in blood and bound with Dark enchantments. That could possibly sting.

Kees glanced from McQuaid to Harker and back again, assessing which presented the bigger threat. Then Mc-

Quaid leapt forward and made the decision for him. The fair-haired *nocturnis* slashed his dagger across Kees's forearm, carving deep enough to draw blood. The wound wasn't serious, but it distracted him enough that he didn't see Harker move until it was nearly too late.

While McQuaid bellowed and attacked again, the stocky Dark mage moved quickly into the room, circling the armchair until he could see behind the sofa to where Ella crouched, her eyes glued to the violent struggle between the gargoyle and the *nocturnis*.

Kees roared in fury and fear. He drew his arm back and struck out at McQuaid, his claws raking across the man's shoulder before he clenched his fist and struck another heavy blow to his chest. The demon's servant flew back and crashed into the apartment door, crumpling to the floor in a heap.

But it was too late to stop Harker.

The *nocturnis* had Ella directly in his sights and his spell was complete. Kees screamed a denial, but his gut clenched in terror. He knew he was too late.

Time seemed to slow down. He watched, horrified, and the Dark mage raised his hands and sent a bolt of thick black energy straight at Ella's heart.

Then his little human astounded him.

Whether alerted by his cry or some sixth sense of her own, Ella turned in time to see Harker lift his hands, already glowing with black light. Her own hands flew up, as if they could ward off a magical attack. But Ella had hidden depths even Kees hadn't yet plumbed. Instead of waiting for the Dark bolt to hit her, Ella briefly clasped her hands together, then pulled them apart and with sudden force, slamming her hands against the air before her with her fingers spread wide.

"Speculum intentus!" she shouted, and a flare of

blue-white energy rippled between her hands just before the bolt made impact.

The *nocturnis* spell slammed into Ella's sheet of magic and stuck like pitch. For an instant it writhed like a fly in a spider web; then the bright energy wrapped itself around the darkness and went winging back toward Harker.

The man didn't even have time to scream.

The combined magics hit him square in the chest, and he collapsed in a dead weight.

Ella gasped and fell to her knees. Kees instinctively moved to catch her, cursing when his mistake gave the fallen McQuaid time to regain his feet. But instead of renewing his attack, the *nocturnis* detective wrenched the door open and pounded down the stairs and out into the street.

Kees swore again and went to Ella.

"Are you all right?" he demanded, taking hold of her arms and raising her gently to her feet. "Were you hurt?"

She shook her head, but she didn't look at him. Her gaze was fixed at beyond him on the motionless figure on her floor. "What about him? What did I do to him?"

Kees didn't bother to look. He knew the spellcaster was dead. "You did nothing wrong, Ella. Nothing. He was *nocturnis,* and he tried to kill you."

"So I killed him instead." She nodded and shuddered violently. "I didn't know that's what would happen. I swear I didn't. I read the spell last night, and the book said it would only return the other person's original intent. It wasn't supposed to kill him."

Kees yanked her against his body and wrapped her up in his arms. Instinctively, his wings curled around his sides to enclose her more fully in this embrace. To shelter her from the world.

"It killed him because his intent was to kill you, sweet girl. You did nothing wrong," he repeated.

She nodded and buried her face against his chest, but her body wouldn't stop shaking, and Kees knew from experience that they had decisions to make.

"Ella, look at me," he commanded, and she raised her face to his, her eyes wet with tears, her lips trembling despite her tightly clenched jaw. His little human had such a tender heart. "We can't stay here. McQuaid ran out before I could stop him. That means the *nocturnis* now know what I am and that I'm with you. They also know that you have at least some magical ability, enough to cast that spell. They'll come back, and soon."

Ella groaned. "Oh, God, and McQuaid said he really is a police officer. What if Harker was, too? What if I killed a cop, Kees? Harker's dead, and even without a body, they could still come after me. They'll put me in prison. What if McQuaid comes back with more police?"

"Just another reason why we need to get moving. You need to pack a bag, Ella, and I need to think of a safe place for us to stay, at least temporarily."

Kees's mind was already racing. He couldn't contact the Guild for the address of a safe house, so he needed to think creatively.

Ella nodded and stepped back out of his arms. Her palms rubbed up and down against the legs of her jeans and she appeared somehow smaller than usual. The events of the last hour had taken their toll.

"Where are we going?" she asked softly.

"I'm not sure yet. I'll figure it out while you pack. It has to be somewhere out of the way, and someplace that isn't obviously connected to all of us. I'm certain the *nocturnis* can find us eventually—there are spells that can locate people, if nothing else—but there's no reason to make it easy for them."

She stared up at his face, taking in his tense expression and the worry he knew must be flickering in his eyes. He saw her hesitate, and then draw back her shoulders and straighten her spine, as if she were bracing herself for something.

"I think I know a place."

Chapter Fourteen

Ella hadn't been back to the cabin since she was twelve years old, and if she'd had her way, she never would have returned. Too bad Fate kept robbing her of those choices.

She could have blamed Kees for making her go, since he had jumped on the idea as soon as she described the location to him and informed him the property wasn't recorded under her name, but in the name of a trust her parents had set up before their deaths. Because it was remote and untraceable, the Guardian had declared it perfect. Ella wanted to curse him, but she was the one who had brought it up in the first place. It was her own fault, but she hadn't been thinking clearly.

Apparently, killing a man could do that to her.

The clock on the dashboard of her third rental car in a little over a week told Ella that they'd passed midnight along with the little town of Sechelt. Now the struggle to find a four-wheel drive at nine thirty at night would start to prove its value.

Turning off the last paved road, Ella followed the semi-graveled lane for another couple of miles before she pulled onto the even more rugged logging road, which quickly petered into something more appropriately labeled a trail. By the time she pulled to a stop in front of the small, dark structure nestled in the trees, her bones hurt from bouncing up and down over the uneven terrain. Or maybe they just hurt because everything else did, from her head to her heart.

"This is it," she said. There was no reason for the announcement. Clearly, they had arrived at their destination, but Ella was stalling for time. She even knew she was. Maybe it would be better to just get it over with. The first few minutes would be the hardest, right?

Kees climbed out of the now mud-splattered truck and circled the rear of the vehicle to stand beside her. A large human hand settled on her shoulder and squeezed.

"Are you all right, little one?"

Ella forced herself to offer up a weak smile. "I'm fine. I just . . . I haven't been here for a while. That's all. I hope everything's still working. Someone's supposed to maintain the place, but—" She shrugged. "I should check the generator first."

That way, she could avoid going into the cabin for another two minutes, at least.

Kees said nothing else, but he followed her to the small lean-to at the rear of the log structure and waited while she checked the gauge on the propane tank, then started the machine. It roared to life quickly and efficiently, fast enough that Ella had to beat back the memories.

"Looks good," she murmured, closing the door and heading back to the front of the cabin. So much for delaying tactics. Time to bite the bullet.

She led Kees up the steps of the wide front porch and stood on her tiptoes to reach the top of the doorframe. The key, balanced on the ledge of wood as always, slid easily into her hand. She felt the gargoyle's curious gaze and shrugged.

"Nothing all that valuable ever gets left up here. Besides, if some lost hiker or injured kayaker ever needed help and found the place, they'd be welcome to come in and use the radio to call for assistance. Out in the woods, people have to help each other out sometimes."

A twist of her wrist made the cabin door swing open on well-oiled hinges. Looked like the caretaker was doing his job.

Ella stepped forward into the dark space and inhaled. She felt assaulted by the familiar odors of cedar and pine, beeswax and lemon. Even the trace of dust in the air smelled natural, the same scent that had greeted her family at the start of every summer when they first opened the cabin for the season. It was just as she remembered.

Her hand trembled as she reached out, her fingers going unerringly to the light switch just inside the door. The single light fixture in the center of the room blinked on and illuminated Ella's childhood in all its braided rug and battered wooden glory.

Her heart squeezed painfully.

Behind her, Kees stood—a large, silent, and somehow comforting presence—but she couldn't turn to look at him. Not yet. She needed a minute to think, to process, to get ahold of herself.

She never thought she'd be coming back here.

"I'll go outside and get our things," he said in his low, gravelly I'm-being-nice voice.

Ella just nodded until she heard his footsteps move off the porch and onto the pine-needled earth of the tiny front yard clearing.

Every summer of her childhood, from her earlier memories until her parents died, Ella had spent days and weeks in this very spot. The small cabin on the east coast of the Sechelt Peninsula, north of the eponymous town, sat nestled in the forest, opposite Seal Cove at the base of Mount

Richardson. It lay on the other side of the almost island from the Sunshine Coast that flooded with tourists and outdoors lovers every time the weather warmed, but it occupied a world away in almost every manner imaginable.

Ella's grandfather had built the cabin in the 1950s, taking years to complete the work of digging a well and contriving a septic system in the remote, nearly inaccessible area. He'd forgone electricity and all but the most basic plumbing for the peace and beauty of the Canadian woodlands. Ella's mother used to say she'd fallen in like with the place the first time she saw it. The addition of the generator and screens on the windows to keep out the insects had sent "like" blooming into full-blown love.

Her parents had been happiest out here, away from their serious academic careers, with nothing to do but be and think and breathe in the peace all around them. Ella's dad said some of his best research grew out of ideas that came to him at the cabin, while he walked or fished or just sat watching the seals and the oystermen across the inlet. Nature, he had said, was the mother of all scientific thought.

Stephen Harrow had been a scientist to his core, a man who believed in what he could see or what he could prove with tidy equations printed on crisp white paper. He had never believed in magic. Neither had his wife. Marian had the soul of a teacher, and she believed in what she could analyze and explain. Neither of them had quite believed in Ella.

They had loved her. She always knew they loved her, but they had never quite believed her.

Kees reentered the cabin with Ella's duffel swung over his shoulder and one arm balancing a box full of grocery staples that Ella knew for a fact had to weigh close to forty pounds. He held it like it contained nothing more than a loaf of bread and a bag of air-popped popcorn.

"Where do I put these?"

Ella pointed to the right to the small kitchen half tucked away behind the front closet. "In there. It will take a little while before the fridge cools down, but now that the generator is on, we can start using it. There should be plenty of room in the cupboards, if they're not completely empty. I suppose there could be a can of chili or something hiding up there, but it should be fine."

She was babbling, and she knew it, but she couldn't help it. She was running on the last punchy fumes of adrenaline, yet she didn't know how she was going to sleep tonight, not after what had happened in her apartment earlier.

Not here.

She heard cabinet doors flipped open and closed, heard the sound of items settling on the wire refrigerator racks, then the door of the appliance sealing shut. Kees stepped back into the main room and found her standing exactly where he'd left her.

A shiver ran through her, and he frowned. "You're cold."

Ella started to protest that she was fine, but thought better of it. The cabin had no central heating, so even if she wasn't registering the temperature now, she knew she would eventually, and unless they got a fire started, that temperature would be *cold*.

"Right." She nodded. "There's kindling in the firebox but the woodshed's out back, on the opposite side from the generator. I'll go get some."

"I'll get it. Sit down." He pinned her with an intent gaze. "You look like you're about to fall over."

"Gee, thanks," Ella grumped, but she sat.

Kees left the cabin again, and she huddled on the edge of the sofa wondering what the hell had happened to her life. Thinking about the surreal horror movie her present had turned into at least kept her mind off the past.

Ella had killed a man today, and no matter what Kees

told her, no matter what logic or reason told her, living with that truth would never be easy. She understood that the man had been a servant of the Darkness; she understood that he had intended to kill her and that after he killed her, he had intended to help summon a pack of demons that would subsequently kill the rest of humanity. She even understood that she had killed him only because the murderous spell he'd cast at her had rebounded on him. But she was the one who'd sent that spell back, and he was the one who'd died. She didn't quite know how to process that.

In truth, she felt mostly numb at the moment. Maybe it was shock, maybe it was exhaustion, and maybe it was just her mind finally rebelling after having spent the last week plus trying to wrap itself around the reality of too many things that shouldn't have been real. Or it could be a combination of all those things, but all Ella knew was that at the moment all she could feel was a great big blank, like a hole in the center of her body. It stretched from her heart to her belly, encompassing everything in its path and sucking the sensation out of all of it.

Guilty, she realized it was almost a relief.

If she couldn't feel guilt over killing a man or grief over the memory of her lost parents or fear at being hunted by the *nocturnis,* at least she also couldn't feel confusion over her relationship with Kees. Provided it even was a relationship. Her head felt too foggy and too heavy to answer even that simple question. Well, deceptively simple maybe.

Ella knew that she had run from the apartment that morning—God, had it only been that morning?—out of fear. What she and Kees shared during the night had been glorious, and she couldn't stand taking the chance that he would turn cold again. Her heart couldn't take giving itself to him so completely if he woke up a second time and told her he felt nothing for her. It had hurt too much before; a repetition might have killed her.

So she had run, like a frightened little bunny, thinking that if she put up the walls instead of him, maybe it wouldn't feel like one of the barriers had collapsed on top of her.

It hadn't worked.

Instead of being tormented by being pushed away, now Ella felt the torment of doubt. What if he hadn't intended to push her away? What if their lovemaking had finally convinced him that he did feel something for her and she had ruined it by pulling the same stupid stunt he'd used on her?

Exhaustion made her brain too tired to answer those questions. She knew that Kees had greeted her eagerly and possessively when she returned from work that night, but had he meant it, or had that been a show he put on for the benefit of the police? He remained mostly quiet on the drive up from Vancouver, but he'd never been much of a talker. Had that been the silent treatment, or just the taciturn nature of a man who spent most of his existence locked in a cage of stone?

And, God, was there even the slightest chance she would figure any of this out before she fell flat on her face with weariness?

She had just enough energy to look toward the door and watch as Kees stepped back inside carrying what looked like half the woodpile. One of the benefits of supernatural strength, she supposed.

He deposited his burden in the box beside the hearth and began to stack kindling in the grate.

Ella braced her hands on the sofa cushions and gathered her strength to rise. "I can do that," she offered. "You carried everything in. The least I can do is build a fire."

He shot her a straight-lipped glance over his shoulder, amusement glinting in his eyes. "I think I can handle it. Having lived in more than one age when fire was the only available source of either light or heat."

"Right. Sometimes I forget about that."

She watched as he efficiently got the kindling blazing and added the smallest pieces of wood. He had shifted sometime since their arrival at the cabin, and Ella realized with foggy-headed surprise that she hadn't even noticed. She knew he had remained in his human form in the car, both in case anyone saw them during the drive and because that way he just fit better within the small, confined space. Now, though, he knelt before the hearth in his natural shape, which meant Ella had missed his shift. She wondered if he had just done it on the last trip outside, and then realized that it didn't matter, which was precisely why she hadn't noticed.

To Ella, Kees was Kees, no matter what form he took. To her, it was all the same, just as she told him before they had made love. Her heart didn't recognize the difference in his forms, and apparently her eyes and her mind had followed suit. She loved her Guardian no matter what he looked like, horns and all.

Hearing her own giggle burst into the quiet cabin told Ella better than words how bone-tired she really was. She'd gone from merely exhausted to positively loopy.

Apparently, Kees had noticed as well.

She felt his arms slide around her, one curling against her back, the other curving behind her knees. He lifted her off the sofa and cradled her against his chest before Ella noticed that she hadn't seen him coming. This time, she knew exactly why she'd missed the important details— because her eyes had drifted shut. She was already half asleep.

She thought about telling him where the bedroom was,

but realized that in a four-room cabin, he wasn't likely to miss it. Her faith proved justified when he lowered her onto the wide, soft mattress and laid her back against the pillows. Ella immediately snuggled onto her side and reached for the blankets. The bedroom was chilly without the fire, though she knew it would warm up quickly provided the bedroom door remained open.

Her last conscious memories were of her gargoyle carefully pulling her shoes from her feet and tucking the quilts up around her. It felt good, sweet and tender and loving. As she drifted off to sleep, the only thing she could have wished for was that he actually meant it.

Ella woke screaming. Choking. Suffocating. Pinned beneath heavy debris, her senses overwhelmed with the smells of burned rubber, gasoline, and blood.

She was twelve years old again, and she had just killed her parents.

"Ella! Ella!"

Someone shouted her name. The sound of it registered because it shouldn't exist. No one had called for her. Everyone who knew her name was dead. She had killed them.

"Ella, wake up. Now!"

Her eyes opened, and she whimpered. She saw no trees, no sky, no twisted pieces of metal. The smell of blood faded. Nothing pained her. Her flesh bore no cuts, no bone-deep contusions. She was awake, she was twenty-seven, and she was back at her parents' cabin.

Her stomach lurched and she shoved hard at the figure hovering over her. She needed the bathroom. Now.

She ran, knelt, heaved. Her stomach revolted, attempting over and over to throw itself out her open mouth. Or, at least, that was what it felt like. She had nothing much to vomit. She'd never gotten dinner last night. She'd been too busy killing a man.

Again, she heaved.

Behind her, she felt Kees's presence. The gargoyle stood in the door to the small bathroom, barely squeezing himself inside. She wanted to shout at him to leave her alone. To go away. To take the car and go, drive himself somewhere else and leave her here, out in the woods. Where she couldn't hurt anyone else. Ever.

Tears streamed down her face, and she knew they weren't caused only by the violent spasms of nausea. She tried to choke back the sobs, but that only made her sick again. Her arms clasped the rim of the toilet bowl and she wanted, more than anything else, to die.

A hand, huge but achingly gentle, reached out and gathered the strands of her hair, pulling it out of the way. The side of a lethally sharp claw scraped tenderly against her skin as it moved the tendrils that tears and saliva had glued to her cheeks. The touch felt like a benediction, cool against her flushed face, gentle and loving, and that only made Ella weep harder.

She didn't deserve it. She didn't deserve to be loved.

She retched again, her empty stomach convulsing painfully, but she had nothing left to bring up now. Not even bile came out. She spit weakly and sank back onto her heels. Laying her forehead against the cool toilet seat, she shook and ached and wept.

"Shh, sweet girl," Kees crooned. "Poor little human. Come on, now. I've got you."

His arms came around her, gathering her up against his chest. She fought his touch at first, but she felt drained of strength, and he seemed not to even notice her feeble struggles. He cradled her close and carried her back into the bedroom. Once again, he laid her down on the cool, crisp sheets and stood.

Ella lay still. She had her eyes closed, blocking out everything. She felt chilled, almost freezing, but she didn't reach for the quilt, didn't try to cover herself. She just lay there, stiff and silent, and the tears continued to roll down her cheeks.

An instant later, she felt the bed dip. Kees sat down beside her and slid an arm beneath her shoulders, raising her slightly. The cool edge of a drinking glass touched her lips.

"Sip. Slowly."

She turned her head away, but the glass followed. In the end, she sipped. It was just easier.

The water flowed over her tongue, helping to wash away the taste of bile. She waited for her stomach to contract, but it felt as if even the internal organ were weary. The trickle went down smoothly, and she accepted another.

Kees eased her back onto the pillows. She heard the click of the glass settling on the bedside table, then felt the rough nap of a wet washcloth against her forehead. He bathed her face like a child's, then abandoned the cloth and shifted her across the mattress. She didn't open her eyes, but she felt him stretch out beside her and did nothing.

Not until his arms came around her and he pulled her into his embrace did she renew her struggles.

Once again, he ignored them. He let her buck and writhe, beat his chest and kick his knees and shins. He paid no attention to her foul language as she cursed him in every way she could think of. He simply held her, pressed close to his chest, until she ran out of steam.

When she quieted, he shifted their positions, rolling onto his back and dragging her on top of him. He settled her head on his shoulder and brought his wings forward, wrapping them around her like a living blanket. She let him, too tired to fight, too tired to move.

Too tired for anything.

She felt him lift his head, felt the tender press of his

lips against her forehead, then heard the words rumble up from his chest.

"Tell me."

And for the first time in her life, Ella told someone her darkest secret.

"I killed my parents."

Kees said nothing. He didn't even twitch. He simply continued to cradle her like a precious burden, one enormous clawed hand stroking her hair as if she were a tame, affectionate house pet.

Ella waited for the condemnation. When it didn't come she continued on in the same weary monotone.

"I was twelve. It was nearly summer, and I wanted to come here, to the cabin. I kept asking, begging. Nagging. But mom kept putting me off, telling me 'soon.' I got sick of hearing 'soon,' but my parents never gave in to tantrums. They were both logical, intellectual people. They believed in reasoning with me, and if I wasn't being reasonable, they ignored the behavior until it stopped. I learned to really, really hate being ignored.

"They loved me, a lot. I was an only child, and they both had wanted me badly, but I don't think I was quite the child they were expecting. Not only were they logical, they were scientists. Mom taught biology; Dad was a physicist. They probably thought they'd get a little Einstein, or at least a top-tier engineer. Instead they got a little girl who loved fairy tales, art, and music and could barely handle long division. Boy, did I confuse them.

"But I know they loved me. They just had no idea what to do with me."

She paused and opened her eyes. All she could see were shadows. Kees's wings enveloped her in a dark cocoon. She could make out his chest next to her face, the back of her own hand where it lay curled against his skin, and the leathery, veined inner surface of his wings. It felt like being in a confessional, only warmer. Safer.

Kees remained silent, only steadily, softly stroking her hair. Ella flattened her hand on his chest and resumed her story.

"I think I was just a toddler when I told them I saw things differently. They wanted to chalk it up to my 'artistic vision,' but I guess that's hard to do when your kid tells you that Mr. Harrington down the street has ugly green branches growing out of his head. I thought everyone could see it. Now I know it was part of the mage sight, but then, I just thought that was the way it was. When I started drawing the things I saw, they really freaked out. No more watercolors for Ella."

She sighed.

"They ignored it as best they could, discouraged me from talking about it. Tried to tell me that none of it was real. Since no one ever believed me, not even other children, and all the adults I talked to looked horrified whenever I brought it up, I stopped talking about it. And mostly, I stopped seeing it. By the time I was seven or eight, I could do a decent impression of a normal kid.

"Then puberty hit."

Ella stopped again and tried to fight back the tears. How she even had any left, she couldn't understand, but there they were. And they wanted out.

"Tell me," Kees repeated, and his hand stroked over her hair all the way down her back.

The touch soothed her, gave her strength. She even felt a warm glow and wondered if this was part of the energy exchange the binding spell had caused. If it was, she could have used it earlier, when she'd been about to throw up her spleen.

She sighed. "Right before I turned twelve, I got my

first period, and I started to see things again. Only this time, there was more. Stuff started to happen around me. light bulbs blew out, TVs changed channels, computers crashed. Sometimes, stuff even moved. If my parents had been religious instead of scientific, they probably would have decided we had a poltergeist."

"It was the magic."

"Yeah. Sometimes I could see it and see that it was coming from me, but I had absolutely no control over it. I happened even when I was trying to hold it back. In fact, when I least wanted it to happen was when it always seemed to."

Kees squeezed her gently. "Stress. And hormones, I hear. The average teenaged mage does quite a bit of property damage before he learns self-control."

"Tell me about it."

He chuckled, then waited quietly for her to go on.

"Since my parents didn't believe in ghosts, they thought there had to be a perfectly logical explanation for everything that was going on. They also agreed that I was causing everything. Which, in a way, I was, I guess."

"You were a child, Ella." He rumbled softly.

"Anyway, they decided they needed to find an explanation, and then a solution. So when I was twelve, they took me to see a psychiatrist."

Kees stiffened. The hand on her back went still. "Your parents thought you were mad?"

She snorted softly. "My parents thought I was acting out. The psychiatrist was the one who thought I was crazy."

She heard another low sound of displeasure, which seemed to start in Kees's toes and climb into his throat, building intensity all the way. She marveled at the idea that his immediate reaction to the story was to believe in her, to defend her, to be outraged in her behalf. She savored it, because she knew that soon enough, he would hear what she had done, and he wouldn't ever feel the same way again.

"They found an expert in child psychology in Coquitlam. He came highly recommended." Her tone, she knew, indicated her opinion of those recommendations. "I didn't like him. I don't remember much about the evaluation interview. I remember that he spent a lot of time just watching me, not talking, and I remember that he looked dark to me, and cold. But I don't remember what questions he asked me, or how I answered. For a child psychiatrist, I don't think he liked kids very much. He didn't seem to like me."

Ella knew she was stalling. She felt so comfortable, so safe, curled up in Kees's embrace. She felt loved. He was being so sweet, so patient and protective, that she wanted to put off telling him the truth. She was afraid that when he pushed her away again, she would break.

He stroked her back again, his fingers kneading her shoulders with gentle strength. "Tell me," he repeated a third time.

"After the doctor spoke to me, he wanted to speak to my parents right away. He took them into another room, so I never heard exactly what he told them, but when they came out, I could tell they were upset. I didn't care. I just wanted to get out of there and go home. The appointment was on a Thursday, and Friday, the next day, we were supposed to head up to the cabin. I could hardly wait.

"I fell asleep in the car on the way home. I used to take a lot of naps that year. All the stuff that was happening—" She corrected herself. "All the *magic* used to wear me out. I'd be exhausted just staying conscious some days."

Kees made a sound, something understanding, but he didn't speak. He just waited for her to continue.

"I woke up because they were arguing. It had just gotten dark, because we'd been stuck in traffic leaving

Coquitlam after a wreck or something. Dad was driving, but he and Mom were fighting. They never fought, so I guess their voices woke me. And then I realized they were fighting over me."

Her throat tightened, and she tried to swallow. "They didn't think I was listening, and I heard that the doctor had told them I needed to be committed. Not only did he think I was crazy, he thought I was a danger to myself and others and that I needed to be put in the hospital."

She heard his snarl and knew he was about to rush to her defense, but she didn't want to hear it. If she didn't finish the story, if she didn't get through this now, she never would. Ella pushed against his chest until he released her. Sitting up, she shifted away from him and drew her knees up against her chest.

"The thing was," she continued tightly, "they weren't arguing about the diagnosis. One of them didn't disagree, or want a second opinion; they both agreed with him that I was crazy. They just couldn't agree on when I should go to the hospital. The doctor had wanted to commit me immediately, that afternoon, but Dad had held out. He wanted us to have the weekend together, up here, at the cabin. He said next week was soon enough for the hospital. My mother was arguing with him. The doctor had scared her, and she was afraid something might happen if they didn't bring me back right away."

Ella shuddered and closed her eyes tight as the memories flooded her. "I got so damned *angry*. It made me furious. I thought they loved me, that they were there to protect me, and they were talking about sending me away, about locking me up in a mental hospital. It wasn't even a question of 'if' from them. All they had to decide was when."

She buried her face in her drawn-up knees and curled her hands into fists. She wanted to scream, to hit something, which was exactly how she'd felt that night. She'd been betrayed by the people she trusted most in the world. She'd thought they loved her, but now they were pushing her away, abandoning her.

"I lost it." She didn't lift her head. She knew her voice was muffled by her position, but she couldn't look at him. She couldn't look at his face while she told him the truth. With his supernatural senses, she knew he could hear her. "I completely lost it. I started screaming in the backseat. Dad nearly swerved off the road, and Mom went a little bonkers. At first she tried to calm me down, but I wouldn't shut up. I couldn't. I'd never been so angry in my life. I wanted to hurt them, because they'd just hurt me so damned badly."

She fought back the sobs, but she couldn't control the shaking. "Mom was yelling, and then Dad started yelling, just trying to be heard over the two of us, I think. He was trying to calm us down, but I was completely out of control. And then the magic just . . . exploded."

Ella shuddered, trapped in her memory. She could see the blinding flash of light, feel the almost painful release as the power overwhelmed her and shot forth from her body, like the way it had when she released it at Kees that first night. But when she was a kid it had felt even wilder, more dangerous, more out of control. It had filled the car.

She remembered the screaming, the sound of car horns, a second flash of light. She felt the impact all over again, the violent grasp of her seat belt against her hips and chest, the horrible crunch of metal on metal. The blood.

She would never forget the smell of blood.

"I killed them," she whispered. "I killed my parents. I lost control and the magic took over. There was a huge car wreck. Our station wagon, another car, and a huge cargo truck. My parents both died on impact. We hit the other car head-on. That driver died, too, and the truck plowed into us from behind. It was an old truck, no airbags, only a lap belt restraint. His spine snapped on impact. The cargo compartment of the station wagon completely crumpled, but the backseat remained intact. I was the only one who walked away.

"And it was all my fault."

Chapter Fifteen

Kees looked down at his little human and knew once and for all that he had a heart, because he felt it break.

He reached out for her and winced when she flinched away from his touch. The sound of her sobbing cut him deeper than the *nocturnis*'s enchanted dagger. That wound had already closed and was well on the way to healing. He thought he might feel this blow forever.

The next time he reached for her, he ignored the way she recoiled. He didn't care if she wanted to be touched. Whether she wanted it or not, his little human needed to be held.

She also needed to understand that what she had told him about killing her parents had been complete and utter nonsense.

First, though, he needed to calm her down again.

He sat on the edge of the bed and pulled her into his lap, arranging her once again against his chest. He felt a surge of amusement as he realized the familiar position was quickly becoming a habit, one he had no hesitation in enjoying. Kees liked the way his little human felt in his arms. He wanted to keep her there.

Ella continued to cry while he held her. After her earlier bout, he wondered where all the moisture came from, then reached for the abandoned glass of water and made her drink some more. She must be getting dehydrated.

Again she fought him, and again he persisted until she gave in and sipped. This time, he didn't let up until she'd drained the glass.

She had obviously worn herself out again. He could tell by the way she wasn't banging her toes or heels against his lower leg or trying futilely to force his arms to unwrap from around her. Instead, she just lay quietly against his chest until her sobs faded into quiet.

Kees waited until he felt her muscles begin to unclench before he hooked a finger under her chin and raised her face to his.

"Look at me, little human," he commanded. Reluctantly, she met his gaze. "Understand this. I listened to every word you just told me. I heard everything you said, and I want you to know that you are a fool."

Ella jerked and nearly fell off his lap. Kees merely tightened his grip.

"You don't understand—"

He cut her off. "I understand perfectly. You think that the magic inside you killed your parents. You think that you bear responsibility for their deaths and that because of that, you are an evil person. It's all nonsense."

"I did kill them," she ground out, her hands fisted as he held her implacably on his lap, ignoring any attempt to move away. "I was there. I remember. Everything was fine until I lost control. I'm the reason we crashed, and I'm the reason they died."

Her conviction echoed in her words. She truly believed herself to be a killer, some sort of monstrous creature capable of killing even those she loved the most. He remembered her reaction to the death of the *nocturnis* and wanted to laugh. He had never met a human—met any creature—as far from murderous as his little human. She had the softest heart and the tenderest soul he had ever encountered.

That fact helped explain why she carried such guilt over the deaths of her parents, and why she had woken in the night screaming. Tonight, she had seen another human die, and once again, she blamed herself. Taking a life must have dredged up all her painful old memories and only confirmed the opinion she had of herself.

Kees understood completely. The only question was if he could convince Ella.

"You know that I have slept for a long time," he began slowly, "and I admit that my understanding of the way human authorities operate is not necessarily complete, but I believe that vehicular accidents like the one you describe are routinely investigated. Are they not?"

She nodded, clearly wary of his train of thought.

"Then did the human authorities conclude that you caused your parents' deaths? And that of the other drivers as well? Were you blamed? Did they tell you the accident was your fault?"

"They didn't need to. I lived through it. I was the only one who lived through it." Her voice held a wealth of bitterness, and not the slightest hint of forgiveness for the little girl she had been, nor for the woman she was today.

Kees bit back a sigh. So stubborn, his little human.

"Tell me what they said to you. When they found you, and later after they completed their investigation."

She stiffened and shrugged awkwardly. "It was a long time ago. I don't remember everything."

"You remember some things. I know, because I saw you reliving them. You remember the accident, little Ella. You told me you were in the backseat, trapped, it sounded like, while you parents had died in the front of the car."

She shuddered. "Yes."

"Then how did you get out? Who came to rescue you?"

He watched her pretty mouth turn down in a frown. Her brow furrowed in concentration.

"The police, I guess," she said after a minute. "No, wait. I guess it must have been firemen. I remember those suits they wear, with the fire retardant material. And the suspenders. I'd never seen a man wear suspenders before that."

Kees nodded encouragingly. "They must have had some trouble getting you out, if the car was so severely damaged."

"They did. They had to cut through the metal with some big machine." Her eyes went unfocused as she looked backwards into her memories. "I guess when I think about it now, it was probably the Jaws of Life, or whatever they call it. I remember the noise it made cutting through the metal. At first I thought it was a monster or a devil coming to eat me and take me down to hell."

Kees wanted nothing more than to tell her he'd seen hell, and that it was no place she would ever have to fear, because nothing went there but the foulest of demons. Not even a vengeful god would be cruel enough to send a human there. And certainly not this sweet, sad woman.

Instead, he just nodded and gently prompted her. She was bringing back the memories now, and as painful as he knew they must be for her, he needed her to see them through the eyes of a logical adult, not a frightened, injured, grieving child.

"Do you remember them talking?"

"I remember the sounds of their voices, but not a lot of what they said. I didn't understand a lot of the technical and medical things they were talking about."

"Didn't they talk to you? Let you know that they worked to save you?"

"They told me they were coming for me. They said I was being brave, and that everything would be okay, but I knew they were lying."

Even then, she had stubbornly held on to her own beliefs, no matter how foolish. Why was he not surprised?

He changed strategies a little. His human required a slightly less gentle nudge, it seemed. "Were the firefighters the ones who told you the others were dead?"

"I knew my parents were dead. No one had to tell me."

"But you couldn't have known about the others. You couldn't see everyone, could you?"

"I could see Mom and Dad. They were covered in blood and so pale and . . . crushed looking. And the driver of the other car. He'd . . . he'd come through his windshield and partway through ours. He wasn't wearing a seatbelt. He didn't die right away, though. I remember his face. It didn't even look human. It was all bloody and half-caved in." She shuddered and closed her eyes. "God, the smell of blood still makes me sick. Blood and cheap beer."

Kees went still.

"Cheap beer," he repeated, careful to keep his voice low and even despite the desire to shout at her to open her eyes and remember the accident instead of reliving it. If she could just give herself a little distance, maybe she would finally start to see the picture she'd just painted for him.

"Oh, but it stank. Almost worse than the blood. Just yeasty and sour and horrible. Like the floor around the cheap seats at a baseball stadium."

She still didn't seem to understand, but Kees had heard enough. He'd also had enough of her torturing herself. It had been fifteen years of guilt and self-disgust. Even if she hadn't just proved herself innocent, he thought she'd paid a sufficient penance. She just needed to let go of the past and realize it.

Easier said than done.

Kees sighed. He'd tried leading her to see the truth on her own, but that clearly wasn't going to work. Perhaps this called for more drastic measures.

"You are a fool, little human, but worse than that, you've made yourself into a martyr."

His harsh words and unforgiving tone seemed to snap Ella out of the prison of her memories. Her gaze flew to his face, at first confused, then hurt.

"What?"

"You heard me. You just told me that your parents were killed by a drunk who lost control of the vehicle he operated. Even if you haven't yet allowed me to drive a car, I have the intelligence to understand that for a human to dull his senses, slow his reflexes, and depress his awareness with alcohol before driving would be a suicidal, or in this case homicidal, decision. Yet you try to take responsibility for what happened. I am disappointed by such selfishness. Why do you believe the world is centered on your actions and yours alone?"

Her mouth gaped open and the confusion faded from her eyes to be replaced by anger. The hurt remained. "Did you just call me selfish? Did you tell me I was stuck on myself? I just told you about the worst thing that ever happened to me, the worst thing that can happen to any child, and you have the nerve to blame me for it? You fucking arrogant prick!"

"No." Kees remained firm. "I don't blame you for anything that occurred that night. Why should I bother? You've been blaming yourself for fifteen years. Actually, you've been blaming the child, your twelve-year-old self, for what reason I cannot fathom. The only explanation I can find is that your arrogance deludes you into thinking your actions have infinitely more power than any human in history could possibly claim."

"I can't frickin' believe you. How dare you tell me I'm arrogant for taking responsibility for my own actions! I'm the one who's had to live with them for all these years. Do you have any idea what it's been like? Could you even begin to understand? Losing my parents was the worst thing that has ever happened to me, and I had to go to sleep every night knowing it was my fault. Knowing that if I hadn't lost my temper, if I hadn't gotten angry at my parents for trying to take care of me, my father wouldn't have lost control, and—"

Her voice broke and he could see the sobs threatening once more. He could see her begin to struggle for breath, and he was not going to let her sink back into that black bit of guilt again. Not now.

"If you hadn't poured an unreasonable number of beers down the throat of that stranger who hit your family's vehicle head-on, none of it would have happened. Is that what you're telling me, Ella?"

"What? No." She denied it, making it reflexive and sharp. "I had nothing to do with the other driver, but the magic was what made my father lose control. I remember the light filling the car and my parents screaming—"

"It was night. The drunk was driving straight at you. You remember headlights. And screams from people who knew they might not survive the impact."

Still, Ella refused to cooperate. "No. The magic filled up the car. My mother even ducked, but I couldn't pull it back. I was so angry with them. I thought they were betraying me, but they were only doing the best they could. They just wanted to help me."

"You didn't need help, Ella. You needed training. You told your parents nothing but the truth about what you saw or what you could do. They just didn't believe you. Maybe they were doing their best for you by treating you for some sort of mental disease, but I can tell you that what they planned would not have helped you. It would have made things worse. Drugs, disbelief, constantly being told you were wrong or insane, that you couldn't really see or do what you knew you could. Even if they had convinced you, brainwashed you into believing it, you can't lock the magic away forever. It will always find a way out. They could have killed you."

She dropped her head and pressed the heels of her hands against her eyes. "But they'd be alive. My parents would still be alive."

"Would they?" Kees pushed harder. She needed to open her eyes and let go or she would never truly heal. She would never be strong enough for what they might have to face. Together. "If they had left you at the hospital that night and driven back home without you, would they have survived the trip? Or would the drunk still have swerved off his side of the road and hit them? Would they be dead anyway, with you left to the mercies of doctors who neither understood you nor loved you? No one would have been there to advocate for you, Ella. Your chances of surviving that ordeal would have been even lower.

"And if you hadn't survived, what would be happening right now?"

Ella dropped her hands and wrapped her arms around her own waist. She looked cold and weary and utterly confused. Kees wanted nothing more than to tell her everything was all right and rock her back to sleep, but he couldn't do it. Not yet. She was almost there, but he needed to push her just the last little way.

"What are you talking about?" she asked wearily.

"If you had been lost to the world because of psychiatric treatments that did more harm than good, or even if you had simply become permanently institutionalized, would you have been at the museum on that Friday night?

Would I have woken, feeling a pull toward you that I have never felt in all my centuries? Or would I still be asleep?"

"I don't know. It doesn't matter."

"It does matter," he snarled, startling her into looking at his face. "It matters a great deal. Wardens are dying every day, and the Guild has crumbled. The *nocturnis* gain strength every hour, and still my brothers sleep. The Order is attempting to keep them from waking by destroying those with the power to rouse us. If they succeed, eventually they will have the time and freedom to discover how to destroy us. Once the Guardians are no more, the Seven will rise, and the world will fall."

She stared at him, her brows drawn together in a frown of confusions.

"You woke me, Ella, and because you did, I have been able to learn of the threat the *nocturnis* already pose to humanity. Because you woke me, we know what we are up against, and we have already begun the task of finding and waking my brothers. With Guardians to counter this threat, the Order may not succeed in their plans." His voice softened. "You might very well save the world, little human."

"That's crazy. We don't—I mean . . . We don't even know for sure that I really woke you. I didn't do anything to make it happen, I was just there. It was an accident, and we have no way of knowing if I'll be able to do it again with another Guardian."

"But you give us hope," he said, cupping her cheek in his palm. She looked so fragile, her skin milky pale against his dark gray hand, his claws almost obscenely hard and sharp next to her softness. "You have made it possible for us to try to save ourselves, Ella. Without the sacrifices made that night during your childhood, we might already be doomed."

Ella snorted and bowed her head. "That's some way of telling me to stop taking responsibility for the car wreck. By telling me to take responsibility for the possible end of the world."

She shuddered, and Kees drew her into his arms, cradling her against him. Her face pressed against his chest and he felt her tears wet his skin, but no sobs accompanied them. These tears came cleanly, finally bringing not more pain but acceptance.

"No, little one," he murmured, lowering his head. He wanted to curl himself around her, to keep her warm and safe forever. To show her she was loved. "You are responsible for neither. The accident that took your parents from you was just that—an accident. And while you can help save the world, the weight of that can never rest on your shoulders. The Guardians bear that responsibility. It is the very reason for our existence, why we were summoned, and why we remain in this realm."

Ella gave a half laugh and pulled back enough to look up at him. "So I'm not allowed to take responsibility for the whole world, but you are, huh?"

Kees felt the corners of his mouth twitch and his heart squeeze and then melt. His Ella was coming back to him.

"I am bigger," he growled.

And she laughed.

Chapter Sixteen

Ella slept most of the day. Since she'd had her soul wrung out like wet laundry by a very determined gargoyle in the wee hours around dawn, she had needed the extra rest. She would apparently need even more of it by the time Kees got finished with her.

He had given her approximately half an hour after she'd crawled out of bed just before two in the afternoon to suck down a cup of coffee and remember her own name. As soon as she could answer that question, he pulled out the stack of books Alan had given her and began picking out spells.

Her stomach had clenched reflexively when he told her they would use whatever time they had at the cabin until Fil contacted them with more info working on Ella's spell-casting. Her mind instinctively screamed a denial. After all, the only two times she ever directed her magic with purpose, people had ended up dying. She didn't ever want to risk doing that again.

She had opened her mouth to refuse and found Kees watching her with steady, patient eyes, ones that glowed with both understanding and resolve. His eyes told her that he knew exactly what he was asking of her, and he had known what her first reaction would be. He would give her the time and the space to either disappoint him or make him proud.

When she looked at the choice in those terms, it became easy.

It became even easier when she remembered the *nocturnis* attacking him in her apartment. She couldn't let herself become just a liability to her Guardian. She knew he had the skills to fight like a sharply honed instrument of destruction, and she also knew that if he had to worry about her all the time, he risked making himself vulnerable in the midst of a battle. If he were to be injured—or, God forbid, killed—because of her, Ella didn't think she could take that guilt. Not again. Not after her parents. It would haunt her into the afterlife.

She had dreamed vividly last night—this morning, really—and she knew it was her brain's way of processing through all the emotion and memories she had dredged up last night. She had dreamed about the accident before, but this time, for the first time, instead of reliving the horror, she had been outside of the events, looking down with the clinical detachment of a neutral observer. Details that she had missed as a furious and wounded twelve-year-old had jumped out at her. She had seen the approach of the other car, made note of the way it swerved and weaved in and out of traffic on the other side of the road. The driver had obviously been seriously impaired.

Her heart had hurt when she saw the way her father had jerked and looked terrified when her magic spilled into the front seat, but he hadn't lost control of the car. No, he had been trying to calm down Ella's mother, talking to her soothingly when the drunk in the other car had crossed into the opposite lanes and come hurtling toward them. For the first time, Ella truly saw that the wreck had not been her fault. It had been just a tragic even that coincided with the worst moment of her life and managed to make it a million times worse.

But Ella was not responsible. She never had been.

So she had nodded to Kees, gathered herself, and picked up a spell book.

When she'd first woken and remembered her dreams, along with the events of the night and the dawn, Ella considered thanking Kees for helping her through the memories and her own muddled emotions. That impulse faded quickly when he proceeded to become the most demanding taskmaster she had ever known.

He worked her like a rented chain saw, pushing her from one spell to the next, giving her only minutes to familiarize herself with the intent and the wording before making her perform it. Then he would have her practice each spell over and over until she thought he ought to be worried about the idea of going to bed with her again. She'd probably be muttering spells and curses in her sleep after this.

Hours flew by while Ella learned how to create and throw fire, how to deflect the energy of incoming spells—he threw frickin' *rocks* at her for that one—and how to create a magical cage that could hold a person trapped within bars of energy visible only with mage sight. She still didn't want to learn any death magic. Killing spells were off her list. She told Kees she could perform her rebound spell again, but to deliberately use magic to kill still made her uncomfortable, so he let it slide.

He did, however, insist that she learn a few basic moves of physical self-defense. Using his human shape, he taught her how to break out of a captor's grip in a number of common holds. He showed her the vulnerable spots on a human's anatomy—both male and female, even though Ella had started to assume that like the Wardens, the *nocturnis* were a bunch of backwards chauvinists—and taught her how to make a blow count in spite of her small size and limited physical strength.

All Ella could think was that she should have gone to the gym more often.

The sun had begun to dip toward the treetops when Kees gave his last lesson. He began to talk to her about demons.

"The Seven, pray to the Light, you will never see. They are the oldest of their kind, and the most dangerous. They have no thoughts, no emotions, no shape but pure evil. When they join together, they form the Darkness, and if that happens, our war is all but lost.

"But there are demons of other sorts, ones less powerful and more easily controlled. These are the ones the *nocturnis* may draw into our realm to aid in their plans. These beings should not be underestimated. Though their power cannot be compared to one of the Seven, they still have the ability to kill even a squad of well-armed human soldiers without thought or mercy."

Ella shot him a peevish glance. "Gee, and I could wind up meeting one? Bully for me."

"If you do meet one, you should call for me. I will stand against it and slay it. That is my purpose."

"Right, but what if you're busy? What do I do then? Politely ask it to wait until you're free to come deal with it?"

"You think I would abandon you in battle? That I would not stay right by your side and protect you from all danger?"

His insulted roar made Ella roll her eyes. "No, that's not what I think. What I do think is that shit happens and after watching one or two movies in my life, I think even more shit happens in the heat of battle. So I'd just like a little more to go on than, 'If you see a demon, wait for me to rescue you.' Sorry if that offends."

Kees's expression hardened. "You cannot stand alone

against a demon. Even a fully trained Warden would not try without two or three others by his side. Even for the weakest of their kind. The most minor demons can be destroyed, but it requires enormous power."

"Fine, then I won't try to destroy it, but I would like to have the option of holding it off by some method more reliable than running away. I'm not that fast, or that graceful. With my luck, I'd trip over something and end up demon chow before you could swoop in and save the day."

Kees growled something under his breath, but he relented and found two spells in the texts and one in the grimoire that might prove useful. One was a variation on a warding spell, and that one looked easy, considering she already had a pretty good handle on standard wards and barriers. Rather than sealing off a space that others could not enter, the spell created a boundary others could not exit. It was like a magic invisible bubble that trapped the user inside. And even better, it had a reflective interior, so magic cast from inside could not pierce the boundary. Put it around another mage, and that mage couldn't cast a counterspell to dissolve it. On demons, it worked like a summoning circle, keeping them inside, but it didn't last as long as with mages and mortals. Eventually the demon's evil would eat away at the barrier and allow it to slip free.

The second spell allowed the mage who cast it to close a portal on a summoned demon. That one was trickier, because it still left you facing an angry demon. Or even parts of an angry demon, since there was a note that said if a demon had partially made it through the portal, that part would remain on earth with a level of power commensurate with the amount of it not contained on the other plane.

That just sounded gross.

The third spell came from the grimoire, and sounded

both the most effective and the most dangerous. In it, the caster bound the demon to something on the mortal plane, like a rock or a tree or a man-made object. Once the demon was bound, it would share the vulnerabilities of the object. It if were bound to glass, it could be shattered; to wood, it could be burned. And remains, like shards or ask, could be swept up and stored in a container, then buried in a hole filled with salt. The demon would be trapped in that prison forever.

Ella immediately committed all three spells to memory. She would have liked to practice them as well, but by the time she looked up from the books, the sun was already sinking below the trees. No wonder the text had been so hard to make out.

"Come." Kees picked up the other books and their sparring tools and turned toward the cabin. "We should eat. Later you can continue to practice."

"Right. Because I'm not just a regular human anymore, so I don't need to worry about stuff like rest and recuperation."

Her words had been muttered under her breath, but the damned gargoyle heard her anyway.

"You can rest later. For now, practice."

She stuck her tongue out at his retreating back.

Trudging up the steps and into the cabin, she almost missed the faint sound of her cell phone ringing as it drifted from the bedroom. She had to dash to reach it before the voice mail picked up. The screen told her who was on the other end of the line.

"Fil," she said. "You there?"

"I'm here. Just starting to wonder if you were, though."

"Sorry, I was in the other room and I forgot to bring the phone with me. D'you have news for me?"

"Sure do. I found your piece!"

Ella immediately looked around for Kees and waved

him over. He finished lighting the fire in the hearth and joined her next to the cabin entrance. "Fil, you are amazing. Where is it?"

Kees watched her closely, and she could see from his expression that he was picking up both sides of the conversation.

"Well, it's not on display anywhere, but I lucked out and stumbled on it by accident. That's the only reason I'm able to get back to you so fast. Turns out it just arrived in town. The Ste. Celeste Museum acquired it from a private seller in Budapest like two months ago. The plane carrying it literally landed on Friday. It's still going through prep and waiting for the display space to be ready. I think they plan to place it in their gardens."

"You're the best. Seriously. I owe you so big for this."

"Hey, we already worked out the price, sweetie. Don't go trying to haggle now."

"Trust me, I'll pay it and still be in your debt."

"Cool. Hey, listen." There was a pause, and Felicity's voice came back sounding slightly unsure. "I can see why your director would be upset to lose a piece like this, El. It's . . . well, it's pretty amazing. The condition is unbelievable. If it didn't come with a stack of provenance paperwork thicker than my front door, I'd be sure it was a fake. I mean, that thing needs not a single bit of restoration that I could see. It's almost creepy."

Ella forced a laugh. "Creepy? Why? Because if more art were like that, you'd be out of a job, right?"

"Har-har. No, I mean it, El. This thing is weird. You gotta trust me on this." She paused, and her voice lowered. "The way I trusted you."

Memories of that night after the library sneaked up on Ella. She remembered Felicity's calm reaction, her easy acceptance. Was there more to easy, breezy Fil Shaltis than Ella had thought?

"Anyway, just be careful," Fil said, her tone returning to normal. "On general principle, if nothing else."

"You got it."

"Good. So is there anything else I can do for you? I've been saving up vacation time, so I can extort you for another couple of weeks, easy."

Ella met Kees's gaze. He frowned and whispered to her. She repeated the question to Felicity. "Can you do me another favor and go back to get a picture? I'd love to have something visual to back up my notes."

"Already taken care of. I took a handful with my cell once I realized that was the one. I'll shoot 'em over to your e-mail."

"Thanks again. And again. Seriously, if I had kids, you'd get pick of the litter."

"No way. Now, if you were talking puppies . . ."

Ella laughed. Fil had a soft spot for furry things, especially furry babies. She'd never met a juvenile mammal she didn't like. Ella opened her mouth to tease, but the words were drowned out by something outside.

Something that sounded like an explosion.

"Holy shit!" Fil yelled into the phone. "What the hell was that? Ella? El, are you okay?"

Kees had pushed Ella to the floor and crouched over her to peer out the front window of the cabin.

"I'm fine," Ella said, struggling to keep the panic out of her voice and knowing she was only half successful. "I, um . . . I think a tree might have gotten hit by lightning," she improvised. "I have to go check it out, make sure it's not gonna hit the house. I'll call you later, Fil. Thanks."

She hung up on her friend's loud protests.

"What was that?" Ella demanded, looking up at Kees.

"We have company."

Judging by his tone, he wasn't referring to a few pals dropping by for dinner.

Ella felt a chill sweep through her. "How many?"

"I can see five. With our friend McQuaid standing right out in front. This other looks familiar, as well."

Squirming, she managed to raise her torso far enough to peer out the very bottom of the window. Despite the sill and the porch railing trying to obscure her view, she could make out the forms Kees had mentioned. She saw three blurry shapes back along the tree line, but the sight that drew her eye was of the bonfire now burning in the center of the front clearing and the two men standing just beyond it. With the flickering light glowing against their features, they weren't hard to recognize.

Detective Michael "Sorry I Didn't Mention I Was Evil" McQuaid, and . . .

"Shitshitshit," Ella whispered. "Patrick Stanley."

Kees grunted and gave a brief nod. "I had forgotten his name. But rest assured I remember his words. And his actions. He was the man you struggled with in the gardens the night I awoke."

"Yeah. I mean, I knew he was a slimy asshole, but I never thought he might be a demonic servant." She paused, remembering her words to Bea that night. "Okay, I didn't seriously think it. But it turns out he's *nocturnis*? That's just . . . It's almost too obvious. He should have pretended to be nice, like the cop did."

"Not every human who looks good is, and not everyone who looks evil isn't."

Ella rolled her eyes. "Thanks, Yoda."

He looked at her oddly, but didn't comment. She was guessing he hadn't seen a movie in a while. Or, you know, ever.

"Come out, come out, wherever you are!"

Stanley called out the order in a creepy singsong voice that raised the hairs on the back of Ella's neck. It sounded full of glee and madness, like the maniacal killer in an old Hollywood horror flick. Which, she admitted, made a lot of sense.

It also explained a bunch of things. Stanley's determined arrogance and implacable belief in his own irresistibility made a lot more sense when you factored in a nice dose of insanity.

"Come on, Ella-bella," the voice cajoled. "I'm not going to hurt you." He cackled. "Well, actually, I am, but I might hurt you a little less if you don't make me come in there looking for you."

Kees growled so low and fierce, he seemed to vibrate above her. Ella laid a hand on his shoulder and squeezed.

"Ignore him," she whispered. "The bad guys always try to piss off the good guys, right? It's like a distraction technique."

And it was damned well working.

Despite her reassurance, Kees could feel his human's unease. Stanley made her nervous and the surprise of learning him to be one of the *nocturnis* had knocked Ella off balance. He wanted to knock the Dark mage's head off in return.

He had hoped the Order would have a harder time finding them. He'd wanted at least a few days to prepare for an assault. A week or two would have been better. He knew that every moment until they woke another Guardian or located more Wardens equaled another day of vulnerability, so the goal had been to hide out until Ella's friend sent word on the location of the first of his brothers. Then he and Ella would immediately travel there and attempt to wake him. They would find strength in numbers.

A single Guardian was a formidable opponent for any

mortal and the lesser demons as well, but if the *nocturnis* attacked him in numbers, he could still be taken down. Worse than that, if he had to fight off too many at once, he would leave Ella unprotected, and that was unacceptable. Without him, she could too easily be hurt or even killed.

She needed more training. As impressed as he had been, as he continued to be, by her talent, she still knew no more than a handful of the most basic spells. Up against an experienced Dark mage or even a warded human, she would stand little chance in a confrontation. One day, he knew, she would make her enemies tremble at the thought of her abilities, but that wouldn't happen today. Today, she needed him to do his job.

"Well, five isn't so bad," she said, her voice rising up to him from where she still half-lay on the floor beneath him. "We can take five, right? Especially if I can disable a couple from a distance. I mean, you could probably handle them yourself if I wasn't here."

He could have, but he didn't confirm her supposition. He didn't want to tell her he would prefer that she wasn't here, because she might misunderstand. He didn't ever want her near danger, but he thought he would always want her.

"I can fight a number at once, but I am suspicious they bring only five, especially when we knew the detective is not a magic-user," he told her. "He must have informed his friends that you had a Guardian by your side. They should have brought more to fight me."

"You mean there might be more? But why didn't you see them when you looked out front?" Her eyes narrowed and she swore. "Be right back."

Before he could stop her, she was scuttling across the floor on her hands and knees, carefully keeping out of sight of the windows. She made it into the bedroom and back in less than five minutes.

"You were right," she panted when she returned to his side. "They're trying to surround us. My vision may not be as good as yours, but I saw at least three more around the back of the house. For all we know, they might have brought a dozen or more *nocturnis* after us."

Kees nodded grimly. He wasn't surprised. He also wouldn't place any bets on a dozen *nocturnis* making up the full extent of their forces. Ella had told him how removed this cabin was from her life. She hadn't visited in fifteen years, had left its deed in the name of the trust that had managed it until she came of age after her parents' deaths, and the only people who ever came here were workers from the company that was paid to maintain it and keep everything in working order. For someone to have found them this quickly meant that their pursuers were not stupid. They would know that even with a dozen Dark mages, they would have a hard time bringing down a Guardian, especially one with something to protect.

No, he suspected they had something more up their sleeves, but he didn't voice the concern. His little human had been so brave and determined so far that he couldn't bring himself to frighten her. They would simply have to be careful.

"Kees, what do we do?" she whispered. "We can't just sit in here forever and wait to see if they go away. Sooner or later, they'll either find a way to make us come out, or they'll get tired of waiting and come in. You are the warfare expert. I kind of need you to tell me which of those options gives us a better chance."

Neither, as far as he was concerned. Both gave the advantage to their enemies. With the cabin surrounded, none of the options were good ones. If they left it, they exposed themselves immediately, but if they waited for the *nocturnis* to breach the walls, the wooden structure would be too easy to burn down around their ears. The bonfire out front demonstrated they knew how to use fire, and the man behind it showed they were crazy enough to do so.

"We go out," Kees finally said, his voice grim. "But first, you need to get to work."

Chapter Seventeen

Ella worked quickly and hard. Setting wards wasn't difficult work, but it did take energy. Rather than risk using her own magic when she might need it later, she tapped into the Source to build the boundaries that would keep the *nocturnis* from using the cabin as cover to sneak up behind them. If they tried to enter the structure through any means other than sliding down the chimney, they would get a nasty magical shock, and Kees and Ella would get an advanced warning.

If they went for the chimney route . . . well, the fire was blazing, so they'd damned well better be dressed in red and packing presents.

She sealed the last ward at the front door, making it the strongest because at least at first, it would be the one directly at their backs. Using the dagger Kees provided, she blooded it with pricks to both their palms to ensure either of them could pass it easily without disturbing the spell. Blood magic wasn't big with the Wardens, but it had its uses, provided it wasn't abused.

The *nocturnis* had a particular fondness for blood

magic, and they did nothing but abuse it. No way did Ella want to go down that path.

She tried to hand the dagger back to Kees.

"Keep it," he told her gruffly. "Don't use it unless you have no other choice. Remember that a weapon is no more than a danger if it can be taken and used against you. You'll need a lot more practice before you can be confident of holding on to it in a real fight."

"I know. I remember the lessons. I fight to get away and get to you. If I can't get to you, I use magic. If I can't use magic, I run. If I can't run, that's when I fight."

He nodded. "Let's go."

Ella pulled up the hem of her baggy T-shirt and hooked the knife sheath to her belt. She also tucked the small pouch of leftover salt into her pocket with an absent gesture. She really hoped she and Kees won this one. She was wearing her "I'm going to get worked really hard, sweat like a pig, and want to kick Kees in the nuts" clothes, not her "It's okay if I die in this because at least I look hot" clothes.

A girl had her pride.

She followed close on Kees's heels as he opened the door and stepped onto the porch. The clear area in front of the cabin was so small that she clearly felt the heat of the fire on her face. It burned just three feet or so beyond the front steps, its base nestled into a small crater that hadn't been there this afternoon. That must have been part of the explosion they had heard. One of the *nocturnis* had thrown a fireball, so big it had carved a divot in the earth before settling in to burn like the centerpiece of a Boy Scouts jamboree.

It almost made Ella wish for some marshmallows.

"Ella, you brought a friend to the party. Did your invitation say plus one?" Stanley laughed, his smile illuminated by the red glow of the fire into something hellish. In the flame-lit darkness, his aristocratic features took on the cast of a devil, handsome but cruel and hard. "No matter. As it turns out, your guest is someone we would have invited out sooner or later. I could almost thank you for bringing him to us. But I won't."

"Why is that, Patrick?" she asked, projecting into her voice a defiant confidence at odds with the butterflies currently learning to mambo in her belly. "Because you know Kees is going to kick your ass?"

Stanley's sinister smile didn't fade, but his eyes flashed with hatred. "Stupid girl. You would have been so better off if you had just given me what I wanted, Ella. After I fucked you, I would have shown you what real power is. If you had behaved, I might even have shared it. I sensed the ability in you from the beginning, and Uhlthor is always looking for a few good men."

He laughed at his own joke. Right, because his demon boss was like the Marine Corps. At least, Ella assumed that name belonged to the demon. It sounded guttural and ugly when he said it, and the sound made Kees stiffen and hiss beside her.

"Thanks, Paddy, but I have to pass. I'm afraid I don't like that signing bonus you guys offer."

"Ah, that." The *nocturnis* clucked his tongue. "I'm afraid you're not the first to quibble over such things. Not to worry. You'll die just as they did."

Everything happened at once.

Kees shoved Ella to the floor of the porch with a furious roar. The fire blazed and leapt into the sky far above the roof of the cabin, above even the surrounding treetops. Stanley's voice shrieked out a command, and a bullet whizzed past the spot where Ella's head had been just a split second before. She caught a glimpse of McQuaid holding his drawn gun just before the impact with the floorboards made her grunt.

"Stay down," Kees growled, and launched himself into the night.

Literally.

He stepped to the edge of the porch and jumped vertically into the air, spreading his enormous wings and catching the night breeze. A few heavy beats lifted him above the fire and Ella knew he was heading for Stanley.

Before he could fall on the millionaire-slash-demon worshipper, Ella saw a bolt of black energy hammer into him. She traced its path back to the edge of the woods to the right of the track to the cabin and swore. Three *nocturnis* mages had combined forces against her Guardian. That was so no fair.

She turned, intending to crawl to the other side of the porch and let the evil bastards know she did not appreciate anyone attacking Kees, let alone sniveling cowards who thought it would be cool to gang up on him. Even if he could undoubtedly handle it himself, there was a principle to consider here.

The pop of another bullet stopped her. Damn it, how had she forgotten about the gun?

Maybe it was more important to take care of McQuaid first. Bullets might ping right off Kees's tough hide, but she didn't think she'd be quite so lucky if she got hit.

"Kill her!" she heard Stanley shout. "Kill her first and then concentrate on the Guardian! She's weak. Nothing but a human whore. Take her out of the picture."

Ella didn't wait for a third bullet. She threw herself behind the cedar trunk her family had always used to store sandbags for when the creek behind the cabin decided to rise. She would definitely prefer not to get shot tonight.

"Damn, I wish the police were coming," she muttered

as she tried to think. Unfortunately, she knew the chances of anyone hearing the shots out here and calling the authorities to investigate were practically nil. There was a better chance of someone reporting the fire, but it had already shrunk back to normal proportions, and at this time of year, it wasn't dry enough to cause concern unless it flared again.

She and Kees were almost certainly on their own.

Too bad the same couldn't be said for McQuaid and Stanley.

A high-pitched screeching sound told her someone had tried to open the back door of the cabin. The wards had done their job of alerting her, and she felt pretty confident that they would have thrown the intruder back a few feet for good measure. No one demon-touched was getting into that building, but that didn't prevent them from coming around the sides.

Movement from the left side of the cabin told her she'd guessed correctly. She also thought she recognized the height and weight of two of the three figures she'd spied earlier out of the bedroom window. Hopefully, the third was still lying on his back in the dirt and trying to remember his name. Both the men approaching were crawling with Dark magic. Mages for certain.

Time for Ella's final exams.

Drawing on her will, Ella centered the two figures in her sight and gathered up the energy inside her. Quickly, she formed it into a ball, raised her hand, and threw it directly at the two men.

"Locus ubi exire!" she screamed, and only then stopped to wonder if the spell would work on two people at once.

Peeking over the top of the chest, she saw an enormous ball of her blue-white magic, at least fifteen feet in diameter. Through the shimmering surface, she could just make out the shadow of two *nocturnis*-shaped figures.

"Yes!" She wished she could give herself a high five.

Instead, she shifted, hoping to get a bead on how Kees was doing with the other three spellcasters. With the ones from the back and McQuaid and Stanley added to the list, they had a total of eight bad guys to take care of. Well, six now, thanks to the bouncy ball cage she'd just set up.

Ella should have known better to gloat. Even mentally. She'd barely had time to process the thought when a rough hand grabbed her by the hair and jerked her to her feet. Screaming, she took a swing at her attacker only to freeze when she felt the barrel of a gun press hard against her temple.

McQuaid laughed, low and mean, and pressed his cheek up against hers until she could almost taste his hot breath. Her stomach heaved. "Bet you wish you'd called me now, bitch."

She froze and waited for the bullet to end everything.

"Wait! Don't kill her!" Stanley shouted. "Bring her here. I've thought of a new use for our pretty prize."

Kees bellowed, and Ella automatically turned in his direction. The sight of him scared her almost more than the gun had. He bled from dozens of shallow cuts all over his body, as if he'd walked through a tornado of razor blades. His claws shone dark and slick with more blood, but at least she could assume that came from the dead *nocturnis* at his feet. Three more continued to attack him with spell after spell. Ella recognized the third as the man she'd hoped had passed out behind the cabin.

Stanley laughed, hoarse and cruel like a hyena. "I don't think your Guardian is going to like my idea, Ella-bella. Some creatures just can't take the sight of blood, but yours is going to taste very, very good to the one you're going to help me raise." He waved to McQuaid. "Bring her here, into the circle."

"Ooh, looks like we're having a party, girl, and you get

to invite the guest of honor." McQuaid chuckled. "Too bad you have to die before he can get here."

Ella fought like an angry badger. She struck out with fists and feet, teeth and nails. Unfortunately, the cop had gone through professional training. He countered every one of the tricks Kees had taught her and kept hold of her as he dragged her the few feet to the circle Stanley had carved into the ground with the tip of a knife. When she began impeding his progress with her writhing and bucking, he struck her on the side of the head hard enough to make her see stars. Involuntarily, she went limp, dazed by the blow.

As soon as she passed the boundary, Stanley sealed it, completing the summoning circle. Ella lay in a crumpled heap in the dirt, on her stomach, her hands caught beneath her. The mage had trapped the three of them inside. And Kees outside.

Despite the three mages still bombarding him with Dark magic, the Guardian threw himself after Ella, but he was bogged down with wounds and tendrils of evil energy. His fists pounded against the magical barrier, but all Ella could hear was a faint ping.

Then even that was drowned out by the sound of his rage.

Ignoring the furious gargoyle, McQuaid frowned at the other man. "You really think it's a good idea for us to be in here with her? I don't recall your 'special friends' being real discriminating about their dinners."

Stanley rolled his eyes. "You'd rather be out there with him? Don't be a fool. The demon I'll summon will be minor, and by spilling her blood to do it, I'll bind it under my control. He'll have to obey me, and I'll order it not to eat you. Provided you stop pissing me off."

Ella lay still and listened, pretending to be stunned by the blow. She knew she wouldn't be able to get out of the circle unless the boundary was broken. She thought about the salt in her pocket. Salt would ground the spell and break the circle, but she had two men standing almost on top of her. If she wanted to make good on an escape attempt, her timing would have to be perfect.

"Well, what the hell use is a minor demon?"

"Minor is a relative term. It will still be strong enough to take care of the Guardian. Summoning one of the Old Ones takes more than a ramshackle circle and a single High Priest. We'd need most of the Order to accomplish such a thing." Turning his gaze to Ella, Stanley's eyes narrowed and his fingers tightened on the long, thin ritual blade he held in his hand. "Now, shut up and hold her down. It's time to make her bleed."

Oh, hell *no.*

Again, Kees roared. It sounded like a pride of angry lions chewing on a bagpipe, loud, fierce, predatory, and slightly otherworldly. He had turned his back on the three mages he was fighting, and the fools thought they would take advantage of his inattention. They converged on him from behind, two throwing spells with manic abandon while the third drew a dagger black with evil magic and shoved it hard into the Guardian's side.

It took every ounce of willpower Ella possessed not to scream and jump to her feet. The *nocturnis* had dared to injure her Guardian, and she burned to make him pay. She would never get the chance. In a move of eerie preternatural grace, Kees whirled around, claws extended, and tore the dagger-wielding mage's head clean off his shoulders. It fell to the ground with a solid, wet thud, but Kees just continued to move. The other two facing him went down in seconds, throats and bellies town open and spilling to the ground in hot rivulets of gore.

Even Ella shivered a little. She knew the Guardian raged in her behalf. The possessiveness and rage were easy to pick out, but the panic startled her. Any Guardian would be angry if a human were threatened, and the fact that he considered her to be under his care would make it even worse for Kees. He would feel as if he were failing her to see her facing death, but why would he panic? Panic implied that he would be emotionally hurt if she were to die, and for that, he needed to care.

For that, he needed to love her.

It looked like she and her Guardian would need to have a little chat after this.

Provided there was an "after this."

Wiggling the fingers of her left hand, Ella caught the drawstring of the small pouch that held her salt and hooked it around her pinkie, then closed her palm into a fist. Her right hand was still a good three inches away from her knife hilt, so she would have to give this everything she had.

And pray.

She waited a long, creeping instant until she felt McQuaid reach for her hair. A slit throat, she knew, would spill the most blood, and blood was what would power the summoning, so McQuaid would want to pull back her head to expose all those convenient veins.

The moment she felt fingers brush the back of her head, Ella sprang. Her left hand shot out, spraying salt across the boundary of the circle, breaking the magical plane. Her right hand snatched her knife from the sheath on her belt and in the same motion swung it toward the detective, drawing a smooth arc across the surface of his stomach.

She didn't wait to see if she'd injured him. She threw herself forward, following the path of the salt and hurling herself out of the circle with every bit of her strength. She heard a man scream and assumed it was McQuaid because over the top of the pained cry, Stanley cursed in foul, angry language.

Ella landed hard enough to knock the wind out of herself and lay there, momentarily dazed. She felt hands reach for her and immediately knew from the size and familiar touch to whom they belonged. Kees rolled her gently to her back and raked his gaze over her with frantic concern.

"Are you all right? Where are you hurt? Tell me."

She opened her mouth to reassure him, to let him know that aside from having trouble catching her equilibrium and feeling as drained as if she'd just run back-to-back marathons, she felt fine. Then she heard the scream.

She and Kees turned as one and saw immediately what had happened. Patrick Stanley stood inside the boundary of his destroyed circle, his face lit with fire and madness. Blood covered his hands and dripped down the blade of his knife to soak into the earth beside the body of Detective McQuaid.

Ella swallowed hard as nausea and understanding rushed through her. Deprived of his blood sacrifice by Ella's escape, Stanley had been unwilling to abandon the summoning. Instead, he had turned on his associate and made McQuaid a victim of opportunity. The *nocturnis* High Priest was determined to have his demon, and for that he needed more blood.

"Shit. Kees!" She grabbed his arm and tugged as the sound of Stanley's chanted spell welled up into the clearing. "The blood sacrifice. He's summoning a demon. Right now. He's doing it right fucking *now*."

Kees swore and Ella looked up at his face. She could see the exhaustion in his eyes. The battle with the mages and the injuries that still bled sluggishly all over his body had taken their toll. She realized in a flash that she didn't know for certain if he would survive a fight with a demon.

The air inside the circle shimmered with a slimy blackness that resembled nothing so much as a toxic oil spill on ocean water. Ella cursed and tried to push to her feet even as the Dark power began to take shape. She saw an arm emerge, then what looked like the top of a head began pressing against the blackness like a moving animal trapped under a blanket.

Kees held out an arm and tried to push Ella backwards. Furious, she grabbed the edge of his wing and yanked. Hard. He snarled and looked down at her.

"You can't do this, Kees. You're tired, and you're hurt. I can see it. You can't take on a demon. Not right now. Let me do this."

"Are you insane, woman?" He barked, "Let you, a human, an untrained mage, take on a demon by yourself? That blow to the head I saw you take must have caused more damage than I thought. I will never let you put yourself in such danger. I cannot. Your lack of faith in me aside, it is my duty to put myself in front of you, and if I were to die there, so be it."

"But I don't want you to die," she told him, gazing up at him with everything she felt for him glowing on her face. She knew it had to be there; she could practically feel it. "I want you to live, Kees. I want us both to live, for a very long time, and I'm afraid that this will be too much for you."

"Fate will out."

Ella rolled her eyes. "Screw Fate. I'm not going to stand aside and hope She's in a good mood tonight. I'll make you a deal. If you want to face down a demon, fine, but you do it beside me, not in front of me." She placed her hand against his, the same hands the Warden Alan pressed together when he'd performed the binding spell just days before. "We're stronger together, remember?"

She saw that he wanted to argue, saw the fierce battle he fought not to simply steamroll right over her. When she squeezed his hand and gave a little push of magic—just a reminder, really, that while human, she wasn't helpless—he groaned. Then he collected himself and nodded.

"Together," he growled.

They turned back to the circle as one. The demon's head and shoulders had made it through the portal. It had both hands on the ground and its black claws dug into the earth as it tried to drag the rest of itself forward out of the oily blackness.

It was a vile-looking creature, stretched out and misshapen, with spines growing out of its back like extensions of its vertebrae. Its arms appeared disproportionately long compared to the width of its shoulders and had an additional joint in the middle, like an extra elbow. It had the head of something primitive and featureless, like a lamprey, just a giant maw with rows and rows of teeth. It didn't even appear to have eyes or a nose, just that mouth, gaping wide and drooling.

Ella suppressed a shudder.

The demon struggled forward, and Stanley's chanting grew even louder, almost frantic in both tone and volume. Ella could feel Kees tensing beside her, preparing himself for an attack, and she knew she couldn't wait. She had to try now.

Dropping his hand, she lifted hers in front of her and reached for the last of the energy inside her. She wished she could take the time to dig down and call upon the Source, but she knew she'd already waited as long as she dared. She couldn't take the time. Pulling together every strand and scrap, Ella hastily built her spell and cast it toward the shimmering gate.

"Claudite ostium!"

Stanley's concentration broke and the demonic portal closed. The demon shrieked, a sound so bloodcurdling, Ella actually had to clasp her hands over her ears and swallow hard to keep from echoing the scream. Even muffled, she could hear it, and she could feel it in her bones, like spikes of icy metal shooting through her marrow. There was nothing human in the sound, and even Kees looked pained to hear it.

Just as Ella suspected, the spell had some gruesome consequences. Cut off from the plane it had been summoned from, the demon had fallen to the ground, where it continued to writhe and shriek. Thick, black blood poured from the stumps of its severed legs and pooled on the ground. Unlike with McQuaid's blood, which while evil had ultimately been human, the earth seemed to recognize the corruption in the demon's blood and reject it. Smoke rose from the spots where the blood touched, and instead of soaking in, it appeared to boil off like water in a pan.

"You meddling bitch!" Stanley screamed, nearly foaming at the mouth in his rage. He stepped forward and raised his hands in Ella's direction, but whatever spell he had intended never materialized. Maybe he had assumed the demon was as good as destroyed, or maybe fury and arrogance had simply clouded his judgment; either way, his movements brought him a fraction too close to the wounded demon.

In a blinding instant, the demon struck. Legless or not, the demon was injured, weakened, and instinct would dictate it needed strength to survive. For that, it would have to feed. It darted out a hand and curled it around Stanley's ankle, jerking the man off his feet. The *nocturnis* screamed, a sound of mingled surprise and terror just before the creature fell on him. Its hands ripped open his chest cavity, and it reached forward, plucking out the still-beating heart. It devoured the organ in a loud, slurping gulp.

Ella turned away, her stomach heaving.

Kees cursed and threw himself forward, and Ella knew things had gotten very, very bad.

She spun back toward the circle to see Kees and the

demon clash head-on over the body of Patrick Stanley. Apparently demons healed quickly, at least when they ate human hearts, because the creature now stood on two partially formed legs. Ella didn't know if the creature normally had lower limbs less than half the length of the upper or if its healing had been incomplete. What she did know was that it was mobile and that its ugly black claws had already carved a deep gash in Kees's shoulder.

God, would this night never end?

Ella searched her recollection for the final spell she had committed to memory that afternoon—the demon binding. The other two had worked out pretty well so far, so she might as well go for the trifecta.

She reached deep again, frowned, and then reached deeper. She swore and felt herself grow pale. Her well was dry. Expending all that energy had drained her. It explained her faint dizziness and the shakes she had been ignoring because now was not the time to fall to pieces. She couldn't stand by and let the demon tear Kees apart the way it had done to Stanley, not when he was already tired and weakened. She had to cast that spell and it had to be now.

Which left her only one choice.

"Forgive me, big guy," she muttered, and lifted her hands.

This time, she didn't reach down into herself; she reached out to the nearly intangible connection Alan had created between her and Kees. She could feel his exhaustion, but a Guardian was made of magic, and as long as he lived, he had power she could tap. What she had to do might drain him, but it would end the demon, and possibly save his life.

Kees had told her a thousand times that his mission was to destroy demons or die in the attempt. She really hoped she wasn't about to help with option number two.

She saw Kees jerk when he felt her pull on him and winced when the momentary distraction allowed the demon to land another solid blow, this one to Kees's back just over his kidneys. If he had kidneys. She'd learned a lot about gargoyle external anatomy in the past week, but it looked like she had some questions to ask about what went on inside. Yet another reason to keep alive the guy with all the answers.

The magic flowed into Ella and took her by surprise. It felt different from what she was used to, different from the magic that lived inside her and different from the kind that could be pulled from the Source. This was . . . richer. She couldn't quite describe it, but it was like the magic had a flavor, and this kind tasted thick and spicy. She wished she had time to savor it.

Kees reeled to the side, the demon's long, multi-hinged arm catching him under a horn and sending him stumbling. He fell to one knee and his chest heaved with exertion.

Ella cried out. Reaching down, she scooped up the dagger she had dropped after escaping the circle and grasped the hilt. With a quick prayer for accuracy, she drew her arm back and threw the knife. She wasn't throwing from the blade as she'd seen in the movies, and she wasn't stupid enough to think she'd hit her target and drop it instantly. She just needed to get close.

The dagger whooshed through the air and slapped the demon harmlessly in the chest before sliding to the ground at its feet. It didn't even seem to notice, but Ella saw, and it was close enough.

Wrenching Kees's magic to her, Ella hurled it toward the dagger and screamed, *"Tenetur ad hanc rem!"*

The explosion of light blinded her.

Ella reflexively raised an arm to cover her eyes but not

before she saw Kees collapse. Her stomach dropped and her blood froze. Dear Lord, what had she done?

Then there was an enormous rush of air, like the earth itself had sighed, and the light faded.

The demon was gone.

Ella barely noticed. She flew to Kees's side and knelt next to his limp form. He was so still, silent and unmoving. She couldn't even tell if he was breathing. Her hands shook as she reached for his head and tried to lift it into her lap, but it was heavier than she could have imagined. Eventually, she grasped his horns and tugged with all her might and managed to shift it. He moaned when he landed hard against her thigh.

It was the sweetest sound she had ever heard.

"Kees." Her voice sounded hoarse and choked in her own ears. "Kees, baby, please. Please tell me you're okay." His eyelids flickered but didn't open. Ella shook him and wiped away the tear that dropped onto his cheek. "Kees, please. I need you to be okay."

The gargoyle moaned again but still didn't open his eyes. Instead, his lips parted and he growled, "I'll be fine as soon as you stop trying to kill me."

Ella half collapsed and started to laugh, her body curling around him in sheer joy and relief.

"Seriously," Kees groaned. "If you don't stop shaking it, my head is going to fall off. I don't know if aspirin works for Guardians—I've never taken them before—but I think I'm about to try. Do we have any in the cabin?"

Ella pulled herself together and tried to suppress the accompanying shudder. Leaning down she pressed a tender kiss to his forehead right between his horns. "Sure, baby. We have as many as you need. Just rest here a minute and then we'll get you inside and get you some. Okay?"

"Okay." Kees heaved a sigh, and finally opened his eyes.

Ella looked into those dark pools and saw the light flickering beneath the surface. It was a new light, different from the ones she'd seen before, deeper and somehow more intense. Her throat tightened, and she felt herself wondering if he finally understood what she had already realized.

"Little human," he murmured, his lips curving tenderly. "I should have known you would be the one to save me, not the other way around. From the very first moment you pierced the fog of my sleep, you have done nothing that I expected. At every turn, you continue to surprise me. But not so much as I surprise myself.

She drew her bottom lip between her teeth and tried not to cry again. For a girl who had lost everything, she felt as if every single wish she'd ever had was about to come true.

"Sweet girl, I truly believed that I came into this world whole, with everything I needed to do my duty and fight back the Darkness. And for centuries I completed my missions. I served the Light and protected the world and not once did I experience any feeling more than the fury of battle or the satisfaction of a job well done.

"Until I met you."

Ella's heart stuttered. Kees raised a hand to cup her cheek and she turned into it, savoring the warmth of his rough, leathery skin against hers.

"You have shown me that I was a fool, a bigger fool than I called you. You tried to shut away the magic because you believed it has cost you the people you loved, but I tried to shut away emotion because I didn't believe a Guardian needed to feel in order to do his duty. I thought emotion was a weakness, but how can it be when two bound together are so obviously more than either is alone?"

He smiled, slowly, tenderly, and brushed his thumb across her lips. "Little human, I love you."

Ella felt new tears rolling down her cheeks and smiled.

She felt as if her heart had just cracked—not painfully, but because it could no longer stretch wide enough to contain her joy. It had cracked open, like the stone skin that had held Kees frozen in place for centuries. In both instances, the result was perfect freedom, Kees from sleep and Ella from pain.

"I love you, too," she whispered, and leaned down to press her lips gently against his. "Forever."

"Ah, sweet girl," he purred, his eyes sparking brightly, "do I have some things to tell you about forever. . . ."

Chapter Eighteen

When Ella finally checked her cell phone the next morning, she had twelve messages, all from Felicity, but it was hours before she could return them. First, she and Kees had a little cleaning up to do.

They took care of the demon first. Ella collected the dagger with carefully gloved hands and laid it in the hole Kees had dug a good half mile behind the cabin, deep in the deserted woods. She used an entire box of salt, both as a bed and a covering for the cursed item, making sure every last inch of it was covered in the stuff. Then they covered it with three feet of heavy, rocky soil.

Straightening up the yard turned out not to be quite so simple.

She felt a little like a mafioso, looking out over her front yard and picturing the faces of the people she'd destroyed in the spots where they had died, but unlike the average character on *The Sopranos,* she at least didn't have to get rid of the bodies..

Magic obviously had its benefits, even if it felt weird to be happy about the all-consuming nature of the Darkness.

The one thing they did have to deal with was the practicalities of the cars the *nocturnis* had used to get to the cabin. They had been parked on the road a half mile from the cabin. She and Kees ferried them to a remote parking area at Porpoise Bay. When the authorities finally investigate the abandoned vehicles, they would wonder what had happened to the owners, but the location would point toward lost hikers or kayakers, not to a group attacking the Harrow cabin.

Dealing with the practicalities here had made Ella nervous about returning to Vancouver. Ever. By now, she felt certain the police would have begun looking for Detective McQuaid and his partner, assuming Harker had also been with the force. Kees told her not to worry. For one thing, he pointed out, the men had clearly not sought her out on official business, so there was unlikely to be any record of their visit to her apartment, and therefore nothing to link their disappearance to her. For another, there were ways—magical ways—to alter the memories of people if they did start poking around.

Ella clearly had a lot to learn about the potential inherent in her powers. She got the feeling she'd be hitting the books pretty hard in the near future.

When they had moved the last of the cars and returned to the cabin late in the afternoon, Ella finally brought up the one thing that had begun to bother her since the night before.

Forever.

"We can't be together forever," she blurted out while Kees built a fire in the hearth.

She'd told him she was too tired to bother with lighting one, but it got cold this time of year, especially at night, so he'd won that argument. When he dropped a giant log on his foot, she realized maybe she should have eased into the discussion.

Rising to his feet, Kees kicked the log away and stalked over to the sofa where she sat. He stopped immediately in front of her and folded his arms across his chest, forcing her to look up and up and up to see his face. The jerk had intimidation techniques down pat.

"What are you talking about?" His snarl tipped her off that she definitely should have eased in.

"You know I'm right," she said, glaring at him. In for a penny, and all that. "There's no way we can be together forever. I can't be forever, period. You might be a Guardian, but I'm just a human. I don't get to be immortal. I'm going to get older and older and uglier and uglier, and you're going to stay gorgeous and perfect just the way you are now. And it's not even like in the vampire novels, where you can bite me and make me like you so I can stay young and live with you forever. Frankly, it just blows."

Then he laughed, and she wondered if she wanted him around forever anyway.

Kees saw her eyes narrow dangerously and struggled to wipe away his smile. She could see him do it. For a man who'd been created with a stony expression, he had an awful hard time keeping a straight face these days.

Reaching out, Kees scooped her into his arms and took a seat on the sofa, settling her into his lap. Rather than cuddling close as she usually did, Ella held herself stiff as a board and continued to glower at him.

"Little human, sometimes I think you just enjoy having something to worry about," he teased, pulling her close in spite of her rigid resistance. "You're right that this is not like the stories humans have written about vampires. I cannot change you into something like me, nor would I want to. You know how I have lived, trapped in endless centuries of sleep, just waiting for the call to battle to stir me awake. Always alone. Never experiencing even the most simple human emotions. I would do anything to prevent you from living that torment."

Ella frowned. This was the first time Kees had described his life as "torment," even though she, personally, had always thought it sounded like a pretty lousy deal.

"But if that's true, what kind of future do we have? There's a threat growing right now, sure, but if we can do what we have planned, we'll be able to put a stop to it. We'll knock the *nocturnis* back into the Stone Age, the Seven will stay confined to their prisons, and the threat will be gone. And then, what? You say, 'So long,' and turn back to stone? That sounds like a pretty crappy version of forever."

Kees pressed a kiss to her forehead and laughed softly. "Such a baby mage you are. You always forget about the magic, silly girl."

Ella thumped him in the horn. "Don't patronize. Tell me what you're talking about. Is there a spell that can make me live as long as you do?"

"No, but there is a spell that can make *me* live as long as *you* do."

"You mean the thing that Alan did? Will that last forever?"

"Little human, you know that I was summoned to stop the threat of the Seven and to guard against its return, but I am not the first Guardian, and I will not be the last. My brothers and I might be immortal, but as you yourself saw, we are not invulnerable. At times, one of us will fall, and when that happens, the Guild gathers together and another Guardian is summoned to take his place."

"So?"

"So, while I cannot and will not abandon my duty while a threat looms, I have served humanity for over a thousand years. I believe I have earned my rest." He met her gaze and hugged her close. "Once this threat is defeated and the Guild is back on its feet, I will request to be released from my duties. I will step down from the Guardians and ask that another be summoned to take my place."

Ella stared. "Can you do that? Is it even possible?"

"I believe that it is. I have never seen it, nor even heard of it, but I read something very interesting in the grimoire that Alan Parsons passed on to you. The mage who authored that volume wrote that he had heard an unusual story once, a rumor that intrigued him so deeply, he spent years pursuing it and still did not fully understand what it meant."

"What was it?" She poked him impatiently.

"The mage wrote that some people said that the first Guardians ever summoned had been truly cold and unfeeling, emotionless as I had pretended to be."

Ella snorted, but Kees simply ignored her and continued.

"They were very good at battling demons, but they lacked the understanding of why they fought because they felt no attachment to the humans or the world they defended. Many argued that this was not a problem until one day when there was need, the Guardians would not wake. Because they felt no motivation to protect the humans, the threat of the demons did not register and they slept through the call of the Wardens."

"See? What did I tell you? Feelings are good for you. They're a strength, not a weakness."

"Hush and let me finish my story."

She humphed, but subsided.

"There was great panic because demons had begun pouring through into the human world and still the Guardians did not wake. Even the Seven began to stir, and the Wardens knew that humanity would not survive unless the

Guardians awoke, so they searched frantically for another way to rouse them.

"Eventually, and completely by accident, the Wardens stumbled on a solution. Or rather, they stumbled on someone who had stumbled on a solution. A woman, a woman of power, had come to the Guild offering her help to wake the Guardians, but the Wardens turned her away."

"I knew they were misogynists. Everything anyone says involving the Guild or the Wardens or the Guardians, it's always 'he,' 'his,' 'him,' like women don't even exist."

Kees ignored her grumbling. "They turned her away, but she wouldn't go quite so easily. She demanded the opportunity to kneel before the chief Guardian and pray to the Light for his release so that he could fight the demonic threat. They agreed with great reluctance because—"

"Because they were male chauvinist pigs."

"—because the woman gave them no choice. Her power held them at bay as she walked herself to the feet of the Guardian. She knelt before the figure and asked the Light for aid, but before she could complete her prayer, there was a tremendous noise and the stone encasing the Guardian cracked and he stepped forward and seized the woman."

She looked at him, the beginnings of a smile teasing the corners of her lips. "Hm, I wonder where this is going. . . ."

"Hush," he scolded. "Let me finish. He seized the woman and claimed her as his own. He dared the Wardens and demons alike to take her from him and vowed to slay any creature that threatened her. When she told him of the threat not just to her but to her family and friends, to all the humans living in the world, he felt rage for the first time and knew the demons must be defeated."

"It always takes a woman to point out what needs to be done."

"And it appears that I have a mouthy one," Kees growled, nipping her lips teasingly. "The Guardian went out to assess the threat and realized he would need his brothers to help with this battle, so the woman called together all the women of power she could reach, and each knelt and prayed at the feet of a son of the stone. Some walked away having failed, but Fate had woven her threads and one by one, the right woman appeared and the Guardian she was destined to bond with woke. Each in turn they repeated the actions of the first. Together, they went to battle and drove the demons back, imprisoning them in the barren planes where they belonged.

"When they had finished and the world was safe, the Guardians brought their women before the Guild and demanded to be released from their duties. Each had fought honorably and done a great service to humanity, and now they wanted to live beside the women they had claimed, their mates, for as long as Fate allowed."

"And did they?" Ella bit her lip and crossed her fingers.

Kees smiled. "They did. The Wardens released the Guardians, although the action demanded sacrifice. No longer would they be able to shift forms. They remained bound to their human forms, but retained their strength and senses, because the threat of the demonic is never truly absent, and they demanded that they still be able to protect their mates from any who would harm them. Their human forms aged, and eventually, like their mates, their lives ended, but none of them ever expressed a single regret for the choices they had made."

Ella reached up and cupped Kees's face in her hands. She looked at him, soaking in the sight of his gray skin and black eyes, his devilish horns and the fangs that flashed when he spoke or smiled or laughed. She loved everything about him in this form, and in the other. His form was just a form. She loved Kees, no matter how he looked.

And he loved her.

Still, she asked, "What about you? Will you regret it?"

"Never." He spoke firmly and without hesitation, and love blazed in his eyes, a bright, crimson fire that glowed whenever he looked at her. "I love you, Ella. You are my mate, and I will love you forever, alive or dead, Guardian or human. There is nothing for me without you, not in any time, not in any place."

She smiled. "In that case, I think I should make a phone call."

Kees pulled back and looked confused. "A phone call?"

"To my friend Fil. Not only do I need to tell her I'm still alive, but I also need to ask her for one more favor."

"Oh? What do you need to ask her that is more important than telling me that you love me?"

"You know very well I love you, and I'm going to be telling you often, every day of our lives. I even promise to tell you again as soon as I'm done with this conversation, but this is important."

Kees sighed. "Why?"

"Because now that Fil has found the next Guardian, I think I need to convince her to kneel."

"And pray?"

"Baby, we should all pray."